Let him kiss her if that was what he wanted! Alexandrine was adamant she would not answer him. Yet scarcely had his lips touched hers than her own flared to life with an eagerness that shocked her. It had not been like this when Luc had held her in his arms and tried to make love to her—and he had more right than this man! Yet, of the two, she knew, had she been free, she would have given not only her heart, but her body, to Alain Ratan. If this strange sensation within her was love, she had no will-power with which to fight him.

Valentina Luellen was born in London in 1938, and educated in Gloucestershire and London. She began writing at school—mainly because she loathed maths! It took her twelve years of writing before she had a book accepted, but she has now had over forty stories published. Historical romances are her favourite to write, because she loves researching into so many different countries, learning about customs and costumes and the way people lived hundreds of years ago.

Valentina Luellen and her husband moved to Portugal eight years ago when he became seriously ill. There his health began to improve and they now live in a renovated farmhouse on the Algarve with their twenty-one-year-old son, twenty-one cats, two Portuguese dogs, and around 100 trees—almonds, olives, figs, plums, lemons and oranges—most of which they planted themselves.

Valentina Luellen has written twenty-three Masquerade Historical Romances. Recent titles include *Where the Heart Leads*, *The Passionate Pirate*, *The Devil of Talland* and *My Lady Melisande*.

LOVE AND PRIDE

VALENTINA LUELLEN

MILLS & BOON LIMITED
ETON HOUSE   18-24 PARADISE ROAD
RICHMOND   SURREY   TW9 1SR

First published in Great Britain 1988
by Mills & Boon Limited

© Valentina Luellen 1988

Australian copyright 1988
Philippine copyright 1988
This edition 1988

ISBN 0 263 76280 7

Set in Times Roman 10 on 10 pt.
04-8812-93463 C

Made and printed in Great Britain

CHAPTER ONE

'WAKE UP, my dear. We have arrived. Open your eyes and take the first look at your new home.' The voice of her husband roused Alexandrine from a deep sleep, and he laughed softly as she sat bolt upright, thrusting back her tousled hair beneath the cowl of her cloak and leaned forward eagerly for a glimpse of the house to which he had brought her, only to find it was as black as pitch outside. The disappointment on her young face prompted him to add gently, 'I promise I shall take you on a grand tour of Paris. We have arrived later than I anticipated, but I did send word ahead that we were coming, so everything should be prepared. Damn that son of mine! As rebellious as always!'

The last words, muttered in a low tone, made Alexandrine stare at him in surprise. Son? She knew of no son. She had not seen Luc Boussières, Marquis de Mezière, since she had gone into a convent, and before that only twice in two years. He had come and gone from her parents' house many times over the years, she knew, but his visits were always fleeting, and as she had grown older, she was no longer allowed to sit on the knee of the kindly man and tug his beard and he had become a stranger to her—a silent, distant stranger— now her husband! A fond memory, but that was all . . . Now she belonged to him!

She was married to a stranger who, as yet, had made no demands on her. He was waiting until she was stronger, she told herself, even though he had insisted that the marriage would be in name only. It was for her protection, nothing more. She did not believe him—how could she? Men of his age, with his vast wealth, did not marry girls of her class. They took them as mistresses, set them up in fashionable houses in Paris or some other large town, and visited them when the fancy took them.

Who was she, after all? The daughter of a well-to-do vineyard owner, a respected man in the small village of Noyen nestled deep in the peaceful Loire Valley. But not wealthy like the Marquis! Yet the two men had been close friends for many years and her mother had always taken great care to make the Marquis welcome in her house. Luc Boussières had bounced her on his knee when she was a tiny child and she had always liked him. Now she was his wife, and inwardly terrified at this new turn her life had taken.

The man who sat opposite her was perhaps in his late fifties—possibly older. Alexandrine had never been able to define his true age and he had only laughed when she had on one occasion asked him. There were times when it seemed to her that he would never age, but now, seeing him this last time, she had to admit to herself that in two years he had aged at least ten. The carefully groomed dark hair was now completely white, as was the neatly trimmed beard he had always worn. The weatherbeaten aristocratic face was deeply lined. Yet still the voice was the same. She found it strange that she had not recognised it during her illness. The brown eyes, like those of a small dog she had once owned, looked at her with something akin to adoration, but she dismissed this instantly as foolishness. Men who were as widely travelled as this man did not adore girls of her age or become infatuated with them enough to marry them. Besides, it would be totally contrary to his character. Yet so was everything he had said and done since she recovered from her long illness.

There was nothing intimidating about him or his manner towards her, yet she still felt no more than a little girl in his presence. Her unease was heightened by his constant companion, the silent, dark-skinned Moor who never left his side and who, she was sure, listened to every word which passed between them. The Marquis's servant, she had thought at first, but as the days passed she was to discover he was more of an equal and his manner was never challenged. She found that strange, perturbing—and frightening. He frightened her with his staring eyes, the implacable mask which was a face, never smiling, never softening for one instant. He accompanied the Marquis everywhere, acting as his body-servant, even putting him to bed at night. What kind of man have I married? Alexandrine wondered for at least the hundredth time since she had stood at the side of the Marquis de Mezière and listened to the village priest proclaiming them man and wife!

The house in Noyen had been closed up and left in the care of an able family who had orders to keep it ready for them to return at any time. They had been amply paid, she recalled, a large amount of money changing hands before they departed. Now she was on her way to Paris!

Like every girl of her age, she had always dreamed of going to Paris, even of being presented at court. Her father could never have afforded such a luxury for his family, let alone for a girl, for she was only expected to help about the house and prepare herself for marriage and the rearing of a family. That had never stopped her from dreaming, however. At night, alone in the narrow bed in the room she had shared with her sister, she would drift into sleep in the arms of some handsome young man—one of many that wished to court her, to whisk her away from the country to a life of splendour in the vastness of Paris. She knew so little of the life there, for few people ever considered Noyen interesting enough to linger more than one day—if that. What she had heard centred on the King and his court, Louis XV, grandson of the 'Sun King' who had built Versailles. One day, she promised herself in those nightly encounters, she would go there…she would be dressed in silk and fine lace…she would dance until her feet ached… She would see the King and the Dauphin, and the King's mistresses whom, it was rumoured, he took and dismissed in rapid succession—each one more beautiful than the one before.

She would wake in a bed with silken sheets, a maid at her side awaiting her orders. She would laze in bed until noon and then peruse her letters at great leisure before deciding whose invitations she would accept. She would go to the theatre to enjoy a play by Molière, or accompany her escort for that evening in a barge along one of the many small canals that made Versailles so picturesque. They would gaze at each other beneath a

brilliant moon and pledge their undying love to each
other...

But now her dreams would never come true. She was
a wife, yet not a wife—the Marquise de Mezière—and
beginning to wonder if this world in which she found
herself were not as unreal as that of her foolish dreams.
Nothing had been real since her wedding day! The service
had been endured, but she had hardly taken in a word
and had made her vows like some wooden doll, afraid
to look into the face of the man who stood at her side,
and suddenly the friend had become a stranger who now
owned her. And afterwards, when he had come to her
bedchamber—to claim his rights, she had thought—she
had been terrified! Instead, he had brought her a small
chest of jewels which had made her eyes almost start
from her head. Necklaces, rings, bracelets, earrings of
diamonds and pearls; rubies, their deep colour glowing
alongside the brightness of sapphires and pale ameth-
ysts; jewels fit for a queen. Her husband had laughed
at her reluctance to touch them and try them about her
skin. In the end he had placed a necklace of rubies about
her slender throat, matching rings on her fingers and
diamonds for her ears and had sat in a long silence inspecting the new vision which presented itself to him—
much to her embarrassment. The way he had begun to
stare made her increasingly nervous, yet he did not touch
her and in no way attempted to assert his authority.
Indeed, after such generosity, she had been expecting to
pay something. But nothing! No demands, no intrusion
on her privacy in the following days leading up to their
departure. It puzzled her—frustrated her—and at night,
as she lay awake in bed awaiting the sound of footsteps
outside her door, it terrified her!

As if sensing the disquiet in her, her husband leaned
across the space separating them and patted the painfully thin, white hands locked tightly together in her lap.
'Do not look so apprehensive, my child. You have
nothing to fear. I understand that everything has happened very suddenly for you, but it is for the best, believe me. Accept it. The alternative was to leave you in
some boring, painfully restricting convent where your
beauty would lie hidden until it faded and died and there

would never be anyone to appreciate it. I could not do that, could I?' He gave a soft laugh as Alexandrine blushed profusely. Beautiful? She? She was as thin as a beanpole and her once beautiful hair had lost its natural lustre while she had been ill. No one would look twice at her! 'There now, at least I have brought a little colour to those cheeks. You are still very pale and not yourself, but that will soon change. You must begin to think of your new status. The old life is dead and gone. You must accept that and try to put away in some part of your mind all the terrible things that happened before I found you. The days ahead are going to be filled with new things, exciting things. New faces, places...I shall expect my wife to be the most beautiful woman in Paris. The most dutiful and the most faithful.'

'I think perhaps you are mocking me just a little,' Alexandrine whispered miserably. She was seventeen years old, and had spent two of those years being educated in a local convent so that when she emerged once again into the world, she would be ready to take wedding vows and accept the role of wife and mother. She had been betrothed when she was fourteen, deprived of the normal everyday things that most children enjoyed, and the memory of the strictness of the nuns who had cared for her, despite their well-meaning intentions, made her shudder at the thought of ever having to experience convent life again. There had been no time for play, no idle chatter with other young girls of her age, to indulge in girlish dreams about the men they would some day marry. Work—learn—pray, the routine never changed day after day.

And then to emerge like a butterfly from a chrysalis, eager to assume the role for which she had been schooled, to have her betrothed taken from her by the plague and, after him, her family! Was this God's reward for all her hard work? Now the Marquis de Mezière had thrust the same role upon her almost before she knew what was happening to her. But, she was forced to admit, life with him, however strange it was at the moment and might be in the future, could not be any worse than that in the convent. At least, now, she was free!

'Alexandrine, believe me, that was the last thing on my mind. Child, why will you not believe I care for you very much? I want you to be happy. You are afraid, is that it? Of me? Of old Luc, whose beard you used to tug when you were a tiny scrap? Do you not think it only right and proper that, as a family friend, since you have no one else to care for you, I should do so? You will like Paris. And you shall have new clothes, the finest money can buy. I shall be so proud when you walk by my side.'

Alexandrine managed a smile before she quickly looked away, noticing as she did so that the attention of Selim the Moor was focused on her. With such a strange expression in those jet black eyes! Did he too find an oddness about his master's words? To Alexandrine's way of thinking, he was speaking of her as though she was some ornament he had acquired and wished to display for the admiration of his friends. He would have many, she surmised, rich and powerful like himself. She would be on show! It was not a pleasant thought.

'How—How old is your son?' She found herself stammering as Luc helped her to alight from the carriage, and she did not miss the look that passed between her husband and the ebony-skinned Moor climbing down behind her.

'Paul is twenty-five. Did I not mention him? No, perhaps not. I was too concerned for your wellbeing after your long illness,' came the non-committal answer which left her speechless. Twenty-five! She was now the stepmother of a son eight years her senior!

'He—He knows we are married?' she gasped.

'I tell my son only sufficient for him to be able to cope with a few hours at a time, my dear,' Luc returned drily. 'No lights? Damn him! Selim, rouse the servants and have them attend us. If he has sent them to bed, I'll flay him alive! Now, man! Can you not see that the poor child needs her bed?' he snapped, as the Moor did not move.

The man touched his forehead in the usual gesture of obedience she had witnessed many times, yet she sensed there was nothing subservient in his manner towards her husband, and he hurried into the house. Luc gave an oath as he began to help her up the darkened steps and she slipped on the wet stone, turning her ankle.

'It's nothing,' she said quickly as he bent to examine her bruised foot. 'I am tired, that's all. Perhaps your son has gone to bed.'

'If I know Paul, he's gambling with his friends in one of the upstairs rooms. That will end now that I am home. I will not have the likes of them about you! I shall protect you from the evils of Paris and show you only the beauty.'

How strange his voice sounded, Alexandrine thought, straining her eyes to see his face, but it was too dark. He spoke as if the city was a decadent place, yet *he* lived here and allowed his son to do so... and he had brought her here to live, so it could not be so very bad. Perhaps he really did care for her. It was somehow a very comforting thought as he led her into the darkened house. She was a stranger here and she did not feel at all welcome. Paul, his son, knew of their impending arrival, yet there had been no one, not even a servant, to greet them. Did he not welcome his father's return? Or was it the new wife who was not welcome?

Liveried servants suddenly appeared with candles to light their way and seemed as taken aback to discover that Luc had returned as they were to see the pale-faced, tired-eyed girl at his side.

'I sent word ahead of our arrival,' the Marquis snapped. 'Why is the place in darkness?'

'We were not told, sir,' one of them stammered as he thrust out his candle to light Alexandrine's way upstairs. 'Monsieur Paul is entertaining friends and sent us to bed.'

'The young scoundrel! I'll take a whip to him,' Luc growled, and Alexandrine did not miss the apprehensive looks which passed between the servants. She had never considered Luc a violent man. Never once had she known him to raise his voice above its normal quiet tone—at least not until this evening. 'Where is he?'

'In his apartments, with five other young gentlemen. Playing cards, I believe.' The answer was supplied with some reluctance.

'Gambling away money he doesn't possess, you mean, don't you, Pierre? And in the morning I'll be presented with his IOUs and expected to pay them like a good father. Damn the boy. I won't do it!'

The sound of raised voices and raucous laughter reached them, halting Luc abruptly in his tracks. His mouth tightened into a bleak line as his gaze swept down the corridor in front of them.

'Forgive me, my dear. I do not think the time is right for you and Paul to meet. He is probably drunk, and he can be quite abusive when he is in such a condition.'

'I think perhaps he has already decided not to accept me,' Alexandrine said miserably.

'Paul is a very high-spirited and rebellious young man,' Luc replied, silently cursing the offspring who plagued his life. 'My fault, perhaps. After the death of his mother I did not spend as much time with him as I should. I was always travelling.' Travelling—searching—hoping— returning again to France, his mission unfulfilled, his quest uncompleted. It never would be. He accepted that now. Married to Alexandrine, he would never leave the shores of France again. He had committed himself to her for the rest of his miserable existence. 'Tomorrow he will receive you with all the respect due to my wife. Pierre, escort the Marquise to the Jade Apartment and see that she has everything she wants before you rouse a suitable girl to attend her. And be quick about it. My wife is tired and in need of her bed.'

'At once, sir.' Pierre, Alexandrine recognised, must be in charge of the household, for he turned to issue rapid instructions to those about him, scattering them in all directions and leaving just one man to escort Luc with a light. Then he bowed before her, and said in an awed tone, 'If Madame la Marquise will follow me.'

She obeyed as if in a dream, following him through darkened corridors with the glow from the sconce he held throwing ghostly, weird patterns over the tapestried walls and the faces which stared at her from age-old portraits. No sound but that of their footsteps upon the marbled floors. The house rejected her as strongly as Luc's son did, she suspected. She could never be happy here in this dull mausoleum. She did not belong.

'I hope these rooms meet with your approval, madame.' Pierre showed her into a large sitting-room with dark oak-panelled walls. There was a huge fire-place, which had not been used in many months, she surmised, seeing how clean everything was in the hearth. The long sofa and matching chairs were all covered in a beautiful jade velvet with gold trimmings. The curtains were a perfect match. The man opened another door, and she followed him into a bedroom beyond her wildest dreams. A massive canopied bed, big enough for at least five people, hung with the same deep shade of green velvet and gold tassels. A coat-of-arms was embroidered along the overhang of the canopy and, seeing her enquiring look, Pierre said with a faint smile, 'The master's coat-of-arms, madame. Yours now also. It was his father's, and his father's before him. A very old and distinguished family.'

His words told Alexandrine that he did not know why someone of Luc's rank should have taken to wife a girl young enough to be his daughter. The house tonight would be rife with speculation and rumours, she suspected, but she was too tired to care. The bed looked so inviting. With a sigh, she sank on to the deep feather mattress. Tonight, nothing and no one could disturb her.

'I shall have your trunks brought up at once, madame. Is there anything you require? Some refreshments? A bath?'

A bath! The magic words revived her flagging spirits. 'Oh, yes, please. A bath would be very welcome,' she breathed. 'But it will be so much trouble. It is so late.'

'If Madame la Marquise wishes to bathe now, she shall have her wish.' His glance at her was puzzled. 'You have only to command.'

Command! *She*, command? Alexandrine d'Albret, daughter of a merchant—albeit a prosperous one—to command and have her every desire fulfilled? It would take her a long time to accustom herself to this new life.

'Yes, Pierre,' she said with a vigorous nod of her head.

'I shall bring madame something to drink while she is waiting for the water to be heated. If you will excuse me, I shall leave you to find a suitable person to attend you until your own maid arrives.'

'But…' Alexandrine broke off, biting her lip. She had no maid. Beneath another penetrating look, she forced a smile to stiff lips. 'Thank you, Pierre, that will do nicely.'

Left alone in the huge room, she relaxed back on the bed and allowed her gaze to wander slowly around. Beyond was another, smaller, room with the door half open. Through it she could see an exquisitely decorated porcelain tub. Such luxury—her very own bath!

She had not known what to expect when she entered the house. She knew for a fact that Luc Boussières was very rich. Just how rich her mother and father never seemed to know, but they always spoke of him with great respect, and when he visited them, he brought gifts that took her breath away. Once it had been a gold necklace for her mother and gold rings for herself and her sister, or a curved oriental dagger for her brother and six engraved goblets of pure silver for her father. They had never been able to give anything so grand in return, only their hospitality—and that was all it seemed he ever wanted.

She knew he had travelled abroad for most of his life. Often he would enthral them all with his tales of new countries and peoples, of being abandoned by his guides one day in the desert only to be found by a band of wandering nomads who took him into their tents and nursed him back to health, treating him as they would a brother. From each place he had collected a memory that remained, some trinket or item of importance to him. Are they all here in this house? Alexandrine wondered, as she stretched her aching limbs. The bed was so comfortable. If someone did not bring the hot water soon, she would fall asleep!

With an effort she roused herself and climbed to her feet. Just as she did so, the door opened and another servant appeared, dragging after him her one and only trunk. It was a huge thing, well worn with age, and it contained, not as it should, an assortment of fine gowns and the like—for she possessed very few clothes—but personal articles that she could not bear to be parted from. It had amused Luc to watch her try to cram so many things into it until the lid would scarcely close and she had been forced to put aside the remainder. If they were important to her, he would have them collected from the house at a later time, he assured her.

So many things had she wanted to bring with her, to ease the loneliness she felt after the loss of her family. The tiny miniatures of her parents would take pride of place on the table beside the bed and she would keep for ever the few items of jewellery her mother had possessed and her father's beautifully engraved timepiece. Never would she part with anything so precious; they held too many happy memories. When she looked at them, she would remember Noyen and how her life had once been. It would never be the same again!

A moment after the man had departed, Pierre himself brought her a glass of warm milk spiced with cinnamon and a plate of small sugared biscuits, and informed her that hot water would arrive shortly, also a maid to help with her toilette. The moment he had gone, Alexandrine fell upon the biscuits with relish. Her appetite momentarily satisfied, the milk consumed, she wandered about the room, growing apprehensive at Luc's continued absence. Was she waiting for her to refresh herself after the journey before he came to her, or was he quarrelling with his son over the reception they had received—or rather the lack of it? Paul had known of their arrival, yet had deliberately ignored the homecoming of his father and the new bride. A show of rebellion—or distaste at his father's decision to marry again?

She paused to consider her reflection in a wall-length mirror and despaired of ever becoming the elegant, perfectly groomed creature she knew Luc expected to be at his side. She had lost a great deal of weight during her illness, and the travelling-dress of grey velvet, the best she possessed, hung on her like a sack. Her skin still retained a sallow, unhealthy tinge, and her hair! Slowly she raised a hand to touch the short curls about her forehead and ears. When she had recovered her senses and discovered she had been shorn like a sheep, it had plunged her into another abyss of depression. She had never been pretty, but she had possessed beautiful long golden hair which had always been admired. Morning and night she brushed it until it shone and it hung past her waist in unbroken waves. But now! Whoever had

wielded the scissors had done so without any consider-
ation for her feelings. It was uneven and ragged, and
the sight of it had brought her almost to tears.

How could she face Paul Boussières looking like this?
Or anyone? She was what she was, a country girl, and
would never be anything else. Why had Luc not left her
where she was? She could have cared for herself. At least
she would have been among friends, people who had
known her all her life, and in her own home with her
own belongings about her. Her thoughts flew back to
Noyen on that day when the fever had left her and she
had fully recovered her senses. How it had gladdened
her heart to know she had at last emerged from that
other unfriendly, frightening, world of shadows and
death. She was alive! She had survived the terrible plague
that had struck down first her father and the handsome
young man she was to have married. Then her sister and
brother, before wrenching her beloved mother from her.
She had lost everyone—her whole family—yet she was
too weak, too wretched at that moment to shed even one
tear. With an effort she had managed to open her eyes,
to regard two shadowy figures close by the bed.

'She is awake.' A strange accent. Not French. Or
English. What manner of man was it who stood out of
her blurred vision, tall, so dark, almost menacing?

'Good. Gently now, Selim, don't frighten the poor
child. Draw back the curtains a little more. The sun may
cheer her. God knows, she needs something after all she
has been through.'

That voice again! So gentle. So soft.

'Do you think her mind has suffered?'

'I pray not. We shall see in a moment.'

They spoke of her as if she were some madwoman.
She had been ill, very ill, but she was not mad! She knew
what had happened—the heartbreaking events that had
taken place before she collapsed. She remembered the
dreadful feeling of cold that had numbed her body, and
from the dark recesses of her mind came another memory
of being stifled by intense heat, when her body had run
with perspiration and she had pushed away the bedclothes, gasping for breath. Her skin had felt as if a
thousand red-hot needles were being thrust into her and

she had screamed in agony, fought against the hands seeking to restrain her violent movements, holding her until she quietened. Then, later, it had all seemed like some ghastly nightmare. How long had it been since the day she had collapsed at the bedside of her mother?

A muffled oath, followed by a low amused laugh, sent the past spinning from her mind. Alexandrine wheeled round towards the door and the three men who stood just inside it staring at her with bold eyes.

'*Mon Dieu!* Are you my father's latest little diversion? Impossible! He may be an old lecher, but he has better taste than this. You look as if you have just been dragged from some peasant hovel. That hair! That dress! Gentlemen, can you imagine *this* at Versailles? Perhaps she will catch the King's eye!'

She knew instinctively who the speaker was, and was startled by the hostility blazing from the narrowed brown eyes, so much like those of her husband, despite the amusement in the high-pitched voice. But there the resemblance ended. Luc's features were deeply tanned by sun and wind, whereas Paul's skin was pale, his cheeks tinged with pink—from his drinking, she supposed—and then, as she gazed at him, she was horrified to realise that they were rouged like those of a woman. Of medium build, slim-hipped, he was clad in a coat of rich brocade, with a heavily embroidered waistcoat beneath and coloured stockings, jewelled garters and leather shoes with jewelled buckles.

This—This fop was Luc's son? She could not believe it! She could not move when he slowly advanced and, to the great amusement of the two men accompanying him, circled her, inspecting in great detail her appearance. A jewelled finger examined the lace on the modest bodice of her gown and another chuckle rose in his throat. Colour flooded into Alexandrine's face at his rudeness. He was inspecting her as though she were some breeding mare at an auction. Did he not know who she now was—or was it not important to him? She tried to speak, but was so embarrassed that no words came. Where was her husband? Why did Luc not come to rescue her from this hideous monster and his ogling friends? They made her feel unclean!

'Gentlemen, I tell you my father will have his work cut out with this one. I'll take a wager with you. How long do you think—one month or two—before she is, shall we say, groomed for court? Fifty gold louis.'

'Sixty.' One of his companions laughed, and Alexandrine almost choked in aggravation. How dared they!

'You have had your fun, Paul. Go back to the cards and leave the poor little thing alone. If Luc finds you here, he will flay you,' a voice remarked quietly from the doorway.

A man was lounging easily against the door jamb, his arms folded across a broad chest. Compared to the other three, he was attired very simply in a plain white silk shirt that accentuated the darkness of his skin, and black breeches. For a moment, a pair of pale green eyes surveyed Alexandrine, and she felt as if a cold wind had swept over her whole body. His inspection, although briefer than that of Paul, and without comment, was more penetrating, more uncomfortable, more humiliating. Without a word, a single look stripped her bare, and it was obvious from the contemptuous smile that touched the corners of the lean mouth that he considered her no better than his companions did. Did they think she had trapped Luc into marriage because he was rich? She had no idea what he had told anyone, if anything at all had been disclosed!

Oh, how she regretted the impulsive marriage; but when Luc had sat with her that day in the pleasant sunlit solar at the house and expressed his desire to take care of her, she could think of nothing else but the fact that she was alive! She alone was left to carry on the proud name of d'Albret! How she wished she had been born a boy, so that she would not have needed—or indeed been offered—help. She would grow stronger, and could in time manage the gaunt old house by herself. But what had she to look forward to? Luc made marriage sound so attractive. What else do young women think of? he had asked her with a soft laugh. She would have her own household, innumerable servants at her beck and call, and unlimited funds to purchase whatever she wanted.

What *do* I want? she had wondered, dazed by the proposal, and aware, as always, of Selim the Moor hovering in the shadows. Was nothing sacred? He was even present at Luc's marriage proposal, and to hear the fantastic terms he offered! A dream world was opening up to her, if she wished to accept it.

She had accepted because she did not know what else to do, and he, the most eloquent of speakers, had convinced her that she should substitute him for the young handsome man who had been taken from her before they could reach the altar. Now she began to wonder if her decision had been the right one. What was she doing here in this cold, unwelcoming house, faced with a son who at first sight had disliked, if not hated, her and a husband who as yet had not come to her bed? Was she a wife, or a thing that had been obtained like some object with little value, save for the pleasure it gave the owner for a few moments? The thought chilled her.

That was how she was being regarded by each of the men now staring at her. Paul's two friends, with the leering expressions they probably displayed every night when they went on a tour of the local taverns. Paul himself, aloof and yet vulnerable. She sensed a terrible insecurity in him. And the stranger at the door, who was still regarding her with narrowed gaze. How those pale green eyes seemed to bore into her very soul! He, she sensed, without understanding why, was the most dangerous of them all. Paul did not like her; his friends were amused by her, but this man—this man looked at her as if he loathed her!

Slowly she lifted her head and stared into the dark, aquiline face, and something stirred inside her. Unbidden, yet there, something she could not deny. He was handsome and proud, and not afraid to let it show. Yet if a man was a man, should he not be so? she wondered. Arrogant, too! She had never encountered the like of him before. He was so sure of himself, and the other three seemed to respect him, for Paul's two friends withdrew to the corridor and even Paul moved towards the door.

She prayed that he too would leave, but at that moment servants appeared with pails of hot water, and, muttering excuses, filed silently past him into the other room. Alexandrine did not miss the gleam that sprang into his eyes and a sliver of apprehension ran through her. When the last one had gone and the room was empty save for themselves, Paul gave a roar of laughter and advanced towards her again.

'My father may see something in you, wench, but I cannot. Perhaps after a bath and some perfume on you, I may feel otherwise inclined.'

Alexandrine screamed as he scooped her up into her arms. For one so thin and wiry he had exceptional strength, and she found her arms pinioned at her sides as he carried her into the antechamber and dumped her without ceremony, fully clothed, into the porcelain bath. The hot water sank through the cloth of her gown and she struggled to her feet, desperate to clamber out. As she steadied herself, she was aware of Paul's eyes dwelling on the saturated cloth that clung to her body and was horrified—she realised she could have been naked! Every curve of her was outlined for him to stare at! She swung a hand at his grinning face and almost overbalanced. He thrust out a hand in return and sent her sprawling back into the bath. She came up gasping, choking from water in her ears and eyes and mouth, to see Paul being forcibly propelled towards the door by the stranger.

'You damned young fool! When will you ever learn?' he growled, and then the door was closed behind both men, leaving her alone.

Weakly she climbed from the tub and stripped off her wet gown and undergarments. Was this humiliation ever to end? Whoever the man was, he had saved her from a very unpleasant situation, despite his apparent dislike. Was he a friend of Luc? And where was her husband? Why had she been left to face this madhouse alone?

'You will not be disturbed again—unless you wish it.'

She spun round with a gasp when, as she was about to sink beneath the inviting water, those same mocking tones again invaded her privacy. He had come in without her being aware, and was standing with his back against the closed door. Alexandrine did not know what part of her coloured first—or most. Her saturated gown lay on the floor, together with her petticoats and stockings, and she had one leg raised to climb into the tub. Instinctively her hands rose to cover her breasts...her cheeks burned...words froze in her throat. No man had ever seen her body before, not even her father, or her husband. Yet this stranger...!

'My name is Alain Ratan. And yours?'

Mesmerised, she could not move as he came towards her. How those eyes delved deep into her soul. Was he some magician to hold her spellbound in such a state of undress? Had she no shame? She wanted to move, to scream, yet somehow she knew that no one would come. In this house, who was there?

'Surely you have a name?' The voice was so soft, deep, stirring her as none she had ever heard. She could not drag her gaze from the pale glittering eyes that without reservation wandered slowly over her body. 'Luc has always had excellent taste. With you, my dear, he has excelled himself. Where did he find you? What distant shore was he cast upon when you offered him solace and he thought you the answer to all his dreams?'

'You—you insult me, monsieur!' At last Alexandrine found her voice. She looked wildly round for a robe, before realising that it was in the other room with the rest of her clothes. She retreated from the advancing figure, cheeks flaming, stuttering, frightened...And yet, how could she feel excited by the way this man looked at her? It was shameful! Obscene! She was a married woman now, and only her husband should ever have such access to her. 'I demand that you bring me something to wear. It is unseemly for me to stand before you like this. You are no gentleman!'

'Where women such as you are concerned—no, I am not.' The words chilled her. 'My dear, you may have attracted Luc's attention for a little while, but I assure you that in Paris alone you would not arouse one iota of interest in any man. You are too thin, for a start, and so pale. Your hair is... *Mon Dieu,* what has happened to it? Did some farmer shear you, or did a jealous lover take his revenge on a faithless woman? Many do!'

'As you will,' she said, without knowing why the strange words came so easily to her lips, and the man nodded.

'Women like you are the curse of man—soft skinned, milk-white like ewes' milk. Innocent eyes that entrap a man and then betray him by casting their spell elsewhere. Your body has the look of one not yet brought to fulfilment. Has Luc fulfilled you yet? I think not. I find it strange, even in him, to take one as you for a bedmate... He is growing old. Poor Luc!'

'How dare you! He is not old,' Alexandrine protested, knowing even as she uttered the words that he spoke the truth. Luc was old enough to be her father, yet she had not really considered until now the problems that might arise from such a union. This man made her think of them, for he had roused in her something frightening—a tingling sensation in her limbs that would not cease. Here she stood, without a stitch of clothing, and did not scream for help! Even when he came closer, she could not move. When her eyes flew to the closed doorway, he chuckled.

'Beyond is Paul. Are you seeking *his* help?'

Her cry of alarm was stifled as he pulled her against his hard muscular chest and his mouth took possession of hers. He kissed her very slowly and with great expertise, skilfully forcing apart the stiff lips beneath his which refused to yield and answer, darting his tongue inside her mouth until she began to gasp and twist in his embrace, desperately seeking to free herself. But she was a mere child in his grasp, forced to endure his lips on hers that grew more demanding as the moments passed. His fingers slid over the smoothness of one shoulder, his touch burning her like fire. They moved down to one breast and began to caress it, oblivious of the indignant noises coming from her imprisoned lips. She moaned as though in actual pain as he teased her nipple, and she felt a strange awakening inside. No man had ever subjected her to this kind of treatment or subdued her so easily, and this was certainly nothing like the holy Sisters had said it would be between a man and a woman! She was actually beginning to like the feeling he was arousing in her. They had made it sound like duty to be borne at all costs, and her own emotions would never enter into it. A dutiful wife did not comment on anything. What was the matter with her?

As he felt her struggles diminishing, the man became bolder, allowing his hands to wander freely over her body, exploring the firm thighs, the rounded buttocks, the firm, uplifted breasts again and again.

Reality forced its way through the spell he was casting, and, dragging her mouth from beneath his, she gasped, 'If you do not release me this instant, I shall scream for help. My husband will kill you for this outrage!'

His hands fell away without a word, and it was then that she realised what she had said. He had not known! None of them had known! They had believed her to be some little country girl that Luc Boussières had brought back to Paris. Another mistress. How many had he had?

'Get out!' Tears welled down over her chalk-white cheeks. 'Get out!'

Without a word, he turned and left, closing the door. She heard the murmur of voices from the other room, and then Paul's raised in disbelief. Somehow she knew that the man, whoever he was, would not disturb her again—or allow anyone else to do so. Weakly she sank into the bath-water and immersed herself completely, rubbing her face and mouth and skin with perfumed soap... yet nothing seemed strong enough to erase the memory of that burning touch on her lips, her breasts, her soft skin. The devil had left a mark on her which would never be erased—his brand! Would anyone ever make her feel so vulnerable again? Please, Luc, she prayed as she began to dry herself, please let it be you!

The voices grew louder, and now she could hear Luc's angry tones above the others. As the door opened again to admit a maid with her robe and nightgown, she heard Paul say, 'I admit she is somewhat more appealing than some you have brought here in the past, but to *marry* the wench! Father, you have taken leave of your senses! It is a joke. When you grow tired of her, I shall take her off your hands. She will be well paid.'

'You will not speak of Alexandrine in that manner.' Luc sounded as though the words were choking him, she thought as she hastily pulled on some clothes and thrust her feet into well-worn leather slippers.

'Alexandrine? A fancy name for a country girl! Still, in silks and lace, with that hair suitably arranged and a few cheap baubles round her neck, she might pass for a lady of some quality.'

'Alexandrine is my wife! Apologise, dammit!'

Alexandrine opened the door in time to see Luc deliver a stinging blow across his son's cheek. The force behind it sent him reeling into the arms of one of his companions.

'Curse you, old man! Is this your way of shutting me out?' Paul spat the words at him, his eyes dilated with disbelief.

'No. This is my way of protecting someone I care for very deeply,' came the simple reply. He really does care for me, Alexandrine thought, and he is not afraid to proclaim it.

'You could have set her up in a house somewhere!' Paul shouted, raising trembling fingers to a rouged cheek. 'This is my home ... I'll not have her here!'

'No, Paul,' he was reminded coldly. 'This is my home, and Alexandrine is my wife, the Marquise de Mezière. You will be polite to her at all times and you will respect her right to be here. Remember that I tolerate you only because you are of my blood. There is no love between us—no affection of any kind. We both know there never will be. Do not force me to reconsider *your* position beneath *my* roof.'

'Luc, the boy meant no harm. He is as taken aback by the news you have brought as the rest of us.' Alain Ratan stepped between them, and slowly Luc's clenched fist returned to his side. 'Let us have no more harsh words.'

'Pretty words from someone who went back to take a second look!' Paul sneered. 'What did she promise you while you were closeted together, Alain? Her bed when my father was not about?'

Alexandrine gasped at the insult, and immediately brought all eyes to where she stood clutching the robe tightly about her neck. Wet curls clung to her cheeks and forehead, giving her a waifish, lost appearance. What colour are her eyes? Alain thought as he stared into them, fighting to overcome the momentary twinge of pity that encompassed him. Hazel, with a touch of grey? No, more a mixture of brown and blue... He became aware of Luc watching him, a silent question on his leathered features.

Alexandrine was stunned as Alain ignored Paul's words and moved towards her. Lifting one limp hand in his, he touched it to his lips. 'Madame la Marquise, forgive a loud-mouthed boy whose capacity for rudeness is exceeded only by a capacity for too much wine. I hope you will forgive him—forgive us all—for the way in which you have been received.'

Had she not been looking into those pale green eyes and seen the mockery there, she would have been deceived by the flattering words and perhaps even comforted by them. 'A country girl is accustomed to animals, monsieur,' she replied in a low tone that shook with suppressed anger. Paul openly insulted her. This man did so with a look—a gleam in the depths of those fathomless pools—and that kiss! She wrenched her hand free as Paul turned on his heel and slammed noisily out of the room. Somewhat sheepishly, his two companions followed, at least acknowledging her with barely audible goodnights before they, too, beat a hasty retreat. Well, they would all discover she was not to be intimidated!

'Alexandrine, you are tired and overwrought—with good reason, I admit.' Luc's tone reproved her for the remark. 'Go to bed, child. I shall join you in a little while. Tomorrow, I promise, I shall make up for this hideous welcome.'

He sounded as if he were trying to pacify a small child by offering a bribe, Alain thought as he turned towards the door. No sweets or mundane baubles for this one. For her there would be jewels and pretty clothes. Like all the rest, she could be bought! Poor Luc, always searching for perfection, but never finding it. Like himself, he had discovered behind an innocent face the heart of Satan!

'Goodnight, my dear.' Luc bent to kiss Alexandrine on one pale cheek. 'Sleep well. I shall not disturb you. I have things to do before I retire so that this house once more functions as efficiently as before I left it. Paul's lackadaisical ways brought about chaos, from what Pierre has told me.'

He was gone before Alexandrine could utter a word. He had no intention of joining her again tonight. His words had been meant for Alain, as if to convey to the other man that everything between them was as normal as it should be between a man and his wife. But it was not! Nothing about her marriage was normal.

Tomorrow, he promised, he would make up for their reception. She climbed into bed, trying to convince herself that, in the light of a new day, everything would be all right. Paul would be nice to her, Alain Ratan would have left the house and Luc would once more be the kindly old man she knew and loved. Yes, she did love him, she acknowledged as she snuggled beneath the sheets and allowed the maid to remove the warming-pan. Not the kind of love a woman should feel for the man with whom she was to spend the rest of her life, but more the feelings of affection and respect that would be afforded an older, wiser man. Indeed, was that not exactly what Luc was? Perhaps in time another love would grow from their union. When she had a child . . . She had not considered motherhood, because she had scarcely had time to dwell on being a bride—and, heaven forbid, a stepmother! But she supposed he would want a family. Every man wanted that.

Tomorrow she would be less emotional, she promised herself as her eyelids began to droop. She must remember she was now Alexandrine, Marquise de Mezière. No one could take that away. Luc would give her everything a young girl could dream of possessing, and in return she would become the perfect wife he wished for, a hostess to grace his home and entertain his friends. What more could she want? She had been selfish these past days, thinking only of herself. Now it was time to think of her husband. She would make him happy, never betray his trust.

Innocence slept, never once considering a life without love.

'I'm glad you are still awake. We should talk,' Luc said, closing the door of Alain's room behind him. He had knocked and entered without waiting to be admitted, to find Alain stretched out on the bed, still fully clothed. He began to rise, but relaxed again when Luc indicated that he should not disturb himself.

'There is no need—not between us,' Alain answered, searching for some sign on the other man's face to indicate that Alexandrine had told him what had happened between them. If she had, he would have apologised to his friend and accepted that perhaps he had actually outraged the girl, but he saw nothing there and knew that nothing had been said. His first assessment of her had been right, after all. 'Who am I to sit in judgement of your actions? Your life is your own.'

Luc's gaze rested for a brief moment on the bottle of wine and the half-empty glass on the bedside table, and knew the man had forsaken the company of Paul and his friends, and probably an invitation to tour the Beggars' Quarter of the city where women were cheap and plentiful—a common pastime among the young and idle—to drink alone as he had done for many, many long nights. He had known for several years of Alain's solitary, self-imposed exile from the circles in which he had once moved. He had heard the first rumours of the beautiful woman he had adored and married and who was betraying him with every man who took her fancy, and then had seen for himself the slender, flame-haired witch and understood Alain's frustrations, his despair, the love that was slowly turning to hate. He had watched a carefree young man turned into an embittered misogynist and had heard for himself one night, when the two of them got drunk together, of the agony of mind he had suffered until a hunting accident took her from him.

A year later, when Luc returned from a trip to Constantinople, it was to discover that Alain Ratan, Duc de Belaincourt, had gained himself the reputation of having more interest in horses than in women, and whose solitary existence on his country estate was broken only by occasional visits to Paris, where he drank and gambled with old friends, but always managed to elude the wily traps of the desirable women who pursued him, determined to prove that he was as vulnerable as any other man to their charms.

'I have never understood your friendship with my son,' Luc said, pouring himself a glass of wine. One eyebrow arched as he sipped it and discovered it was a taste he knew well. 'A good year,' he added with a half-smile.

'His father keeps the best cellars in Paris,' Alain returned, unabashed that he had been discovered enjoying Luc's favourite wine and one of the last bottles. 'Does that answer your question?'

'Because I enjoy flattery, I shall accept it.'

Alain came up on one elbow and regarded him with narrowed gaze. 'Are you really married to that young thing?'

'I am. You are thinking it was she who did the chasing, perhaps? You are wrong. Do you think I would have been caught unless I wanted it—at my age? I have known Alexandrine all her life. Her parents were my friends for over fifteen years. The plague took them. I found her ill at the house, almost dead herself from exhaustion. The child had nursed them all in turn with no thought to her own plight. How she was spared the sickness is beyond me. It must have been a miracle.'

'God has been known to smile on the righteous,' Alain replied sarcastically. Luc had taken pity on her. No doubt she had fed him a pretty tale of a harrowing ordeal and he, soft-hearted old fool that he was, had fallen for it.

'I used to bounce her on my knee,' Luc continued, as if he had not been interrupted, 'and she would pull my beard.' He touched the growth at his chin, his features softening slightly. There were not many memories as enjoyable as that one.

'While you still might be able to bounce her on your knee, I rather think the beard-pulling will no longer apply,' came another dry comment.

'She will not betray me, Alain.'

'Good God, man, she's a child!' Alain snapped, mindful of his own bitter experiences. 'And you...'

'I am an old man. Old enough to be her father. I am aware of that. I *am* old—sixty-two, to be exact. I am also lonely. Alexandrine will brighten what days are left to me on this earth. She is quite innocent of the world, having been in a convent for the past two years. Under my guidance, she will blossom and grow.'

'And when you have given her new confidence in herself, she will slip into bed with the first handsome man who smiles at her. If I believed in sorcery, I would say she has given you a love-potion to blind those old eyes!'

'I am neither bewitched nor blind, and because I understand the concern that prompted such uncalled-for remarks, I shall overlook them. But be warned, Alain, I shall not tolerate the slightest insult to Alexandrine! From anyone. As it happens, I am exceedingly fond of the child. I might even go so far as to say I love her— as far as I am capable of love.'

'Then I wish you well.' Alain shrugged broad shoulders. 'I hope she turns out to be everything you want her to be.'

'I shall ensure that she is.' Luc finished his wine and then refilled the other man's glass. 'I have found something I have been searching for for a very long time. Perhaps, if you began to look about you again...'

'I'll stay with the wine, my friend,' Alain retorted with a harsh laugh. 'If I wake up with a headache in the morning, I can treat it. Not so a broken heart, and only wine erases the memories.'

'Time will temper those,' Luc assured him, turning towards the door. 'Be patient. Who knows, perhaps somewhere in the world, in this very city, there is a woman to make you forget. Will you be leaving in the morning, or shall you stay a while?'

'You mean that I haven't outstayed my welcome yet?' Why did he not say that he had made plans to leave? Paul's gambling parties and the late-night excursions to seek women were beginning to bore him. He longed for the fresh air of the country and the feel of his stallion beneath him as he raced across the open fields. The wind in his face would soon dispel the moodiness upon him now. Yet he hesitated to speak what was in his mind, not knowing why.

'Stay a few more days,' Luc urged. 'Watch as my little flower begins to blossom. You might find it quite interesting.'

·'After tonight's little fiasco, I shall be surprised if your wife even speaks to me tomorrow! But, very well...a day or two longer, to watch the master at work.'

For several minutes after Luc had gone, Alain did not move. The invitation had surprised him. Here was a man on his honeymoon who did not want to be alone with his wife? Yet he had spoken of caring for her—even loving her. He sprang from the bed and quietly eased the door open again. At the far end of the corridor a light gleamed as Luc made his way towards the wide staircase to the upper floors. He was going in the wrong direction, Alain realised. The Jade Apartment, where Alexandrine was supposedly awaiting her husband, was in the other direction. A shadow materialised from one of the many alcoves lining the corridor and began to follow Luc at a distance. Alain caught a glimpse of a hawk-like profile as Selim turned to look just once over his shoulder before vanishing from sight.

Luc's shadow! The stealth of that man was unbelievable. The relationship had always puzzled him, but there were some things which should never be asked. How would his closeness to Luc be affected now that Alexandrine was to take first place in his life? It was none of his business. Nor was she! Luc would surely within a very short time find out for himself the high price he must pay for his well-intentioned but foolish gesture.

Alain Ratan awoke in the early hours of the morning. He had finished the bottle of wine and fallen asleep, still dressed, on the bed. With a grimace he clambered to his feet and went to the marble wash-stand to splash cold water on his face and erase the dream that had awakened him. He had been with her—Alexandrine! She had been not in the arms of her husband—but in *his*!

CHAPTER TWO

ALEXANDRINE AWOKE to the sound of voices coming from the sitting-room next door. She lay for a moment not knowing quite where she was and then, as memory returned, and with it the promise she had made herself before falling asleep, she sat up and reached for her robe. She would not be intimidated by Paul Boussières, or humiliated by Alain Ratan—thank goodness, at least he would have quitted the house by now!—one fewer egotistical man to deal with—for *she* was mistress here now and she would not allow herself to forget it, or anyone to take from her the great sense of pride she felt as she once more surveyed her surroundings.

Warm autumn sunshine was flooding into the room through the large french windows that opened on to wrought-iron balconies overlooking the garden. Her bare feet sank into the thick oriental carpet covering most of the floor as she went to open one and allow a pleasant breeze to disperse the stuffiness. Below, a gardener was diligently weeding between the fading summer blooms that had flourished early in the strong sun and preparing new ground alongside. A high wall encircled the garden and the house itself, so high that she could scarcely see over the top. From beyond came the sound of horses and carriages clattering over the cobblestones, the cry of a fruit-vendor plying his wares. Excitement gripped her, and a feverish desire to explore beyond those walls, to see for herself what attracted people to the city like moths to a candle-flame.

'So you are awake at last, my dear. I was beginning to think you might sleep the whole day through!' Luc's amused tones from the doorway brought her wheeling about. 'I hope it all looks different to you this beautiful morning,' he added meaningfully, and Alexandrine ran to him and kissed him warmly on both cheeks.

'Yes, it is a lovely day, isn't it? When can we go out? You did promise to show me Paris. I want to see everything, Luc.' In her eagerness she forgot how difficult it had been to address him thus, and his smile grew at the effervescence bubbling over from her.

'Gently, my dear, you have nothing suitable to wear yet. There is much to be done before I can present you to the outside world again.'

'Oh—of course.' Alexandrine drew back, immediate disappointment registering on her young face. 'You will not want to be ashamed of me in front of your friends.'

'Your spirit is returning—good! Now you are more like the Alexandrine I used to know.'

'Then I shall change immediately,' she declared, remembering how her mother had had cause many times to reprove her for her lack of ladylike finesse. Even the convent had not instilled that in her—not deep down in her heart where it mattered. 'I shall be demure and quiet, offering no conversation until I am asked. I shall smile at your friends.'

'Good God, I hope not!' Luc declared, stifling laughter, and she stared at him in amazement. Taking her hand, he led her out into the other room. Her eyes widened at the sight of the two enormous leather brass-bound chests that stood in the centre, the lids thrown back to reveal their contents. Beside them were several bolts of the finest damask she had ever seen, and cloth of gold, velvets and silk. 'Sit down, child, it's time we talked,' he said, giving her no chance to examine them. 'Never, I repeat never, smile at a strange man at Versailles, or, married or not, he will consider it an invitation to climb into his bed. You will see what I mean when I take you on a tour of the city.'

'No! If it is so wicked, I don't want to see it!'

'You must. It is the first and most important lesson you must learn. Trust no one, however pleasant they might seem, however grand their names. Many faces are worn abroad in this city to hide a multitude of sins.'

'Don't spoil this wonderful time for me, Luc,' Alexandrine protested, horrified by his words. 'I want you to be so proud of me, but I am afraid, now, that I *shall* embarrass you. I *am* a country girl. Paul was right. I shall never be a true lady.'

'My dear, I am too old to be embarrassed, and the mistakes of the innocent such as you make me realise that there is still beauty and innocence in the world as yet untouched by the ugliness of reality. I shall always try to protect you from it.'

'You make the world sound such a terrible place! Can you see no beauty in each day?'

'Only when I look at you. My days are filled with darkness, memories, fears and horrors. No, not all of them. Not now, thanks to you.'

'I wish Paul felt the same as you do. Have—Have you spoken to him this morning?' she asked hesitantly, not understanding the strangeness of his words.

'My son—out of bed before noon?' Luc gave a dry chuckle, but she saw there was no amusement in the brown eyes. 'He will stay there until late afternoon and then no doubt go out gambling with his friends. He is an indolent young fool. I despair of him!'

'I suppose I should try and understand. It must be very humiliating to be presented with a stepmother younger than yourself,' Alexandrine said quietly. 'And, I promise, I shall try—but I fear he will never accept me.' The way his eyes had roved over her, stripping her of clothes! Barely did she supress a shudder of distaste.

'Then he can live elsewhere,' her husband returned with a shrug of his shoulders.

'But he is your son!' One wrong word, she suspected, and Paul Boussières would be thrown out of the house. Was that what she wanted?

'And you are my wife. It is you, and only you, that I care about. You will give me what no woman ever has before.'

'What is that?' The time has come when he is going to tell me he has been patient long enough, Alexandrine thought, steeling herself for the words. What no woman had ever given him before? But he already had a son!

'Devotion. Loyalty. I demand these things of you, Alexandrine.' From the table beside him, Luc picked up a heavy book embossed with gold letters. She saw it was a Bible, and a puzzled look crept into her eyes. Was she expected to swear her loyalty, her devotion, upon that book?

'There is no need for that. Are you so unsure of me? Why then did you marry me?'

'Because you are my salvation. No—there is no need for this.' He placed the Bible back on the table and turned again to her. 'It will be enough to hear the words from your own lips without that. Say them, Alexandrine. Tell me you will be faithful to me until the day I die. It will not be too long, after all . . . and then you will be a very rich widow, able to choose any man who takes your fancy. Until that day, I shall give you anything you desire. In return, I ask only that no other man touches you.'

'None shall, save for my husband.' Alexandrine had paled considerably. It was not a strange request, although she had never thought of him as a jealous man, but the words had been uttered with such vehemence. Did he really believe she would allow her head to be turned by another? That she was too young, too immature, to take her marriage vows seriously? 'You do me an injustice, Luc, to believe I would betray you. I am your wife. We are pledged to each other until death. I—I do not love you, you know that; but I shall pray that comes in time. But I am fond of you. I always shall be . . . and I shall be true. I swear it. None but you shall touch me.'

'Not even I, my dear. I am content to have you as my wife, and to know you are mine.' The shattering answer left her speechless for several minutes. Luc stood watching her in silence, unable to put into words what he felt at her wretched expression. There was so much he could not tell her. He did not want her to turn and flee from him in terror, to watch him as the days passed with fear in her eyes. God had been kind to him for the short while he had left. Nothing, no one, would take it from him.

'What—What are you saying?' Alexandrine managed to gasp, her voice barely audible. Suddenly the day was far from beautiful.

'Perhaps I have not made it clear to you, child. I want to take care of you now that you are alone in the world. Nothing more do I expect from you except that which you have just promised. Poor Alexandrine! Now I

understand the question that has been in those lovely
eyes of late. I shall not force myself upon you.'

'But—But that is not fair...' she was beginning to
stutter again, unable to comprehend fully what he was
saying. A wife, yet not a wife? Never to have him touch
her. To look pretty, to behave like a lady and be given
everything she desired, but to give nothing in return?
'How can you not want...? I mean, I cannot accept
anything from you unless you take what is yours by
right.'

'On the contrary, I shall know contentment.' Luc bent
and squeezed one slender arm. 'Contentment at my age
is very important. You have given that to me. You are
here with me...mine...'

She gasped as his thin fingers, which looked so frail,
bit into her skin with unexpected strength.

'Am I disturbing anything?'

She knew the voice at once—that low, almost mocking
voice that had insulted her the night before, and she sat
with head downbent as Alain Ratan advanced into the
room. She had thought him long gone!

'Of course not, Alain. Come in. I was expecting you
a little later, but no matter.' Luc released Alexandrine
and swung round to greet the newcomer, his lined face
immediately creasing into a welcoming smile. 'How is
the head this morning?'

'Better for the early ride I had through the Bois. I'm
afraid I smell of horses. Perhaps you would prefer me
to come back later?'

'Nonsense! I've smelt worse than you at court, and
Alexandrine was raised in the country. If she can stand
you, I can. Pour us some wine and then let's get down
to business. I need your keen eye and common sense or
I might be inclined to go too quickly with my little flower.
Your eyes will see her differently.'

Indeed they did, Alexandrine thought, gathering sufficient courage to lift her head. Alain's gaze was full
upon her as he advanced to where she sat and kissed
one ringless hand. A gesture which meant nothing to
him, she suspected, hoping Luc did not notice the haste
in which she pulled it free. Were they here to discuss her,
the two of them?

'This afternoon a dressmaker, one of the best in Paris, Madame Heloise, will come to the house to take your measurements. She will furnish you with a new wardrobe, Alexandrine, and all that goes with it. There is no need for you to take a step outside the house until you are ready for court. Madame has made gowns for the King's mistress herself,' Luc added, as he beckoned Alexandrine to join him beside the open trunks. 'The contents of these are for your personal use. Anything you do not require will be packed away again and returned to the attic. Later, I shall show you over the house and you shall pick any extra pieces of furniture to make this apartment more comfortable. Now, to business. With your colouring, let me see...'

He bent to examine a bolt of exquisite white damask, threaded with gold in the pattern of a huge peacock with a magnificent flowing tail. Alexandrine could not drag her eyes away from the contents of the two trunks. Silver and plate of every size and description. Ornate hanging lamps of some strange design which made her think they had come from one of her husband's many trips abroad. Tapestries and carved wooden trinket-boxes, some inlaid with precious stones or ivory. Tall-stemmed Venetian glasses that looked so delicate she was afraid to reach down and pick one up, even though her fingers itched to do so. All this was hers! And so much beneath the items she could see...more treasures for her alone! How could he lavish such wealth on her and ask nothing in return?

'Come here, child.' Obediently she obeyed and stood before him while he laid first the white damask against her and then a heavy, deep green velvet. A nod of satisfaction for both materials, and then a questioning glance in Alain's direction.

'The green suits her best with such fair colouring,' was his candid comment from where he lounged on a sofa. 'The white for a court occasion, perhaps, when she has more colour in those pale cheeks.'

'My sentiments exactly. What about the red?'

'Too harsh. Try the blue. No, not the velvet, something softer...the silk. Trail it a little...Perfect. Perfect!'

Alexandrine felt her cheeks begin to burn as the comments continued back and forth. At no time was she allowed to interrupt with her own opinion, and she realised that she was not to have one of her own—on anything! The colour and styles of gowns were discussed. Accessories, shoes, how her hair should be worn. She began to wish the floor would open and swallow her up. Luc's interest seemed so remote, almost mechanical, as though he were dressing a dummy. Not so that of Alain Ratan! She was aware of his eyes on her at every moment, as if he were waiting for her to break out into a fit of temper over the way the two men were discussing her. Somehow her tongue remained still, her lips pressed tightly together, as she was turned this way and that until Luc was satisfied with his inspection.

'Madame is bringing a few spare dresses to tide you over until your new wardrobe is ready,' Luc said, drawing back from her at last to pick up his glass of wine. 'Tomorrow—yes, tomorrow—we shall take the air in the carriage for an hour or so. Would you like that?'

'Very much. If you do not think it too soon.' Alexandrine could not keep the frostiness from her tone, and one furry eyebrow was arched at her tone.

'This is for your own good, child, remember that. There are many who would destroy me... To face them I have to be strong. As you will be when I have done with you. But we must do something with that hair.'

'No!' He turned in some surprise at the rapid answer from Alain. 'Don't touch it. Soon it will grow, and for any special occasion she can wear a wig. But there is a simplicity about her, Luc, a naïve charm that must not be altered. See how those unruly curls accentuate her high cheekbones. Properly dressed, it could be quite effective. How many women can wear their hair unadorned?'

'Why, Alain, there is a touch of romance left in your soul, after all!' Luc chuckled. 'That woman did not rip out every morsel of gentleness. There is hope for you yet.'

'Save the pretty words for your wife.' Alain came off the sofa like a mountain cat uncurling himself after a sleep, and stretched lithe muscles. 'If you are going to try and save my soul again, I'm going to leave. Madame la Marquise, I hope none of my observations has unduly embarrassed you?' The glittering green eyes were laughing at her as he touched her fingers to his lips. Hers in return were like flinty daggers.

'You have been most kind—and patient, monsieur. I hope we have not kept you from anything important.'

'No. I have ridden this morning, and horses are the only things of interest to me these days. More dependable and less treacherous than the human animal,' Alain remarked, stepping back. Were his words for me or for Luc? Alexandrine wondered as he left them. And who was the woman her husband had mentioned? A wife? Mistress? He would have many of the latter, she decided, no matter what he said to the contrary. He was too handsome to be without a woman, and the way he looked at her told her that, contrary to his scornful words, he was still vulnerable. Why else had he kissed her? Why had he held her hand so tightly, daring her to pull away as she had done when he first joined them? It was as if he was playing some game with her...

'Don't mind Alain, my dear. He suffered rather an unfortunate experience some years back and it has scarred him deeply.' Luc's attention was once more on the contents of the trunks. 'If you care to go through these now, I shall get Pierre to arrange them, and then you shall see the rest of the house.'

The house! How she had resented it when first she stepped foot over the threshold, as she believed it resented her intrusion beneath its roof, but how could she have been so wrong. It was a lonely house, an empty shell only. Little remained of the magnificence Luc spoke of as he led her through it. I shall bring it back to life, Alexandrine vowed, as she went from one shuttered room to the next on the upstairs floors. So many unused, closed for years, with the furniture left to gather dust. So many memories for Luc. Although he said very little, she watched him carefully and saw how his eyes lingered on certain objects: a brass Moorish hanging lamp with coloured glass panels of green and pale pink and yellow, an enormous Persian rug, and small trinkets suspended from the walls or on some huge cabinet gathering more dust.

'Well, my dear?' When they returned to her apartment again, he turned to her enquiringly. 'What do you think of this old mausoleum now?'

Her first description of the place, but not now! Now, she had a mounting desire to make this the most frequented place in Paris. Perhaps she could find a way to repay his kindness and generosity—his faith in her. 'It needs a woman's touch.'

'Indeed! And how exactly do you intend to transform this into something worth while? And for what reason? I must admit that the idea appeals to me.'

'Let me,' she pleaded. 'It is my duty, as your wife, to make this a home for you—for us both.'

'A duty? I want you to enjoy life, Alexandrine. I want to enjoy the sound of your laughter, the pleasure in your eyes when I give you a new jewel or you choose a new gown. Don't you understand? Your pleasures in life will be mine. If I had wanted a housekeeper, I could have hired one.'

'Instead, you bought yourself a young wife.' Alexandrine could have bitten off her tongue at the thoughtless remark. Luc's lined face immediately hardened and a look crept into his eyes which momentarily frightened her. Instantly she was contrite, seeking to undo the harm she had unwittingly wrought.

She felt him tense as she laid a hand on his arm, but did not remove it. It was as if her touch was somehow repulsive to him. Or is he fighting a natural inclination to make me his true wife? she wondered, as she gazed into his closed face and sensed an inner disquiet in him which she did not understand.

'Luc, my husband—for that is what you are to the world, no matter what is between us here in this house.' His lips tightened at the comment, but he made no reply. 'Do you know how happy it would make me to turn this house into a true home for you? *Our* home? You have travelled to so many different shores and returned with such wonderful treasures, which you now share with me. Let me share something with you—my pride, my joy at what you have given me. Let me share all of myself with you. Take from me what you will so long as you too are happy. A smile, a kind word, anything. I shall deny you nothing. That is as it should be. You brought me back to life, and now you treat me as a queen. I am not, and the role you have thrust upon me is a little frightening. But I have my mother's courage and my father's stubbornness. Oh, Luc, let me bring this old house back to life again! You say you have many enemies, but let this place admit friends. You have so much to offer. You are so clever, so worldly.'

'Enough, child, or my head will begin to swell! How can you want to spend your days renovating this old graveyard?'

'Because it will give me pleasure and satisfaction, as you gained pleasure this morning from wanting me to look like a lady so that you will be proud of me. I promise I shall make you proud of me. I shall give a ball such as this house has never known. And we shall receive your friends together. All will see that the Marquise de Mezière and her husband are happy and will not be parted . . . no matter how handsome the young man,' she added with a cheeky smile. 'No matter how beautiful the woman!'

'Alexandrine, child, I am so—blind! I am and always shall be proud of you. Never think otherwise. What I have done has been for your own protection. You will have to hold your own against women who would claw out your eyes because your natural beauty outshines their false fronts. And men who would use you. You do not know what the world is like!'

'I am not a child any longer. I admit I have learned only from the convent Sisters, but—but I am no fool. Luc, your son looked at me as if I was something he might encounter in the street, as did his friends. As did the Duc de Belaincourt.'

'Alain? You have some complaint against him?' Luc's tone was suddenly sharp, and she sensed more anger here than against his own son.

'No, not exactly.' Why did she not confess her fear of this man and the way he had made her feel when he kissed her? How could she? It was obvious that he was a close friend of both Paul and Luc. 'I—I found it disturbing, even embarrassing, to be stared at so intimately by a perfect stranger.'

'You will discover in time that Alain is totally impervious to womanly wiles, even yours, and I say this not unkindly, for I know you will never encourage him after the warning I have given you. Of all people, I would trust you with him. He understands that my wife is out of reach, and I am hoping that he will convey the message elsewhere. One day the fates will once again bestow their favours on that unhappy young man.'

'Do you believe only in fate—not in God?' Alexandrine asked, aghast, having been brought up in the most strict household.

'Is there a difference, my dear? After all, who has seen the faces of any of them?' Luc returned with a casual shrug of his shoulders.

After he had left, Alexandrine sat down to await the arrival of Madame Heloise, her mind in turmoil. Luc had not refused her request to be allowed to do as she wished with the house. She would not fail him. Her success would bring society to them so that they could see her and accept her on her own territory. Then, and only then, she told herself, would she have the necessary confidence to allow herself to be presented at court.

But as to trusting herself with Alain Ratan! Luc might think him trustworthy, but she never would. He was the last man on earth she would want to be alone with!

'Such a tiny waist! Madame, you are a treasure. Every seamstress in Paris dreams of outfitting such a perfect figure. I shall have the first gown ready in a week, and my girls shall work night and day on the remainder of the wardrobe. Such a figure... how it will be admired!'

Alexandrine sat dreaming in bed the next morning, remembering how Madame Heloise had flattered and praised the body she herself considered too thin and without the necessary undulating curves that made a woman look like a woman. *She* could find no fault with the flat stomach, the softly rounded breasts or the lithe hips and the long legs as she stepped out of her petticoats. She was no beauty, yet the woman had made her feel so attractive and sure of herself and of her ability to wear the clothes being made with style and expertise. She had believed it then, but now in the light of another day she was wondering whether Luc had ordered her to be so pleasant and complimentary. Would he do such a thing to bolster her confidence? What am I to Luc Boussières? she wondered. Certainly not an object of pleasure, for he had made it quite plain that he had no intention of making her his wife—in that way. Had he a satisfactory mistress who made it unnecessary? If so, why had he taken Alexandrine from her country home and brought her to Paris? Why did he make her feel as if she were the most important person in his life—even though he did not want her in his bed?

Breakfast was brought to her as she was about to rise. Shall I ever get used to being pampered? she wondered as she relaxed amid the pillows fluffed up behind her back and drank apple juice and then attacked the coddled eggs with relish. Her appetite belonged to the country. Had she been there now, she would have been out of bed and about her daily duties for at least three hours. Her mother was not one to allow her daughters to linger in bed and daydream.

But what were her duties now? To lie abed until nearly noon? To rise and preen herself before a mirror until the late afternoon, when she would take tea with her husband? Then what? The opera? The court? A bal masqué? All these things made her pulse quicken with excitement, for she had never indulged in any of them, but the day would be so long! She was not accustomed to being idle. The house would be her salvation! She would do as she had promised Luc. She would turn it into the most elegant mansion in Paris and make all his friends welcome—and his enemies could remain in the background and grind their teeth like the idiots they were! How could anyone not like Luc? He was the gentlest of creatures—so considerate and accommodating. And so interesting. His enemies, such as they were, must be jealous, she decided as she rose and rang for the maid to come and help her with her toilette. It was an instinctive act, and after she had rung the bell she wondered at the ease with which she had slipped into her new role.

Almost instantly, the pale, glittering green eyes of Alain Ratan rose in her mind. He had expected her to assume this new role with panache! He, despite all his fine words and smiles, regarded her in the same low light as Paul Boussières. How right Luc had been in his warning! She must never smile at a man, no matter how genial he appeared to be. She was the Marquise de Mezière—and proud of it! A little awed, if not frightened, but she had been well schooled, and whatever he wanted from her—then, as his wife, she would comply.

The house was situated in the Place des Vosges, an elegant square built in the reign of Henry IV, which housed many an aristocratic family. Alexandrine was aware of people stopping to stare at their carriage that afternoon, as, true to his word, her husband took her on a short—a very short—excursion in the brilliant sunshine. Luc acknowledged a few people but spoke to none, she noticed, and most were ignored. A look directed at her told her that she was to follow his example. When he considered anyone worth introducing, he would do so, she mused.

After less than an hour the carriage returned to the house, where Madame Heloise and her bevy of young chattering seamstresses were waiting to give her fittings. When they departed, she found herself in possession of a dozen pairs of assorted shoes, petticoats, and night attire so flimsy that it took her breath away, coloured stockings and jewelled garters, the like of which she had never seen before.

'Madame Heloise has promised to have you ready for me in a week, my dear,' Luc declared as they sat at the evening meal. 'I trust you are pleased with her efforts so far?'

She was aware of the eyes of Alain Ratan flicking to where she sat as she raised her head to answer her husband. His presence annoyed her—more than that, it inhibited her. She wondered if Luc ever noticed how sharp her tongue became whenever this man was near. She had prayed for his early departure from the house so that she could relax and enjoy the wonderful days opening up before her, but he had taken his time.

'When you told me she had such high connections at court, I expected her to be a most pompous person, full of her own grandeur, but she is not like that at all,' she replied. 'She has been most helpful to me in every way. I hope you will be satisfied with what she has produced for me, Luc, for I most certainly am. I could not be more so.'

'I am pleased to hear it. At the end of this month there is a court function at Versailles—some reception for a foreign ambassador. Would you like to go? I have no doubt that you will be more than ready by then.'

His last words momentarily dulled Alexandrine's elation. Ready to be shown off to his friends, to be stared at and discussed behind her back? To be ogled at, speculated about and generally torn to pieces. And then, recalling the exquisite ball-gown being made for her, confidence surged through her like wildfire. Let them do their worst! She would look as good as any of the women at Versailles. She would wear the emeralds Luc had given her. No, the pearls would go better with the rich creamy satin and lace or perhaps the blood-red rubies...

'Yes, I would like that very much,' she answered with shining eyes. He was considering her frankly, and she knew by the smile which touched his lips that he was pleased with her appearance. The ill-shorn fair hair had been retrimmed and was a mass of tiny curls, with several wisping across her forehead and about her ears, where diamonds glittered. Her skin was perfumed and softened by one of the many sultry aromatic oils that Luc had brought with him from the East, her nails carefully manicured, the long, slender fingers now adorned with a diamond ring, to match those in her ears, and a huge ruby set in gold.

She wore no other jewellery. She did not need it to grace such petal-soft, milk-white skin, Alain thought, watching her from beneath lowered lids. Every day she was growing more beautiful—and more sure of herself under Luc's guidance. She rarely stammered now when she spoke, and was beginning to treat him—whenever her husband was not about, anyway—with great contempt. She was still afraid he would tell Luc of that kiss

and thus spoil her luxurious existence. But he wondered
if the news would even penetrate Luc's love-sodden
brain. The man was indeed infatuated, Alain saw. He
could not take his eyes from her whenever she was in
the room. For not one day, since they arrived at the
house, had they been apart. He did not like what he saw.
Luc had been his friend for several years and was the
only person to whom he had ever opened his heart. He
did not like this child-woman who had invaded their relationship and could only wreak havoc on an old, vulnerable man. A good man, despite the many ugly
rumours that often circulated about him and his strange
companion the Moor.

'Well, Alain, what do you think of her now?' Luc
asked when Alexandrine had excused herself and left the
room. Every day she had spent a few hours in one of
the upstairs rooms, instructing the servants on how it
should be refurnished or redecorated. When they were
ready, she had made up her mind to have a ball. That—
not Versailles, although the prospect of the forthcoming
event had aroused excitement in her—would establish
her truly as the Marquise de Mezière.

'A transformation! You are to be congratulated. She
is no longer the shy, awkward little thing you brought
here a month ago.'

'Something in your tone tells me that you do not
altogether approve.' Luc raised a speculative eyebrow in
his friend's direction. 'Speak frankly—you always do.'

'For myself, I am delighted with your good fortune,'
Alain replied truthfully. 'But you must accept that there
are others who are not, and who will never, never, accept
her.'

'Paul? Yes, I do accept that he will forever be a thorn
in my side. There are times when I think I would be
doing that young man a favour if I had him bound and
tossed into the Seine,' Luc said, a harsh note creeping
into his voice. How long before his son's defiance became
more? Before his threats became reality? 'I am aware of
the ugly rumours he has been spreading. I am not without
my friends,' he added, as Alain looked down the table
at him. Luc had not left the house except for the one
carriage ride with Alexandrine, and there had been no

other visitors apart from himself. He had returned to his own house at Belaincourt, overlooking the Seine, the week before, but at Luc's insistence he still visited the house several times a week. Much to Alexandrine's chagrin, he surmised. How his presence must offend her!

'And Selim is an excellent spy,' Alain murmured, and his words brought a broad smile to the other's face.

'As you say, a most excellent spy. He is my eyes and my ears—and the most able physician I shall ever encounter upon this earth. Without him, I would have been dead long ago.' He broke off quickly as if he had said too much, and rose from the table to indicate that the conversation was at an end.

An odd fellow, Alain thought as they parted, and he watched Luc ascend the stairs to his room—noting how Selim was at the top of them, waiting as always for his lord and master—given to sudden, temperamental moods that made him disliked in many circles. He went from a charming, intelligent man able to converse on any subject under the sun to a rude, curt egoist who revelled in provoking a quarrel. Perhaps, to a man who had travelled to so many places and seen so much of life elsewhere, it was a way of alleviating the terrible boredom he must feel amid the bewigged, powdered popinjays who infested the court—and the harlots who called themselves ladies, whose morals were worse that those of the lowest street-woman. Alain's shoulders lifted in a silent shrug of acceptance at his friend's often confusing behaviour. He was his friend, and nothing as far as he was concerned would ever change that. Not the wagging tongues, or Paul's cruel remarks about his aged, senile father, or the arrival of a country girl bent on becoming someone at court.

Senile! He laughed aloud as he swung himself on to the back of his waiting horse, and the groom who handed him the reins looked at him as if he had partaken of too much wine. Luc—senile? Not with that she-cat in his bed! That one had long claws. He could feel them itching to get at his own cheeks whenever they were together. She was a challenge to him, a challenge he could not ignore. Luc might never be interested to learn the truth about her, but Alain needed desperately to know, to satisfy his own suspicions and prove to himself that she was no better than any other pretty face who had attracted his attention. And she had done that! Not once had he been able to put from his mind the memory of that slender white body as she stood beside the bath—the proud uplifted breasts, so young, seemingly so virginal. Or the way she had tried to cover herself modestly from his gaze. It had worked! She *had* aroused his interest more with her ploy of innocence. And the taste of her lips, sweet like honey, before she had wrenched them away. Had he been mistaken in believing for a moment—one fraction of a instant—that they had parted willingly beneath his—answered him?

Luc did not pay his usual morning visit to Alexandrine's room the following day, nor did he appear after she had risen and dressed and spent her hour or two upstairs with the servants. Mystified, she found herself beginning to grow anxious as the day progressed and there was no sign of him. Not once, since she had come to the house, had he failed to appear, as she was sitting up in bed, to sit in a chair beside her and discuss what she would be doing that day, or to bring her some little present. Sometimes he would stay for an hour or more, and on those occasions she began to find conversation rather difficult. When all else had been discussed, he would lapse into a strange silence and simply look at her. It was as if he drifted off into another world, she had thought the last time it had happened only a few days earlier, and the one in which she dwelt was shut out. Then, with the same suddenness as he had sunk into the trance-like state, he would come out of it and, with an abruptness she found quite startling, would get to his feet and leave her, often without another word.

The servants assured her that the master had not gone out and was still in his room, and so, that afternoon, she made her way to Luc's apartments on the upper floor. She had been there only once before, on the day he had shown her over the house, and even then she had not entered his private domain. He had merely pointed it out without issuing an invitation to enter. No sooner had she knocked, than the door was opened by Selim.

The room beyond was dark, for the curtains were closed against the pleasant autumn day. It reminded her of her own room at home, when she had first recovered her senses again. A sick-room...illness...death! Was her husband ill?

'Can I do anything for madame?' The Moor made no attempt to move aside, even though she stepped forward to indicate that she wished to enter. A surge of colour rose in her cheeks at his offhand tone. Not exactly disrespectful, but denoting that he possessed an authority which over-ruled hers—in this quarter.

'Yes, Selim, I wish to speak with my husband. Please allow me to enter,' she returned stiffly. It was time to rid herself of this unreasonable obsession about this man. He was a servant and, as such, should do as he was bid. She was mistress here!

'The Marquis does not wish to be disturbed. He is indisposed. Perhaps tomorrow he will send for you, madame.'

Send for her? He made *her* feel the servant! The bright spots of anger burning in her cheeks deepened. She opened her mouth to unloose a tirade, but before she could utter one word, the door was closed in her face and she heard the bolt being distinctly, deliberately thrust home on the other side. He had locked her out! Her clenched fist rose to hammer on the wooden panels, and then, as a maid passed, her arms full of clean linen, Alexandrine realised how undignified it would be for her to have to demand entrance to her husband's rooms. Luc's illness was sudden—and strange—but there was much that she was finding strange and rather bewildering about him.

For the remainder of the day she occupied herself with planning the ball which was to be Luc's surprise, but she did not know who to invite. Paul would know, of course, but she did not want to spend any length of time closeted alone with him, even to obtain such important information. Every moment he was near was odious to her. His comments still greatly upset her although she outwardly ignored them, knowing that Luc needed only the slightest excuse to send his son packing from the house. So she bore his crudity in silence, noting how

careful he was to be at least polite in the presence of his
father. But, out of earshot... How that viperish tongue
lashed her, with accusations so vile that she often cried
herself to sleep at night, wondering how she would ever
face the next day with him still beneath Luc's roof.

She was not allowed entrance to her husband's room
the following day, or on the third day, when she presented herself. Selim was adamant that Luc had issued
instructions not to be disturbed. No one, save the Moor,
was to attend him. He even went down to the kitchens
to prepare special food for his patient.

'What have we here! Will you look at this, Alain? My
poor father lies sick in his bed, and where is his devoted
wife? About to go out in her carriage.'

It was Alexandrine's unfortunate luck to encounter
Paul just returning home late that morning. From the
untidy state of his clothes and the way he reeled towards
the staircase, where she had halted in dismay at the sight
of him, it was clear that he had spent another night gambling or carousing with his wild friends. Beside him,
Alain Ratan looked as clear-eyed and alert as though he
had slept in his bed.

'Madame Heloise is also ill,' she returned icily. 'She
cannot come to give me the last of my fittings, therefore
I am going to her.'

'And leaving my father to languish in his sick-bed
alone? Shame on you! What do you think of a woman
who deserts her husband when he needs her, Alain?' He
wheeled on his companion, whose eyes were still avidly
fixed on the slight figure clutching the banister rail, and
gave a drunken laugh. 'Yes, she does catch the eye now,
doesn't she? It is amazing what good clothes can do.'

Alexandrine felt herself grow cold as Paul advanced
up the stairs to where she stood and his gaze raked her
from head to toe. A perfumed handkerchief was flicked
spitefully at her bare shoulders, as with another laugh
he proceeded past her to his room.

'He's drunk,' Alain said quietly, as she quickly joined
him. 'And a bad loser. This is the fourth night in a row
he's had bad luck. He owes money to half of Paris.'

'And you? What kind of luck did you have?' she enquired, wondering how two men of such differing
characters could be friends.

'I make my own luck, Madame la Marquise. How is
Luc this morning? I hope he regains his health soon, for
I grow bored with playing nursemaid to his idiot son.
Didn't you know he had asked me?' he added, prompted
by the look of surprise on Alexandrine's face.

'I—I have not seen him for several days...since he
became ill. I...Selim thinks it best I do not go near him
for fear the sickness is contagious,' she answered, and
knew by the gleam which sprang into those pale panther's
eyes that the lie did not deceive him.

Once again his gaze returned to her appearance,
studying it with a frankness that was embarrassing, but
somehow exciting. Did he think she had made progress?
After all, he had sat in judgement of what colours suited
her, what materials would best grace her complexion,
what designs would do full justice to her still rather thin
figure. What was she thinking of to wonder such a thing?
It mattered not what *he* thought—or Paul!

Yet she could not help wondering what he thought of
her pale blue satin gown with its pretty fichu of Brussels
lace and the divided skirt that fell gracefully apart to
reveal rows and rows of more frothy lace. Of the wide-
brimmed straw hat now so fashionable, set upon her fair
curls and tied beneath her chin with pale blue ribbons.
Of the matching leather shoes upon her feet, the sapphires at her throat and encircling a slender wrist. Never
had she owned anything so grand, and this was only one
of the gowns that had been quickly made to tide her
over until her proper wardrobe was completed. When
she thought of what was to come...

And that reminded her of the forthcoming ball. Here
was the very man to help her, but dared she ask him,
lest he misconstrue her motives? He had made it horribly clear that he considered her in the same light as
Paul. Would a favour need to be repaid? And what would
he ask? Luc had made her afraid to even smile at a man,
let alone ask for his help.

'Monsieur, I need the assistance of someone who is Luc's friend,' she began, and immediately had Alain's full attention. So much so that she quickly sought to rectify what she suspected had sprung into his mind. 'I intend to give a ball here in a few weeks, as a surprise for my husband, but I confess that I have no idea whom to invite. I have not yet met any of his friends, and I would not like to include anyone he might find offensive.'

'That would include most of Paris and leave few agreeable people to invite,' Alain returned. He had been expecting a request to join her for her excursion to the dressmaker, knowing that as Luc's friend he would be above suspicion as her companion, but certainly not this. A ball! What a clever little thing she was! A perfect way to integrate herself with those who counted. Paul's rumours and half-finished stories of his father's young wife had everyone who knew Luc agog with anticipation. There were some, believing what they had been told of the country girl who had trapped an old, sick, feeble-minded man into marriage, who would come to inspect her and hope she would grow quickly bored with the life she had chosen for herself—as so many wives did. His own had been no exception.

'Of course, if you are too busy, I shall understand.' Alexandrine saw the look that darted across his face and sensed that something had disturbed him, but was at a loss to understand what.

'How could I not agree to such a small request? You shall have your list this evening. We can go over it together so that you are acquainted with your guests before you meet them face to face. This will be quite an undertaking, you understand? For you, I mean. Do you think you are ready?'

'I want to do something for Luc,' Alexandrine said, then broke off when she realised that to explain her reasons she must divulge the true state of their marriage. That she would never do—to anyone! 'And I also hope that when they all see for themselves that I am just an ordinary person in love with her husband, perhaps Paul's wicked lies will go unheeded.'

By the end of the evening, you will have every man eating out of your hand, Alain thought, as he escorted her out to the waiting carriage. Exactly as you have planned . . . and that will be only the beginning!

To her surprise, Alain did not close the door after she had entered, but vaulted nimbly inside also and settled himself into the seat opposite before ordering the driver to move off.

'What do you think you are doing? Stop the carriage immediately and leave! How dare you presume that I am in need of company,' she gasped.

A smile flitted across the dark features, but his voice was quite hard and his reply took her breath away with its audacity. 'I have been appointed as Paul's watchdog, so I can do no less for you, surely, as Luc's wife. It is unconceivable that you be allowed to wander unchaperoned about Paris. I am simply offering you my protection, madame, as your husband's friend. Nothing more.'

'My reputation is unlikely to be enhanced if I am seen in your company,' Alexandrine retorted, aghast that she was helpless to prevent him accompanying her. The only way to do so would be to stop the carriage and get one of the lackeys riding behind to eject him forcibly into the street. What gossip that would cause, if it could be done! She very much doubted if he would allow it. 'Your reputation is not unknown to me, Monsieur le Duc.'

'Oh dear, have I injured your womanly pride?' Alain chuckled. 'Believe me, madame, you hold no interest for me. It suits me to play the gentleman this afternoon, so you can rest easy in your mind. There will be others soon enough to bolster your vanity and make you believe you are something you are not.'

Easing himself back in his seat, he folded his arms across his chest and closed his eyes, not opening them again until they reached the house of Madame Heloise half an hour later. Alexandrine spent that time fighting to regain her shattered composure. Paul had done his evil work well! She had been tried and judged before she had attended her first function. Suddenly Versailles, and the glittering occasion she had allowed to excite her, became an ordeal. Everyone would look at her, as Alain Ratan did, with contempt and suspicion. They would echo his words: 'There will be others soon enough to bolster your vanity...' They would be as blind and prejudiced against her as he was!

CHAPTER THREE

NOT ONCE during the journey did Alain open his eyes and Alexandrine felt that it was a relief not to have those pale glittering green eyes watching her, unnerving her with their scrutiny. For a long while she concentrated her gaze on the streets they travelled along so that she would not look at him, but always, somehow, her eyes were drawn back to the silent man reclining opposite.

He was as immaculately dressed as always in a coat of dark green velvet and white breeches. An abundance of lace at his throat accentuated the extreme darkness of his skin and she remembered Luc telling her how, since his wife's death, he spent most of the year on his country estate in Belaincourt, with his horses. He had grown embittered since that loss, she reasoned, and suspected every woman he encountered of being as faithless as his beautiful wife. But it was nothing to do with her and she must not allow his unreasonable attitude to ruin the elation she had been experiencing these past few days.

She had acquired a new confidence thanks to Luc's attentions and she must maintain it at all costs. Gossip could harm her only if she allowed it to enter into her home, and that she would not do. There, all would be peace and tranquillity. In the weeks and months ahead she would grow even closer to her husband, learn to know his likes and dislikes, his weaknesses, his hopes for the future, and what they would share would be beyond the hurtful remarks of anyone.

How black his hair is, she thought, her eyes dwelling on the raven tendrils curling above the collar of Alain's coat. One had fallen over his forehead and she was seized with a silly impulse to lean forward and brush it back. His hands were strong, with long fingers and well manicured nails, but they were not the hands of a man unaccustomed to manual labour, for several small scars criss-crossed the back of one and another travelled almost the whole length of one little finger. That curl fascinated her. It made his features look almost boyish as it curled above a black eyebrow.

No sooner had the carriage come to a halt than his eyes were open, catching her completely unawares. Abashed that her scrutiny might have been noticed, she said coldly, 'You add insult to injury, monsieur. Not only am I forced to endure your company, but you are rude enough to fall asleep and deprive me of some semblance of conversation.'

'I thought you might wish to evaluate my worth in silence,' Alain murmured. 'Save the sharp tongue for those who come after me and will not, perhaps, feel any sense of obligation or honour when they are in your company. Paris will be at your feet soon enough, Madame la Marquise. Be patient.'

Without thinking, Alexandrine swung her closed fan at his grinning features. It caught him across one cheek as he bent forward to open the door and he wheeled on her, catching her wrist in a grip so tight that she cried out. His expression was so fierce for a moment that she thought he would strike her, and wondered if only the opening of the door by the waiting lackey prevented it. Alain's fingers touched the spot where the fan had grazed his skin, crushing the anger which dictated he should retaliate in kind.

'I shall remember that, and exact payment at a time when we shall not be disturbed,' he said in a low tone that chilled her.

And then he was all smiles again, courteous, the perfect gentleman, helping her from the carriage and escorting her into the salon of Madame Heloise, leaving her with the parting comment that he would be back in two hours to escort her home.

Just like that, Alexandrine thought, as she followed one of the seamstresses into a side room. Had she no say in what she wanted to do? She was alone in Paris for the first time since she had arrived, and wanted to go sightseeing again. Why should Luc mind her spending a few hours away from the house? She would not venture from the carriage and was therefore in no danger. She did not need the unwelcome presence of Alain Ratan overshadowing her little adventure.

'I will be with you in a moment, Madame la Marquise.' Jeanette, Madame's best seamstress, looked in to see that she was comfortable before escorting the woman with her to the door.

Alexandrine glimpsed a most attractive woman, whose skin was like porcelain, attired completely in pink, being given absolute attention by all about her. She was exquisite, not very tall and with a perfect figure, like a fragile doll. Someone of great importance, she decided, leaving her chair to take a closer look. At that moment, the woman looked back over her shoulder and saw her standing in the half-open doorway.

Jeanette whispered something to her, and she turned and moved slowly over to Alexandrine. 'So you are the new Marquise de Mezière.' The soft voice rippled with amusement, but was curious rather than condemning. 'Don't worry, I don't believe everything I hear. Nor must you. Pretty. Very pretty. Do your very best for her, Jeanette. I want you to make all the women at Versailles green with envy when they first see her.'

She was gone in a swirl of pink, leaving the air heady with her perfume and Alexandrine stunned by her frank description. Several of the sewing-girls stared after her, their heads bent together, whispering, until Jeanette sent them scattering in all directions.

'Now, madame...' She ushered Alexandrine back into the room and began to help her to undress. 'Everything is ready for you. One last fitting and we shall pack it all tonight. You shall have every last item in the morning.'

'That will be wonderful! Who was that woman?' Everyone seemed to know who she was, so why should she not have her curiosity fulfilled.

'That? Isn't she the most delightful little thing you have ever seen? Madame Heloise loves making gowns for that one. Her name is Madame Jeanne-Antoinette Poisson d'Etoiles. Doesn't it have a nice sound to it? A great lady. She and her husband have a fine house in the Rue Croix-des-Petits-Champs and a country house near the village of Etoiles. She entertains all the best people there. There is even a rumour... But no, I chatter too much! Madame would never forgive me if I told you idle gossip.'

'I hope Madame is as considerate with my reputation…one I have earned without setting a foot outside my house,' Alexandrine replied. 'D'Etoiles? Perhaps my husband knows her. I shall ask him. I am compiling a list for a ball I intend to give, and I see no reason not to include Madame and her husband on it. I know so few people.'

As a giggle came from one of the girls helping Alexandrine out of her petticoats, Jeanette tutted sharply and dismissed her, making sure that the door was closed tightly before daring to speak.

'I am sure Madame la Marquise will have good advice as to whom to invite. As to Madame d'Etoiles, there is a certain notoriety about her—from her mother's side, I assure you. Some scandal that has never died.' Her voice was lowered. 'Lovers, you understand. Many, many lovers. Now, it appears, Madame is anxious to breach the society which has shunned her for so long because of the unfortunate relationship.'

Jeanette slipped white brocade over her head and pulled it tight about her waist. Alexandrine caught her breath at the low décolletage, without the usual modest addition of a fichu. The bodice curved low over her breasts, pushing them up as the woman tightened the back of the dress, imprisoning her waist. Beneath the divided skirt were wide panniers that stood out on either side.

'The very latest fashion,' she was assured as she voiced a suspicion that she might not be able to pass safely through a doorway. The underskirt of cloth of gold was liberally sewn with tiny diamonds that winked and sparkled in the light. An additional innovation, Alexandrine realised, wondering whose idea they had been. Luc's or that of Alain Ratan? She had known nothing about them, but how striking she looked. She could scarcely believe the reflection in the mirror. Gone was the pale, badly-shorn country girl who had stood at the side of Luc Boussières just six short weeks ago and consented to be his wife. A stranger faced her now. Tall, slender, elegantly gowned, tiny fair curls emphasising the fine bone-structure of her features. Her cheeks now contained a blush of colour that was quite becoming, she thought.

'Madame's eye is beyond reproach,' she breathed, turning this way and that to get a better look at herself. 'She saw what I did not. Am I pretty, Jeanette?'

The woman looked quite shocked. It was obvious that most of her customers did not ask such a question. 'Madame, can you not see for yourself? Whatever made you believe you were not? Pretty? You are beautiful.'

'Or is it just Madame Heloise's lovely gown?' Alexandrine still needed that last little word of praise. Dare she believe in herself? Alexandrine d'Albret, the merchant's daughter from Noyen, who not only looked like a lady now, but felt like one!

'Such a transformation.' Jeanette was staring as if she, too, was taken aback by it. 'Forgive me, madame. I did not mean to imply...'

'Do you think my husband will be as pleased with your efforts as I am?' Alexandrine's question cut across her confusion.'

'How can he not be? Madame looks like—like royalty. Every man who sees you will be at your feet. Who knows—perhaps you will follow in the footsteps of Madame d'Etoiles and catch the eye of the King! He has already noticed her, you know, and apparently made his interest abundantly plain through his equerry, Monsieur de Briges. The whole of Paris is waiting to see what will happen. But Madame d'Etoiles—she treats the whole affair so casually, as if he can be dismissed with a wave of her fan!'

'The King? Is he not married?' Alexandrine asked in all innocence.

'He has not only a wife, but many mistresses. Who knows how many? He is far worse than his great-grandfather.' Jeanette looked at her with some scepticism. What a little innocent she was, after all. Did she not know all men took mistresses, whether they were happily married or not? It was the way men were, and nothing could change them. She would learn soon enough from her own husband! Although, perhaps, for her it would be different. She had heard some very strange rumours about that man.

'Forgive the intrusion.' Madame d'Etoiles stood in the doorway, her fan of ostrich feathers, in a delicate pink to match her gown, fluttering before the smiling face as she surveyed Alexandrine. 'I forgot my gloves and had to come back. And, I confess, I was dying of curiosity to see what Madame Heloise had created for you, madame.'

'Come in, please.' Alexandrine was not at all offended by the outspoken comment and secretly rather pleased at the admiration in the other woman's eyes as she inspected the ball-gown with great thoroughness.

'Madame has surpassed herself. You will greatly add to the grace and elegance of Versailles in that apparel,' Jeanne d'Etoiles added, carefully lowering herself into a nearby chair and arranging her wide-panniered skirts about her. 'Jeanette, ask someone to bring us lemon tea, will you? This heat today has quite fatigued me. I have not known so hot an autumn in years.'

'You have left your sick-bed too soon,' the dressmaker protested, quickly lifting her customer's small feet shod in pink satin on to a stool. 'Madame has only recently lost her first child,' she explained to Alexandrine before leaving them.

'And I should go mad if I were confined any longer to that sick-room, with everyone being so sympathetic and sweet.' Madame d'Etoiles' face dimpled into a grimace. 'They were suffocating me! Besides, I have a new design for Madame, and I shall need the gown very quickly.'

'I am so sorry. It must have been a very difficult time for you.' Shall I ever know the bitter-sweet pain of childbirth? Alexandrine wondered. Luc did not want her as if his wife, so how could she? It had been denied her along with the normality of a married life. Would her beautiful clothes and jewels, the fine carriage and high-stepping horses he had just presented to her, make up for not being a wife and mother, not fulfilling the natural functions of a woman, the duties she had been trained to carry out?

Jeanne Poisson d'Etoiles was indeed very, very lovely, she thought, allowing her gaze to study the slender figure. She was below average height for a woman, unlike Alexandrine herself, but both were reed-slender with tiny waists that needed little or no tightening of a corset about them. The chestnut brown hair fell in a profusion of ringlets about one shoulder, intertwined with ribbons to match those on her wide-brimmed hat, which was turned up on one side and adorned with a glittering brooch. The eyes which met those of Alexandrine, unabashed at her scrutiny, were of an indefinable colour. Blue, yet with a deeper hue that was almost black, and then, as she smiled, there was a touch of grey lurking in the depths. Her smile was delightful, open and honest, and Alexandrine felt immediately at ease, despite the news that she was in the presence of the daughter of an infamous person!

'I am as fascinated by your wardrobe, madame, as I am about your background,' the woman remarked candidly. 'The Marquis has set Paris agog with his marriage. Half the city have you marked as a heartless money-grabber who has taken advantage of an old and senile man, and that opinion is shared by his son Paul, I believe, who has lost no time—no time at all—in spreading his opinion of you. Some consider you a doe-eyed innocent swept off your feet by the thought of rank and wealth...'

'And the others?' Alexandrine asked, stiffly.

'The sensible ones, myself among them, are waiting to see how you conduct yourself in the future. Did I not tell you I do not believe everything I hear?'

'Thank goodness there are still some people who are reserving judgement on me! I was hoping Paul would have accepted me by now, but his animosity is growing, not waning. I am at a loss as to what to do,' Alexandrine confessed.

'Ignore him and those who will seek to spoil what you have found,' she was advised.

'If only I could, but I—I am not used to this kind of life...I am a country girl. Before my marriage to the Marquis—to Luc—I had not been out of a convent for more than a month...'

'I had the feeling we might be soul-mates,' Jeanne d'Etoiles murmured. 'I was brought up in a convent at Poissy. I spent four years there, and drove the poor nuns mad. I was a terrible pupil!'

'So was I,' Alexandrine laughed. The lemon tea was brought and, as they sipped it, Alexandrine found herself unburdening herself to the quiet, attentive person who sat opposite. She told of her engagement and the terrible disaster that had deprived her of fiancé and family in three short weeks. Of the illness which had come upon her, and of Luc's help. She told of the arrival at the house in the Place des Vosges and the unpleasantness of her reception, of Luc's generosity... and hardly before she realised what she was doing, she had blurted out the conditions he had laid down for their marriage.

If her confidences surprised her companion, it did not show in her sympathetic features, and when Alexandrine apologised, blushing profusely, for boring her guest she was told how pleasing it was to be considered a friend on such a short acquaintance.

'We are both outsiders. We shall have to fight, and fight hard, for our survival,' Jeanne d'Etoiles said softly. 'I shall achieve my goal—and soon. I shall pray you also succeed in getting what you want.'

'All I want is to be accepted by my husband's friends,' Alexandrine confessed. 'We are to go to Versailles soon, and I am terrified! Thank goodness, at least I shall know you.'

'Unfortunately I have not been invited...this time. There are certain—difficulties pertaining to my acceptance at court, but they will be overcome.'

How confident she sounded, as if she already knew what lay ahead. Did she really have designs on the King himself? Something must have shown for a moment in Alexandrine's eyes, for the woman laughed, and continued, 'I suspect Jeanette has been talking again, but no matter. It is true that the King has noticed me. One day he will do more than survey from afar. I have a husband who adores me, and maybe one day I shall give him the son he desires, but I cannot ignore my destiny. I have told him I shall never leave him—except for the King,' she declared, as casually as if she was discussing

the weather, not an affair with the most powerful man
in the land. Seeing that Alexandrine was slightly abashed
by her bluntness, she immediately changed the subject
and, learning that she had not yet obtained a maid, suggested they should visit a young girl whom she was trying
to place with a good family.

'She is a clever little thing, with nimble fingers and a
nice manner about her, despite her place of origin. She
lives across the Pont-Neuf in the not-so-pleasant part of
our fair city,' she explained. 'Of course she may not be
what you want...and you should consult your husband
first, perhaps?'

'I am sure Luc will accept my judgement in such a
matter. Are you sure you feel well enough to make the
journey?'

'That part of the city excites me...perhaps it will you.
The people are real, not bewigged fawning courtiers or
powdered cats!' Her lips deepened into a humourless
smile. 'When I have power, I shall remember those who
sought to do me harm.'

Alexandrine suspected that a shrewd brain lay behind
the pretty face and wished she possessed the determination and sense of purpose of her new friend. She accepted the invitation to ride in Jeanne d'Etoiles' carriage
and instructed her own driver to wait until the Duc de
Belaincourt returned and then convey him wherever he
wished to go. She had not asked him to accompany her,
Alexandrine mused, nor did she seek his company. She
had been generous in not sending the carriage straight
back and making him walk home!

She held her breath as the carriage began to cross the
Pont-Neuf, the driver swearing at a group of acrobats
performing in the middle of the road. They pulled faces,
jeered at him with loud cat-calls and peered cheekily into
the interior until one of the lackeys riding behind pushed
them away. Then the smiles disappeared, the jokes ceased
and vulgar language such as she had never heard before
followed them.

Alexandrine soon forgot them, however, and sat
enthralled in her cushioned seat, staring wide-eyed at
the scene outside. Apart from the fact that the bridge
had been started in the year 1578 by Henry III and com-

pleted in 1605, after several interruptions brought about
by religious wars and the usual lack of money when it
had all been taken to pay the armies—all of which she
had learned from history-books in the convent—she
knew nothing about the Pont-Neuf or that part of the
city beyond. Fiercely she concentrated on the people, as
it really was a fascinating area. Four steps, the same on
either side, led up to pavements and open-air shops,
outside which girls waved bunches of flowers under the
noses of passers-by. Money-changers, Jews from the look
of the long curling whiskers and caps, argued over rates
with their customers, waving their hands and gesticu-
lating wildly as they shouted to make themselves heard
above the hubbub of voices. Further on, a group of
strolling minstrels followed pretty girls or ones who
looked able to toss an ample reward into their ever-open
palms, singing songs of love and then love denied, which
made Alexandrine's heart ache as she listened to the
words.

In the middle of the bridge, the carriage passed a statue
of Henry IV gazing sightlessly down on the abundance
of people milling below, aloof and untouched by the
poverty and squalor he could see from his lofty position—perhaps uncaring. The bridge touched the north
bank of the Seine between the Quai du Louvre and the
Quay de la Mégisserie on its right. A revolting smell
reached Alexandrine's nose, causing her to fan herself
vigorously to sweep it away. Sheepskins hung out in
preparation for tanning stank more hideously than the
rotting vegetation littering the roads, which was pro-
ducing its own nauseating smell. It was a relief when the
carriage reached the far side, where the streets although
very narrow were not so crowded and where the air was
somewhat more acceptable—but only just.

Scarred, dirty faces, old before their time, watched
the carriage pass by as their owners begged for a coin
and cursed the occupants when none was forthcoming.
So lurid were the oaths that she held her hands over her
ears as they approached the next deformed figure seated
by the roadside, and Jeanne broke into peals of laughter.
Obviously the sights did not shock nor vex *her*! They
passed a hurdy-gurdy grinder at the end of one street,

a cheeky-faced monkey perched on his shoulders doing tricks for a group of children in tattered clothes, barefooted, who gazed enthralled at the little creature. A seller of birds thrust a wild-looking thing under her nose and begged her to buy it as his wife and children had not eaten in a week. She shook her head, then, consumed with shame and helplessness, delved into her purse and tossed a coin into the road.

'You should not have done that,' Jeanne said softly. 'Look.'

From nowhere appeared three other men who fell on the luckless individual. She heard a scream of pain at the same time as she saw the sunlight glint on a polished blade, and knew that her good deed might very well result in a man being killed.

'How—How much further is it, madame?' she asked, beginning to regret the impulsiveness which had prompted her to accept her companion's offer. Luc was ill in his bed, and here she was on an errand of very little importance. It was true she was in need of a maid, but it could have waited. There again, if she was at home, what would she be doing? She was not allowed access to her own husband during his illness—whatever it was— and perhaps she would not even be missed.

'We are here.' Jeanne smiled across at her as the carriage came to a halt, and Alexandrine looked out of the window. They had stopped in a narrow street where the houses were so close together that they leaned forward over the cobblestones in a most alarming manner. 'The girl I have in mind for you makes her living as a seamstress at the moment. As yet she has been untouched by the world about her, but she earns so little—a pittance which barely keeps her alive—and she is such an independent little thing that she will accept no help from her aunt, her only living relative. Or from her sweetheart. But then Jules is a rogue!' The comment was accompanied by a soft laugh as Jeanne stepped down, and, as she followed, Alexandrine wondered how her friend came to know so much about this part of the city. It was the haunt of the poor, the destitute, cripples and beggars, yet she appeared at ease here as she sent someone scurrying inside a nearby house to find the person she sought.

She was aware of many eyes on her as she followed
Jeanne through a doorway so narrow that she had to
turn sideways to accommodate her skirts. Men and
women came out to look at the monogrammed coach
and comment on the two elegantly dressed women who
had invaded their domain. A dirty-faced urchin came
after Alexandrine and caught at her skirts, tugging at
them insistently and demanding money. She snatched
them free and hurried after her companion, apprehensive in these surroundings. Whatever had she been
thinking of to come here?

The odour of cooking invaded her nostrils as they entered a large untidy kitchen where a huge cauldron was
suspended over an open fire. The room was heavy with
the smell of smoke and whatever it was the pot contained. She was reminded of her old home, of her mother
standing beside a similar fire, cooking the chickens that
had been caught and killed that morning. The sweet smell
of basil and tarragon she recognised immediately, and
somehow she found it reassuring. Now she no longer
felt out of place. Her mother had taught her many culi-
nary skills, none of which she had been able to practice
since her marriage. Now that she was the Marquise de
Mezière, cooks and the kitchen staff did all the essen-
tials. How she had wished many times during the past
weeks that she be allowed to indulge herself in the
kitchen, just a little!

'Madame d'Etoiles! I was not expecting you.' A young
girl, perhaps sixteen, certainly not more than a year older,
sprang up from the chair beside the fire where she had
been engrossed in her sewing. 'And you have brought a
guest. The place is not fit to receive you... Oh dear!'

'Do not distress yourself, Francine. I have brought
someone who has need of your nimble fingers... and
who may offer you employment, if you still wish it,'
Jeanne said smilingly.

Alexandrine found herself under the gaze of a pair of
liquid brown eyes that lacked the lustre they should have
displayed in one so young. Curiosity lurked in their
depths, but suspicion too, she saw, mixed with more than
a fraction of fear. What had she to be afraid of? To be
taken out of this place would be a blessing, Alexandrine

thought, aware of the well-worn furniture, the torn curtains at the windows, many of which lacked glass or were
cracked. There was no comfort here. She could offer
that, and there would be more to eat than a scrawny
chicken. And she would have nice clothes to replace the
patched gown that hung on her thin frame like a sack.
She was terribly thin, as if she had been ill. Alexandrine
remembered how gaunt she had looked when she first
rose from her sick-bed. The girl needed care.

'I am the Marquise de Mezière,' she said, and immediately the girl bobbed a rather unsteady curtsy and
almost lost her balance. Ill and undernourished,
Alexandrine thought in alarm.

'I—I am called Francine, madame. I think I shall be
seventeen in a few weeks' time. I can cook and sew, and
I have served a lady before. I know what is required.'
The words tumbled out in a great rush and then she fell
silent, her huge eyes watching Alexandrine in a most appealing fashion. She was both desperate and frightened.

'Unfortunately her position was made impossible by
the unwelcome attentions of the lady's husband,' Jeanne
remarked drily. 'He regularly abused the poor child, and
when the wife discovered it, she turned Francine out of
the house without a sou. Men! Pah! They should all be
made to pay dearly for their pleasures!'

'She would have nothing to fear in my house, I assure
you,' Alexandrine replied confidently. So that had been
the trouble!

'And what is your word worth, Madame la Marquise?' A man was leaning against the door-jamb,
watching them. He had come upon them so quietly that
no one had heard. He was perhaps the same height as
Alexandrine, with a thin, hard face marred by a deep
scar that completely crossed his right cheek from chin
to hairline. His shock of red hair was as fierce a colour
as the flames licking hungrily about the cauldron. His
eyes were like pieces of jet, and so unfriendly that
Alexandrine was once more apprehensive. There was
contempt and anger in them, and the way they looked
at her brought a blush to her cheeks. Was she always to
be so embarrassed when men looked at her so? First

Paul Boussières, then Alain Ratan...and now this stranger.

Jeanne waved her closed fan in his direction with a sharp tutting sound. 'That's enough of that, Jules le Chat! Madame is here at my invitation and you will be polite to her. To us both. We are exhausted, so bring out some of your good wine and decent glasses before we discuss this any further.'

'There is nothing to discuss.' The man's voice was flat, but he moved to a rickety sideboard and from it produced a cut glass decanter filled with wine the colour of honey and three matching glasses. Alexandrine could scarcely contain her amazement at the sight of such exquisite glassware in this place, and Jeanne threw her an amused look.

'Jules is the best pickpocket in Paris, and Francine's sweetheart.'

'In France,' came the quick retort.

'And what he cannot fit into his pockets, he takes when there is no moon to betray his activities. Keep your doors well locked, my dear Alexandrine. This is a dangerous man...if he does not like you.'

Which he did not, Alexandrine decided, as a glass was thrust out towards her. She thought it best to accept, and did so with a half-smile of thanks, which was ignored.

'Francine stays here,' Jules le Chat said coldly. 'I can take care of her. She needs no fancy lady, even though the husband is too old to bother her. This one knew what she was about when she married him, didn't she?' His mocking laughter brought more colour to Alexandrine's cheeks. The impertinence of the creature! To suggest...

'You do her an injustice, Jules. And you have nothing to say in this matter. I believe Francine will have a good home with Madame la Marquise. If she is willing to go and the Marquise is satisfied, then you will allow it.'

'I am well aware I am in your debt, Madame d'Etoiles, but do not push me too far. It is a long way back to the Pont-Neuf.'

'Would you harm the golden goose? No, my friend, I am too useful to you, and shall be more so in the future. Best you keep me alive and well.'

Alexandrine was amazed at her companion's coolness. If she could have turned and run from the house, she would have done so, but the wiry frame of Jules le Chat blocked the doorway and his slight build could hide strength of an undefined character. Besides, there were people clustered at the open window and more behind him. She would never reach the carriage!

'You have frightened Madame Boussières with your silly words!' Jeanne reproved him. 'Come now, say you approve, and we will leave. Madame's husband is not well and she wishes to return as soon as possible. Give Francine your blessing, if you care for her, and tell her how pleased you are that she will no longer be subjected to this—this indignity you choose to call an existence. After all, *you* have chosen to leave it, so why should she not do likewise?'

The man was silent. Watching him, Alexandrine sensed in him the wildness a caged animal might possess. For some reason he did not want to, nor would, she suspected, go against the wishes of Jeanne d'Etoiles. How two such people had ever come together was beyond her comprehension! Yet he did not like Alexandrine, nor did he want Francine to accompany her, even though he knew she would benefit from the move. He was no fool, she decided, forcing herself to remain calm as his piercing gaze once more raked her, but he *was* dangerous. He despised the nobility, that was sure. How would he react if she told him she was only the daughter of a merchant, who had also known poverty, although not on such a drastic scale as he and his friends endured? And then, remembering his comment on her recent marriage, her lips compressed into a tight line. Those days were over for her. She was a different person now and must always remember her new position.

'On the recommendation of Madame d'Etoiles, I accept Francine into my household, monsieur.' Her frosty tone challenged his authority, and his bushy red eyebrows deepened into a fierce frown. 'Shall we say for a month's trial? If at the end of that time she is not happy, she may leave—with her wages. If I am not happy with her, I shall do my best to find another house for her to reside in. However, I see no reason why we should not become friends.' She smiled at Francine, and was rewarded by an answering softening of the girl's pale features. *She* was agreeable, at least!

'Ladies of quality do not become—friends—with their maids,' came the derisive retort from Jules, which brought another tut of annoyance from Jeanne's carefully rouged pink lips.

'Perhaps I am as in need of a friend as she is,' Alexandrine answered. 'When can she come to me?'

'At once, madame.' Francine uttered the words before she had considered her sweetheart's reaction. With an oath he swung away, but then turned back to stare with narrowed gaze at Alexandrine.

'If anyone—anyone at all—touches her while she is beneath your roof, I shall kill him. Do you understand me, Madame la Marquise? And you—for allowing it to happen. Do you still want her to go with you?' Mutely Alexandrine nodded, too stunned by the threat to utter a word. 'Wait outside in the carriage, then, both of you. I wish to say goodbye to my girl alone,' he demanded insolently.

'She—She is quite at liberty to come and visit you as often as she pleases...' Alexandrine began, and was interrupted by laughter from someone looking on. The smile which twisted the mouth of Jules le Chat etched the scar still deeper into his sallow skin.

'Have no fear! I shall see her when and where I choose, madame, and you will have nothing to say about it.'

'But *I* shall, and you will stop behaving like a fool. It is what we both want for Francine. I am surprised that Madame la Marquise has not changed her mind. You were very rude to her, Jules.'

The woman who came into the room was perhaps in her middle forties, dressed in a heavy, voluminous skirt that swirled about her ankles as she walked, and a pale coloured blouse. Alexandrine could no more define her nationality than she could her age. The skin had an olive tint and her hair was as black as a raven's wing. Long gold chains adorned her bare neck and her wrists, but her voice betrayed no accent. A thoughtful look spread across the flawless features as she came to a halt before Alexandrine, hands resting on her hips.

'No, perhaps not. This one has a mind of her own. A stubborn streak that will not be easily tamed. I am Solange, "the gypsy". Of course I am not really a gypsy, but when you tell fortunes it is expected that you are. Would you like me to tell your fortune, madame?'

'I don't believe in such things,' Alexandrine said with a soft laugh. What a lie that was! For all her strictness of religious upbringing in the convent and at home, she had lived in a small village where superstition and love-potions were a part of the everyday existence of the people, and, as a child, she had kept well away from the hovel on the edge of the village where everyone went who needed a potion to cure an illness or to secure the affections of an indifferent party.

'A disbeliever! Ah, but you are young. Fate has not yet intervened to guide you, or has it? Your hand, madame, if you please.'

Jeanne nodded vigorously at Alexandrine who, with some reluctance, drew off her glove and extended one hand. Long, painted nails examined the back and then the palm, gently stroking the smooth skin. It was only a game, Alexandrine told herself, yet even so a strange tremor seized her and immediately Solange's eyes locked with hers.

'You have recently suffered some great loss, no?'

'Yes. The plague took my family.'

'You have suffered, and there is more to come . . . each of the men who love you will in some way inflict pain upon you.'

'Men, who love me? I am recently married!' Alexandrine gasped.

'Soon you will be a widow, but not before you have come to know love. There will be more than one man in your life, Madame la Marquise. I see them quite clearly.'

'I shall hear no more!' Alexandrine snatched her hand free, her cheeks flaming. More than one man, indeed! What preposterous nonsense!

'You do not believe because you do not want to,'
Solange said, not in the least perturbed by her scepticism. 'If you will leave me something personal I shall
be able to see the future more clearly for you. The Tarot
will reveal everything.'

'Thank you, but no,' Alexandrine said firmly.

'Do it,' Jeanne insisted. 'Solange has a wonderful gift.
I come to her often.'

'There is little I foresee for you, Madame d'Etoiles. I
have but confirmed what you already knew,' the woman
answered with a deep smile.

'Solange told me I would become the King's mistress,'
Jeanne said softly. 'But I was told that when I was nine
years old. So, you see, I have to believe it, don't I?'

'I think we should be leaving.' Alexandrine turned
towards the door and found a dozen or more faces
grinning at her. Everyone had overheard the conversation! More than one man? It was nonsense, and she
knew it, but she prayed none of this would ever reach
Luc's ears. Perhaps he would laugh and dismiss it as she
had—but if he believed... What was it he had said to
her once, when she had asked him if he believed in fate—
or in God? 'Is there a difference? After all, who has seen
the faces of any of them?'

Before Alexandrine could guess Jeanne's intentions,
the latter had plucked the fan from her fingers and given
it to Solange.

'Madame la Marquise lives in the Place des Vosges.
And I want to hear everything she tells you,' she added
to Alexandrine as they left. 'You may be in for a few
surprises—disbeliever or not.'

In that smoky kitchen, surrounded by all those strange
people, Alexandrine might have begun to believe, had
she been foolish enough to remain. As it was, she climbed
back into the carriage with a laugh and dismissed Solange
and her silly predictions without a second thought.

As they sat waiting for Francine to join them, a little
deformed hunchback was hoisted up to the carriage
window by his companion.

'Ah, such two fine-looking fillies, but pink has always
been my favourite colour! Madame, will you not step
down again? I am sure you would find me a better fellow

than Jules le Chat. That one has no manners, whereas I have dined with princes and dukes . . . even a marquise from time to time,' he added with a wink which brought ripples of laughter from the onlookers.

'I thank you for the offer, little man.' Jeanne leaned forward and boldly patted him on his bald head, quickly withdrawing her hand before he could grasp it. 'But I must decline. I have set my sights rather higher.'

On the King of France himself, Alexandrine thought, as she settled back in her seat. Nothing could be higher!

CHAPTER FOUR

SHE WAS quite, quite mad, Alexandrine decided as she bade goodbye to Jeanne d'Etoiles and ascended the steps to the house, Francine following close on her heels, clutching a pathetically small bundle of clothes wrapped in an old curtain. She knew how the girl felt, but she could never tell her. Had she not felt shy and awkward, as the girl now did, when Luc first proposed to her? When she had arrived at the Place des Vosges, feeling out-of-place, an intruder, unwanted.

Pierre met her in the hall with the news that the Marquis had been asking for her for several hours. Luc must be well again! But that morning he had still been indisposed and Selim had flatly refused her entry to the sick-room. Alexandrine was at a loss to understand such a swift recovery, unless her husband had not been as ill as she had been led to believe. But why should he deliberately deceive her?

'This is Francine, who is to be my maid. She is to be treated kindly, do you understand? I want her bathed and given some different clothes. Something from one of the other maids will suffice until I can make other arrangements. Then have her brought to my apartment.'

'As madame wishes.' The steward gave the girl no more than a cursory glance before instructing her to follow him. How I wish I could have read his thoughts, Alexandrine mused as she hurried upstairs. She was hot, and she should have changed before she visited her husband, but she was anxious to assure herself that he was well again and to discover what strange ailment had struck him down so suddenly—and had disappeared with the same remarkable swiftness.

Selim opened the door to Luc's sitting-room and stood back without a word to allow her to enter. Luc was sitting in a high-backed chair by the window, clad in a heavy velvet robe, his legs covered by a plush blanket. Several pillows supported his back and head.

'Oh, Luc, I am so glad to see you well again!' Alexandrine fell to her knees beside his chair, her eyes scanning the lined face. He did not seem unusually pale, as she would have expected, and the hands that grasped hers and drew her to him so that he could kiss her cheek were as strong as always. But his eyes... There was something strange about the eyes that rested on her anxious features. A far-away look lingered there—a lack of awareness of those about him, almost as if he were drugged. And his speech was halting, each word pronounced with great care. What had happened to him?

'My dear child, I was beginning—to—grow concerned about—you. You have—been gone so long...'

'Madame Heloise was indisposed and could not come to give me my last fitting, so I went to her salon. I hope you do not mind,' Alexandrine explained. 'I did try to see you again. In fact, I have been trying to see you every day since you became unwell, but I have been refused entrance,' she added, with a meaningful glance back over her shoulder to where Selim stood by the door. A well-mannered servant would have left the room—or indeed, been ordered to leave—but Luc never told him to go... ever. When he did, it was at his own discretion. If it were not ludicrous, she would have thought him afraid to leave Luc alone with her!

'On my instructions,' she was told in the same slow speech. A seizure, was that what he had suffered? she wondered. She had seen a man in Noyen who had had one, and he had been a month without proper speech. He had mumbled like an idiot and been forced to use sign-language to communicate with his family. After that, all his faculties seemed to return and he once more lived a normal life. He had been about Luc's age, she remembered, in his late fifties.

'Did I not nurse my own parents when they became sick? I am not a child to be turned away from unpleasant things, Luc. I shall nurse you from now on—as a wife should,' she declared firmly, never for one moment expecting her right to be at his side to be denied.

'You will do as I tell you, you foolish child. What ails me is of many years standing and not pleasant...not for me, and certainly not for those about me.' Alexandrine drew back, hurt by the rejection and the sudden harshness in his voice. 'It is a—a weakening thing, child, that forces me to take to my bed for several days. I am subject to fevers and chills, and it is only the knowledge that Selim has stored in his black head that has kept me alive this long. I will not let you see me like that. Besides,' a hand reached out to touch her cheek, trembling as it did so, 'we do not want you to get it, do we?'

'But where did you contract this terrible disease? Have you seen other doctors, here in Paris? There are many good ones you could consult.'

'It is one of the less pleasant—gifts—I brought back from my trips to far-off lands...And yes, I—I have seen other physicians. None, I might add, did me any good. I trust Selim with my life—what is left in this tired, old body. Now, it becomes—hard for me to speak again...' Selim began to move forward, but was waved back again. 'I shall have the medicine in a moment. First I must hear what you have—been—up to today...'

He fell back amid the cushions, waiting for Alexandrine to oblige his curiosity.

'Madame has finished my wardrobe. It is so beautiful, Luc! And my ball-gown.' She pressed the cold hand she held to her cheek. 'Please, please, get well soon! I shall not go to Versailles without you. I would not dare! And it would be no fun without you at my side.'

'I shall not miss it, but I want to see you in your gown. I want to see those lovely eyes shine. Most of all—I want...' He broke off, his lips deepening into a strange smile. 'You have everything you want, then?'

'Everything...and I have a maid now, too. I met Madame d'Etoiles, the wife of Charles-Guillaume le Normant d'Etoiles, a nephew of Monsieur le Tourenhem, who knew a girl who will suit my needs admirably. She is very young, but willing to learn, and she was living in such pitiful conditions across the river...'

'Enough! My head begins to reel. Tell me all about it some other time. So long as you are satisfied, I shall have no objections to her, I am sure. Leave me now, child. I need to rest.'

Obediently Alexandrine kissed the lined brow and rose to her feet. Before she had gone two steps, a soft snore escaped him. Selim opened the door for her but she did not pass through at once. Her eyes locked on the impassive black features, as she said flatly, 'I wish to be called if my husband needs me. At once!'

'You will be sent for, madame. If he needs you.' Again that quiet insolence in the man's tone. She ignored it. What else could she do?

She did not like the man and doubted if she ever would, but at least his skills were making Luc well again. And, from the sound of it, he had been undergoing treatment for some considerable time. It both hurt and annoyed her to know she was not needed. But it would do no good to brood. The best thing was to turn her attention elsewhere. While her husband was ill there was still a great deal to be done to finish the renovations of the *hôtel*, and her plans for its grand reopening.

Her steps quickened as she neared her own apartment, thoughts of the ball once more filling her mind. She would send an invitation to Jeanne d'Etoiles and her husband. Perhaps it would recompense her for not being invited to Versailles.

'I am glad to see you have safely returned from your little expedition across the river. Are you growing bored already that you seek your pleasure in such quarters?'

She froze in shock and horror at the figure who reclined in a chair in her sitting-room. She had entered and closed the door before Alain addressed her. Immediately she wheeled to call a servant and have him escorted downstairs, but the words were never uttered, as he continued coldly, 'Have you told Luc where you went? I do not think he would like it very much, especially if he learned that you were in the company of a woman who, despite her youth, has gained some remarkable degree of notoriety. And you chose to flaunt your identity openly, not even bothering to mask your face, as any woman in her right mind would have done. You seem to care little for your own reputation—or the good name of your husband!'

'Where I go and who I am with is none of your business!' Her hands clenched into tight fists at her side as she turned to look at him, stung by the unjustness of his words. She had not concealed her identity because she had not done anything wrong. To have done so, as he said, would have implied that she had set out to do exactly what he thought. 'I did not ask for your company, monsieur, but it was forced on me, therefore I did not consider myself under any obligation to inform you where I was going, or why. Please leave this room at once. If you do not, I shall be forced to call Pierre and have you removed.'

'That would be unfortunate.' Alain's smile mocked her anger. He reached for the wine-glass at his side, unperturbed by the rising blue fire in her eyes or the hostility in her flushed cheeks. 'The noise that would occur while the poor man was trying to enforce your wishes— and which, I tell you now, he would not succeed in doing—would most certainly reach the ears of your husband. When he enquired why an old friend was being ejected from his house like a common peasant, I should have to tell him, shouldn't I?'

'You are beneath contempt!' Alexandrine cried, restraining the temptation to slap the glass from his hand. He had made himself comfortable in *her* sitting-room as if he belonged there! 'But because you—you are my husband's friend, and for that reason only, I shall overlook your insolence and your invasion of my privacy.' She almost choked over the humiliating words, hating him still more for the contemptuous smile that twisted his lips. He believed she was afraid to tell Luc where she had been, or of her new friendship with Jeanne d'Etoiles. He would learn otherwise, as soon as Luc was well enough to comprehend what she was telling him. She was still of a mind that he had not been quite lucid during their time together.

'How very gracious of you.' Alain reached into his coat and produced a piece of folded paper which he tossed down on the table in front of her. 'You wanted this, I believe.'

She found herself looking at a list of names, and realised he had been as good as his word and had compiled the names of potential guests for the ball.

'I am grateful for the time you have spent on my behalf, monsieur. Thank you.'

'I am curious, madame. Satisfy me. Why did you go across the Pont-Neuf? Only a brazen hussy who seeks to sell her body—or find a man to satisfy it—would venture there in broad daylight. Many ladies do, you know. Like your friend Madame d'Etoiles.'

'As you say—she is my friend and I will not have her name maligned by a man such as you,' Alexandrine said fiercely.

'What kind of man am I, Madame la Marquise?' Alain rose to his feet, his eyes never leaving her face. Why he was so incensed at the knowledge that she had gone into that part of the city was beyond him. Seeking excitement perhaps from boredom at home? She had hardly been outside the door since she arrived. If only she had not chosen to do so when Luc was sick and confined to his bed!

His own treacherous wife had first begun to deceive him in such a sly manner. A visit to a sick friend, endless trips to the dressmaker whenever they were in Paris. So many other reasons he had never suspected were mere ploys to enable her to meet her lovers. Why should he have suspected her? In that first year of their marriage he had been blindly in love. Blind—deaf—and stupid to what she really was. A whore! He saw her in every woman he had met since, and whereas he had never suspected her duplicity and deceptions, he now attributed the same traits to every unfortunate female who crossed his path. Alexandrine was only one of many to bear the brunt of his whiplash tongue, the contempt which was always more intense whenever he felt the slightest attraction. Was that why he felt such animosity towards this woman? he wondered, taken aback by the thought which caught him totally unawares.

'You showed me the kind the first night we met, monsieur, with your disgusting behaviour. And now you have the audacity to suggest that you only have my husband's interests at heart when you force your company on me, and...'

'And what, madame?' Alain prompted quietly. 'If you recall, I did not know who you were then. My motives were purely selfish. What man could have resisted the temptation to kiss you?'

'He would not call you friend if he knew the way you act behind his back!' Alexandrine told him, feeling that she was getting nowhere. Selfish he certainly was. He cared nothing for her anger or her embarrassment—or her dislike of him.

'Do you intend to tell him? That would be most unwise.' Alain's pale eyes gleamed with mockery. 'Whom do you think he will believe?'

'Why me, of course. I am his wife!'

'Really? Innuendos and suspicions can easily destroy a man's self-esteem—and love!' he warned.

'As they did yours, monsieur? Am I to suffer at your hands because *you* were unlucky in love?'

For a moment the handsome face froze in anger and she held her breath, afraid he was about to unloose it upon her head for daring to comment on his personal life. But he said nothing, and his silence was more devastating to her nerves than any words of abuse. She watched the green eyes come to rest on her mouth and grew uncomfortable at the glitter which nestled in their depths. He could not—would not—dare to lay hands on her again!

'I should make you apologise twice. Once for the slap you gave me, and now this unwarranted intrusion into my affairs,' Alain murmured. 'However, I shall collect my due in another way.'

He was going to kiss her! Alexandrine opened her mouth to call for help, but his mouth was suddenly crushing hers, silencing her. She clenched her fists and pounded them against the broad chest until he caught her wrists in one hand and held them fast behind her back. His free hand fastened at the nape of her neck, rendering her immobile. Tears of anger and humiliation welled into her eyes as his lips bruised hers with a relentless pressure until they could no longer withstand his determination and they broke and parted beneath his.

Alain was a master of the art of seduction when he chose. It was a game he had begun in the arms of countless women after his wife's death as a way of forgetting the last remaining vestige of love that still lived inside him. Later, when that had gone and he grew bored, he reversed the rules. He did the hunting, the loving and the leaving, hoping at least to gain some satisfaction from the tears shed when he left. Instead, there was only emptiness. Revenge brought nothing but more sleepless nights and memories that refused to fade. If only Alexandrine were not married to Luc Boussières! He drew back, gazing down into her pale face, and saw it was wet with tears. The expletive which broke from his lips brought Alexandrine out of her stupor.

She stumbled back from him, rubbing her bruised wrists, and then flung a trembling hand towards the door. 'Get out! If you dare to touch me again, I—I will get Luc to forbid you entrance to this house ever again. And I will tell him why it must be so!'

'Never play with fire or a man you can't control, Madame la Marquise,' Alain chuckled. 'And you can't control me! Try at your peril. We might both enjoy it.'

With that parting shot, he left her standing in the middle of the room, fingers held against the lips that still throbbed from his masterful kisses and the words of Solange ringing in her ears: More than one man in her life, she had been told. Was Alain Ratan, Duc de Belaincourt, one of them?

'Are you ready, my dear? The carriage is waiting.' Luc came into Alexandrine's bedroom as Francine was making a last-minute alteration to her hair, substituting a diamond circlet upon the powdered wig instead of pearl combs. 'Turn round. Let me look at you.'

Slowly Alexandrine turned in a full circle before him. She was flushed and excited and, at the same time, overwhelmingly conscious that she would be on show tonight, like an exhibit at a fairground.

'Admirable! I am a very lucky man.'

'I am the lucky one.' Alexandrine went to him and kissed him affectionately. 'I am glad you are pleased with me. But are you sure you are well enough to attend? There will be another time.'

'This is your night. You have hardly been out of the house since we arrived in Paris. I shall not unduly tire myself, so I shall have to surrender you to the arms of a younger man for the dancing, but it will give me pleasure to watch you enjoying yourself.'

'I shall save all my dances until you can partner me,' Alexandrine assured him.

'You will do no such thing. If I know the young rakes at court, they will flock after you like hungry wolves! However, I have no fear that any one of them, no matter how handsome, will turn that pretty head. We have an understanding, have we not, Alexandrine?' She nodded, realising he was reminding her of her promise. Did he really think it necessary? 'And I can trust you to keep your word?'

'Yes, Luc, you can trust me,' she replied truthfully. No matter how many men tried to flatter her with flowery adjectives, or to force their attentions on her like Alain Ratan, she would remain faithful to her husband.

Soon you will be a widow, but not before you have come to know love... The blood drained from her cheeks as the gypsy's words came back into her mind. Not a day went by when they did not haunt her. How she wished she had never gone with Jeanne d'Etoiles, yet, if she had not, she would not now have Francine, and the girl was a treasure. Eager to please, polite, and with an eye for detail that made her the perfect lady's maid.

'Alexandrine, what is it?' Luc's hand was beneath her elbow, steadying her as she swayed. 'You are over-excited. Sit down, child. You, whatever your name is, fetch your mistress some wine from the other room. And a glass for me, too.'

'Her name is Francine, Luc. Do you approve of her now that you know where I found her?'

'I admit it was something of a surprise to learn of your visit to such a place, and with a perfect stranger, too.'

'It was a perfectly innocent visit and I did not know where I was going, did I?' Alexandrine said with a faint smile. The moment he had fully recovered his faculties,

she had told him everything about that day, as much to
justify her right to freedom, to go where she pleased and
with whom, as to combat any attempt Alain Ratan might
have to discredit her in her husband's eyes. Well, she
had told him almost everything. Luc had taken it for
granted that she had gone to Madame Heloise's salon
alone, and she had not corrected him. Neither had she
revealed the outrageous conduct of his so-called friend
when they were alone together in her apartment. How
could she? It was best ignored—*he* was best ignored,
along with those ridiculous predictions of Solange. She
must learn to have greater control over her emotions. A
reserved dignity would keep at bay those she did not
want near her—that and the fact that she intended to
stay very close to Luc tonight. If he did not dance, neither
would she.

Francine placed a cloak of dark blue satin over her
mistress's shoulders and fastened the diamond clasp at
her throat. Alexandrine had deliberately chosen that
colour because blue and gold were predominant in the
house, in her husband's coat-of-arms and the livery of
the servants, and she was doubly pleased at her choice
when she noticed that he was wearing a blue cloak
himself, his own being lavishly embroidered with gold
and silver.

'We make a handsome couple,' she said meaningfully,
and Luc's weathered features softened into a smile at
the affection in her voice. They had already grown closer
than he had ever hoped possible. Now, he knew, for her
sake as well as his own, he must allow the relationship
to develop no further. But how he loved to touch her,
for even the slightest caress roused him instantly. She
was as unaware of the effect she had on him as she would
be of the desire and lust she would arouse in many men
tonight.

'I have not been to court for some considerable time.
I thought I should look my best for what is a very special
occasion. For you, my dear, not for me. This cloak was
a gift to me from the late King. To wear it is considered
almost as great a privilege as being awarded the collar
of the Order of Saint-Louis! Come, it is time we were
leaving. We do not want to be late, or we shall find

nothing left to eat. At these functions, the tedium of standing for hours on end makes me exceedingly hungry!'

As they reached the hall and Pierre moved forward to open the main door, Paul came sauntering out of the Blue Salon. With a shock of surprise, Alexandrine realised he was to accompany them. He was dressed in yellow silk, ribbons cascading from his shoulders and from the tops of his stockings, as was the fashion. He had rather overdone it, she thought, momentarily picturing him with a hat on his head sewn with tiny bells that jingled as he walked, and a jester's stick in his hands. It was an unkind comparison, but when had he ever been nice to her? Her surprise grew as he stopped before her, took one of her hands in his and touched it to his lips. He wore a powered wig and reeked of Cologne, and not one finger did not have a ring on it. He wore more jewellery than she did! She felt Luc's hand tighten over hers, as he waited for some caustic comment to fall from his son's lips.

'Stepmother, you look enchanting! Like a fairy princess. Does she not, Father?' he said, stepping back to examine her in detail until a frown from his father dispensed with the scrutiny.

'Thank you, Paul.' She could think of nothing else to say.

'And what do you think of this?' He twirled before her for inspection, dabbing a lace handkerchief against a rouged cheek as he did so. 'Yellow is the latest fashionable colour. It would suit you, you know. I can tell you where to buy a bolt, if you like?'

'I think I should like that very much. You are most thoughtful,' Alexandrine replied, wondering if this was not some strange dream from which she would awake in a moment. Paul being polite to her? More than polite—helpful! What miracle had taken place? She stole a look into her husband's face as they proceeded out to the waiting carriage. Of course, Luc had spoken to him. What else could have made him change so quickly?

She discovered after only a few minutes in the carriage, however, that Paul had not changed. His pleasant manner was merely a front to appease his father. He was as insulting as ever. He was sitting beside her, while Luc and Selim sat opposite, with Francine beside him. A second surprise—to find that the Moor was also going to Versailles, dressed for the occasion, as they all were, in clothes befitting the most eligible gentleman. He looked more like some foreign dignitary than a manservant.

The carriage was not large and her panniered skirts took up most of the seat, squeezing Paul into one corner. Some of the folds of her magnificent gown had fallen across his knees, totally obscuring the hand which deliberately and quite painfully squeezed her thigh. She dared not move—indeed she could not, and she dared not speak for fear she began an argument between father and son. There had been so many, she knew, because of her presence in the house. How stupid of her to think that Paul would change. He hated her! She saw it in the eyes that considered her amusedly, challenging her to betray him. The fingers groped again, and she flinched visibly.

'Are you uncomfortable, my dear?' Luc enquired, and she shook her head, forcing a smile to stiff lips.

'I thought I felt something on my shoulder, that's all. I keep forgetting I have this thing on my head!' she said, indicating her wig. 'I mustn't make any sudden moves, must I?' How she would have loved to stab Paul's foot with her high-heeled shoe and make him yell like the coward he was! Not content with accosting her in the house, he was now subjecting her to his crudeness in the very presence of his father. How much longer would she be able to hold back her anger and disgust at his behaviour? The moment she told Luc, she knew something terrible would result, and yet in her heart she accepted that it was a situation she would soon have to face. It could not continue.

However, the moment she caught her first glimpse of Versailles, everything was forgotten. Their carriage was caught up in a stream of impressive-looking monogrammed conveyances all heading towards the huge complex of buildings ahead, and progress became so slow that she had plenty of time to see for herself why so

many people in Paris clamoured and bribed and schemed
to be received here.

They passed through the huge gates of the main
courtyard and into the inner one that led to the palace
itself and the many salons adjoining it. Alexandrine had
no time to stand and gaze about her as they alighted,
for the carriage moved off immediately to allow another
to take its place and Luc took her hand and led her inside.
She found herself the centre of attention as he led her
through endless corridors, jostling shoulders with other
guests, who often stood back to watch the couple pass.
He nodded acknowledgement to many people, greeted
only a few cordially, reminding her of the time he had
taken her for a carriage-ride. It was as though he wanted
to remain apart from them. She knew that, had she not
been so magnificently dressed herself, she would have
become embarrassed at the attention being paid her. As
it was, her gown and jewels equalled those of any of the
women. That knowledge and the man at her side, who
from time to time smiled down at her with pride in his
eyes, made her straighten her back and hold her head a
little higher.

Soon she was so fascinated that she forgot the comments and the stares and the whispers which followed
them. She could not drag her eyes from the beautiful
paintings on the panelled walls on either side of them
by artists such as Boucher and Watteau, and the eye-
catching landscapes by Poussin which made her think
of the countryside around Noyen. She was captivated
by the enormous, richly woven tapestries everywhere,
some so large they took up an entire wall, from end to
end, floor to ceiling, and the gilt stucco-work that was
characteristic of Louis XIV's reign brought gasps of admiration from her lips.

Carefully picking up her skirts, she attempted to keep
pace with her husband, whose stride was more like that
of a young man in his prime and in the best of health
than of an ageing man who had recently been confined
to bed for over a week. She suspected he was attempting
to prove to those they passed that he was fit and well
and not at death's door. He was a very proud man, she

decided, and there was still a great deal she did not know
about him.

She craned her neck to look out of the windows at
the gardens which surrounded the main buildings, her
eyes dwelling longingly on the well-laid-out pathways and
arbours and the many fountains by which people were
strolling in the unexpectedly warm sunshine. How she
wished they were out there in the cool instead of inside
where it was unbearably hot! It would only grow worse,
she surmised, once they entered the banquet hall ahead
where the reception for the foreign ambassador was to
be held.

Alexandrine was not sure whether she liked what went
on at Versailles, but the place itself enthralled her, in-
trigued her and held her spellbound, despite the air of
unreality that prevailed. The highest degree of etiquette
was demanded at Versailles, and people cared little that
they would stand for five or six hours in the presence of
the King while he ate breakfast, went to Mass, received
petitioners and then ate lunch and so forth throughout
the day. It was not unusual for them to remain on their
feet until the early hours of the morning, at which time
they would stagger wearily to the apartments allotted to
them. The unlucky ones would find repose where they
could, and pray that the next day they would be noticed
by their monarch. It was a life she did not wish for. She
was content to remain at home at the Place des Vosges,
with only an occasional attendance at court. She would
not miss the noise and the bustle, and certainly not the
attention. She could stay as long as she wished, Luc had
told her that morning, as he had two small rooms which
had been bestowed on him by Louis XIV, when the court
of the Sun King was at its most splendorous.

The noise from the banquet hall as they entered
deafened her. They had to force their way through people
who stood crushing each other about the laden tables
and were reluctant to move the slightest fraction to allow
them to pass. It was unbearably stuffy, but she could
not use her fan for fear of hitting someone as she
squeezed past men and women busy chattering about
the latest pretty face who had caught the King's eye, or
the latest unfortunate to fall from grace. Ordinary con-

versation was non-existent. No one was discussing what
a lovely summer it had been, or if the crops were good
in the fields, or their families and friends. So false, she
thought, relieved when they managed to find a space at
the end of one of the tables and Selim fought his way a
few more feet to scoop two glasses of ice-cold champagne from a tray for them. No, this was not for her!

Alain Ratan could not take his eyes from Alexandrine.
For the first time he found himself looking at her not
as the wife of a friend, or as the opportunist, scheming
female he believed her to be, but as a woman, a beautiful, desirable woman. He was shocked by the effect she
was having on him. His eyes had alighted on her as she
entered, clinging tightly to Luc's arm as they threaded
their way the entire length of the room to seek a place
to stand comfortably. The blood-red rubies at her throat
and ears accentuated the alabaster whiteness of her skin.
The ball-gown was a creation to top all creations fash-
ioned for this evening's event, he thought, noting the
envious glances that followed her. She looked a lady, no
longer the tousle-haired urchin he had seized in his arms
and thoroughly kissed that first night they had met! She
carried herself well, and Luc was damned proud to have
her at his side, that was obvious! She had done him
credit, he could not deny it. He knew that for his own
peace of mind he should turn and leave the room. The
King had not yet arrived, so his bad manners would go
unnoticed, but he could not. Instead, he found himself
moving towards her.

'Luc, I am glad to see you are better,' he said upon
joining them. 'Madame la Marquise, your nursing has
made him a new man.'

Alexandrine allowed him to touch her fingers to his
lips. Slowly she lifted her eyes to his face, expecting to
see there the usual mockery, and found none. Only a
frank admiration as he surveyed her, which was more
devastating than any barbed comment he might have
made. He knew, of course, that she had not been allowed near her husband, that only Selim had attended
him. Like Paul, he was a man with two faces! She must
not trust him.

'I should feel more of a new man if I had another drink,' Luc returned, draining his glass. At his side, Selim frowned at the comment.

'Do you think you should?' Alexandrine asked, concerned that he had not yet eaten. 'Shall I bring you something to eat?'

'Don't fuss, child! I have a head like a rock, and this stuff tastes like water. But you go and get yourself something. Alain, feed her before the vultures devour everything. The King probably won't appear for some time yet. I heard someone say that he went hunting this afternoon and had a bad time. A single deer, that's all they managed to kill, which means he has been in a petulant mood for several hours. Selim, the Comte de Marsin is over there, do you see him? With Madame Le Froix? Bring him to me. I wish to have a few words with him. Well, go on,' he added to Alexandrine, when she did not move.

The last thing she wanted was to be alone with Alain Ratan, but she had no choice, or Luc would question her reluctance to comply with a simple request. In silence she allowed him to lead her to one of the tables and watched as he slipped cold chicken and spiced ham on to a silver platter for her, noticing how people stepped aside to allow him through, even though there were many before him. A man of importance—even power—which made him respected and perhaps a little feared in court circles, she thought. He stood out amid the crowd, even though his clothes were less colourfully conspicuous than many. He was dressed in dark grey. Beneath the open coat with its wide turned-back sleeves, where an abundance of frothy white lace matched that of the jabot beneath his throat, was a waistcoat of pale grey silk, embroidered with silver thread which blended admirably with the darker colour. His shoes were of matching leather with plain silver buckles. No bright yellow or flame reds for him! No streaming ribbons from shoulders or garters, and yet many a head turned to watch him return to Alexandrine's side and she saw a few fans begin to flutter faster.

'It is very uncomfortable in here. Shall we find somewhere cooler to enjoy our food?' Alain asked, looking
about him.

'How gallant you are tonight, monsieur, but I do not
trust you,' she returned bluntly.

'You have every reason! You still have a most tempting
mouth, and alone with you...' His pale eyes danced with
wicked lights. 'But I very much doubt if I could find a
place to be alone with you tonight, so you are quite safe.'

'I should not leave Luc. He will wonder where I am.'

'He is with an old friend. Besides, he trusts me, even
if you do not. And Selim is watching us like a hawk.
That one misses nothing.'

'I know. Sometimes I feel he can see me even if I am
in another room,' Alexandrine answered, and Alain
smiled as he guided her towards the far side of the room,
holding their platters high to avoid the food being
knocked out of their hands.

'He comes from the mystic East, where I am told anything is possible.'

They walked together along a glass-panelled corridor
towards the gardens, where it was blissfully quiet after
the uproar behind them. When Alexandrine made the
excuse that she wanted to stop and sit down in order to
eat her food, Alain's eyebrows rose quizzingly, and she
knew the lame excuse had not deceived him.

'Luc has entrusted you to me, and I repeat that you
are quite safe. Can we not begin again, madame? Let
us pretend we have met tonight for the first time. That
I never kissed you—and that you never enjoyed it. What
do you say?'

'You are impossible!' Alexandrine almost choked over
a piece of ham at his effrontery. 'I shall never trust you
after the way you have acted towards me. And how can
I forget it—or the things you said? Without ever knowing
me! You judged me unfairly—and unjustly.'

'Then, if we begin again, perhaps this time I shall be
able to make a correct assessment and not upset you,'
Alain returned candidly.

A statue of Cupid stared down at them as they passed,
an arrow aimed at her heart. Alain's smile deepened as
he glanced up at the stone figure. The God of Love had

smitten him once with an arrow, but he would take care it did not happen a second time, he thought, as he led her to a seat beside a small fountain.

'We have a truce, then,' he said, as she seated herself and continued to eat, and her eyes instantly locked on his handsome features, scanning them to see what trickery he was up to now. They were not alone, people were milling all about them, but they were mostly too engrossed in themselves to bother with the two seated by the fountain. She was as vulnerable here as she had been alone with him in her sitting-room, yet he had taken care not to sit too close, she noticed, and nothing in his expression betrayed an intention to seize her in his arms and subject her to those soul-searching kisses again. 'If only because I am Luc's friend,' he added, reminding her once again of the last time they had spent together, and she pursed her lips in annoyance. 'I see I am going to have a hard time persuading you of my good intentions. I shall have to try harder! Let us change the subject. What do you think of Versailles?'

'It is—rather overwhelming. It is so big and splendid. I never expected anything like this,' Alexandrine answered truthfully, as she put aside her empty platter. Alain, who had eaten little, offered his to her, and tempted as she was to accept the remaining mouth-watering slices of breast of chicken which had been cooked in a wine and herb sauce, she declined, confessing, 'I'm afraid I still have my country appetite, which I must curb, or none of my new wardrobe will fit me! I do not think Madame Heloise would be too pleased if I allowed that to happen.'

'You have filled out since you arrived, but you will never look like—her, for example!' He grimaced as a heavily perfumed woman bedecked with jewels and a preposterously large face-patch went by on the arm of a man, whose wafting aroma almost smothered her own. 'I prefer a woman to wear her hair naturally and to leave her skin unmarked by those hideous things.'

'What are they?' Alexandrine asked. 'My maid had a tin full of them and she thought I should wear one this evening. She said all ladies did at court.'

'Those that wish to get themselves noticed,' Alain said drily. 'Those so-called beauty-spots do not enhance a woman's features; far from it. Did you know they have a language all of their own? The "passionnée" is worn near the eye. The "coquette" close to the lips—you can draw your own conclusions from that one! The "galante" on the cheek and the "effrontée" on the nose.'

'You know a great deal about what a woman should and should not wear, Monsieur le Duc. I remember how critical you were when Luc was deciding on the right materials for my wardrobe. I am surprised you did not suggest I should always wear a "coquette".'

'*Touché!* I stand duly reprimanded,' Alain acknowledged with a mock bow. He held her gaze for a long moment, and Alexandrine felt as if the ground was moving beneath her feet, so intense was that look.

As she averted her eyes to something over his shoulder, Alain saw a soft touch of colour creeping into her unrouged cheeks. She was blushing. A woman blushing at Versailles! She was so natural and unaffected by all about her, and he was fast finding it difficult to retain his original conception of her. If she was merely acting a part of a shy, reticent wife, awed by the circles in which she now mixed, she was doing a beautiful job...and a convincing one! Even his contempt and mockery had thawed in such pleasant company. And he was remembering how those soft lips had been imprisoned beneath his. As he placed his platter on top of hers and drew back slightly, his hand brushed hers, and instantly her eyes flew once again to his face. What was it: apprehension—or anticipation? His fingers curled over hers. She did not move, but her lips parted slightly as if she wanted to speak, but could not. He found his head bending closer towards her face, uncaring who passed and saw them. He saw the alarm in her eyes, yet she made no sound.

A sudden commotion from the banquet hall brought him upright, and the moment of intimacy between them vanished.

'I think the King is about to arrive,' he said, rising and offering her his arm. She laid her hand on the grey velvet and he was sure he felt a tremor run through it for an instant before she composed herself and opened her fan.

What would I have done if he had kissed me again? Alexandrine wondered as they returned to the crowded room and the people standing on each other's toes in their eagerness to glimpse the arrival of the royal procession. Slapped his face? Ignored it and returned inside alone? No, that would have aroused questions at once. He had not changed! If only she had not been so much affected by his nearness, or wanted once again to feel the touch of his lips on hers. That was the terrible sin for which she could not forgive herself. She had wanted him to kiss her! She would never betray Luc with her body, but she was betraying him in her mind—with Alain Ratan.

CHAPTER FIVE

'PLEASE LET me through. I am trying to get to my husband,' Alexandrine pleaded, but the close web of people in front of her refused to budge. She had scarcely made any progress across the room and already Louis XV and his selected company were making their way towards the table where Luc and Selim stood. Occasionally the King would stop to converse with someone he knew or to introduce the tall, elegant, mouschachioed man at his side.

'Allow me,' Alain whispered. 'This is no time to be polite.' With that, he jabbed his elbow unceremoniously into the ribs of a stout man blocking their path. With a grunt of pain his head swung round, anger and indignation written on the puffed features, but no comment was ever uttered as he looked into the cold features of Alain Ratan.

'Stand aside, there's a good fellow. The Marquise de Mezière is trying to reach her husband,' Alain said pleasantly. Alexandrine had the feeling that had his wish not instantly been complied with, he would have used his elbow again, but harder, and more painfully.

'Thank you.' She slipped through the small space which opened up for her, with Alain close on her heels.

'Step on a few toes,' he said with a broad smile. 'That has the same effect. Or smile sweetly. In your case, equally as devastating.'

'Luc said I should never do that.'

'Your husband is a very wise man, and a protective one. I can understand his disquiet that a simple smile of appreciation could be taken for an invitation, yet it happens all the time here. But when one looks at the excuses for men that we see here, who can really blame a woman for seeking something better?'

'I, for one, am quite content with what I have. I consider myself very lucky to be married to Luc,' Alexandrine replied firmly.

'I thought you might miss the King's little walk, my dear,' Luc said, taking her by the hand and drawing her close.

Protective was not the word he should have used, Alain thought as he watched them, but possessive. It was natural for a husband to think of himself as owning his wife body and soul, but with Luc, he sensed, it went deeper and was far more complex than just the need to touch her and have her near him, or to show the world that he was her lord and master, for he had surrendered her company to his friend without one moment of apprehension. Or so it had appeared.

Of course Selim had been watching them all the time they were away. Alain had seen his attention focused on the corridor where they had walked, but, as always, the black face was impassive. If he suspected that Alain's interest in Alexandrine was not purely impartial, he did not show it.

What is this sudden attraction I feel for her? Alain wondered, still puzzled by his conflicting emotions, apart from the primary one of wanting to get her into his bed and prove to himself that she was just like his wife and every other woman he had made love to. What kind of woman really lay beneath that innocent smiling face? Angel or heartless devil, waiting to destroy him if he allowed his vulnerability to show? Child, who had recently suffered the loss of her family and had clung to Luc like a father when he offered marriage and protection, or scheming woman, well aware of the advantages that would be hers as the wife of such a rich, eminent man? Which? Would he ever know? Did he really want to suffer the agony of disillusionment yet again?

De Briges, the King's equerry, leaned forward to whisper in the monarch's ear as Louis halted a few feet in front of Luc Boussières, frowning as he stared at the long blue embroidered cloak. It was clear he did not remember a name, only that the face or the apparel was familiar. Reminded of the man's identity, he moved closer.

'My dear Marquis, how pleasant to see you at court again. I hear you have been ill since you last returned to our shores.'

'A trifling malady, Sire. Nothing to speak of,' Luc returned with a deep bow. 'I thank Your Majesty for his concern.'

'I am told you have recently married again...' A pair of black eyes turned themselves on Alexandrine, and behind her she heard a flurry of whispers at the King's interest. A new face for the capricious monarch to ogle and contemplate, as he did all newcomers—women that was—who came to his court. What would this one be seeking for herself? Young, Louis mused, staring hard as Alexandrine folded into a curtsy, and not unattractive, and with a freshness that was lacking among other ladies of his company. They were all so knowledgeable, so eager to please him—and it bored him to tears!

His bold gaze would have pleased many a woman had she been subjected to it before the whole court as Alexandrine was, but for her it brought only embarrassment and a fluttering in her heart that was akin to fear. Now she knew what Luc had meant when he told her to be careful with her smiles. She had the impression that one fleeting glimpse of encouragement on her face would have been enough to spur the King on to do more than engage her in polite conversation. What was it Jeanette had said about him?— 'He has not only a wife, but many mistresses. Who knows how many? He is far worse than his great-grandfather.'

Alexandrine knew more about the old King, Louis XIV, who had borne the grand title of 'Sun King' when he reigned resplendent over Versailles, then she did of this one, and she had often thought, during her days in the convent, what a hypocrite he must have been to attend Mass only an hour before going to one of his mistresses. Poor Louise de la Vallière had been acclaimed as his titular mistress, only to be cruelly abandoned when his attentions turned elsewhere. The Marquise de Montespan and countless others, including

Madame de Scarron, whom the King had disliked on sight at their first meeting, were to fall victims to the charm of the Sun King. Only Françoise d'Aubigné, Madame de Scarron, who in later life became Madame la Marquise de Maintenon, was to triumph ultimately. Not only did she become the wife of Louis XIV, remaining with him until he drew his last breath, but she was a controlling influence on affairs of state, especially in his last years when he grew old and dissatisfied with prospective candidates for the throne, since his rightful heirs had all died prematurely. How could a woman live such a life, continually at the command of a man, her future uncertain, her children most probably bastards or fostered out to other parents? Love did not prompt such unions between a monarch and a subject—but lust!

As Louis bent to lift her to her feet again she was aware of Luc's eyes narrowing. She glimpsed a strange look there before he lowered his gaze. Was this what he wanted to happen? Surely not!

'Allow me to introduce my wife, Sire. Alexandrine d'Albret.'

'Alexandrine? It sounds like music. How charming. Your wife will grace our court with her presence again, I trust, Marquis?'

Was it a request or an order? Alexandrine wondered, as the King turned back to her and the fans fluttered a little faster at his continued interest.

'Of course, Sire.' Nothing in Luc's tone betrayed that he was not in full agreement with the suggestion.

'And how do you like your first visit to Versailles, madame? Is is not a fascinating place? A fairytale kingdom where all dreams can come true.' Louis bestowed a charming smile on this stranger to his domain and there was not a woman in the room who would not have changed places with Alexandrine at that moment.

'I must confess I find it rather strange, Your Majesty,' Alexandrine replied, choosing her words with care. She did not want to give the King the impression that she might be willing to exchange her husband's company for his. Nor, she realised, must she offend the royal personage by not agreeing with him. She heard a gasp from behind and could only guess what was being whispered throughout the room.

Versailles, strange? The girl was a simpleton! The King of France spoke to her and she told him she thought his court was strange! 'It is indeed a fairytale kingdom, and it would be so easy to forget that I am a mere mortal, and allow my head to be turned by the beauty and grandeur all about me. But mortal I am, Sire, and a mere shadow amid the splendour that is Versailles.'

'Then you must come again—and again—and again, madame, until you do not feel strange, but that you belong here. And I assure you, before very long, the shadow will become a tantalising will-o'-the-wisp, elusive as all lovely women should be.'

Alexandrine sank into another deep curtsy as the King passed on, followed by the Queen and her entourage and the highest nobles in the land. She did not rise until she felt someone touch her arm, not wishing to see the speculation on the faces that surveyed her as they continued past. He expected to see her again, she realised, and he had more or less hinted that in no time at all she would become as ambitious as everyone else.

'Congratulations, Madame la Marquise,' Alain whispered in her ear. 'You have arrived.'

'I don't know what you mean!' she said indignantly. Of course, he would think she had enjoyed being ogled by the most powerful man in the land. She was being stared at more than ever now, and turned to Luc appealingly. 'Do we have to stay? Can we not go home?'

'Home? My dear, it would be the height of bad manners to leave now, especially as the King has singled us out. We would be *personae non gratae*—and, believe me, that would make life very uncomfortable for you. You would be barred from the best houses in Paris and forbidden attendance at court. Is that what you want? I don't think so. You must stay longer the next time and begin to make friends. Alain, take her away to dance; the poor child is having no fun at all.'

'I am sure that Monsieur le Duc has many friends he wishes to speak to. We must not detain him,' Alexandrine said, directing a look at Alain that told him she would not dance with him under any circumstances.

With a smile he excused himself and left them, and moments later as the musicians began to play and the King opened the dancing by leading the Queen, who was once the daughter of the deposed King of Poland, on to the floor, she saw him take the arm of a strikingly attractive dark-haired woman and follow.

'I did not bring you here to stand at the side of this old goat when you should be enjoying yourself,' Luc reproved when she stubbornly refused many offers to go into the ballroom.

'Have I not been stared at enough?' she asked, shaking her head at another invitation. 'I am glad I have seen the court and Versailles. It is a lovely place. I wish I could say the same for the people here. I do not belong, Luc, and I do not want to come again.'

'You will have to, my dear, or the King will be asking why you are absent. I shall of course accompany you when my health permits, but if that is not possible, you must come alone. There will always be Paul to escort you if you wish... Providing he retains the manners he has found tonight,' he added, as his son appeared at Alexandrine's elbow and requested the next dance.

It was on the tip of her tongue to refuse, when Luc frowned at her and she changed her mind lest he asked her why. It was clear that he thought Paul a reformed character, now doing his best to accept her as his father's wife. He could not have been more wrong!

She endured the torturous moments in silence, replying neither to Paul's sly remarks about the King's interest in her nor to the stares of the lecherous old men round them. Himself included, she thought, as his eyes continually stole to the cleavage of her bodice. She could not return to her husband's side soon enough, which earned her one last taunt: that soon she would grow tired of playing nursemaid to an old man past his prime, and look further afield.

When Alain presented himself moments later to claim her, she again refused, but for a far different reason. She had not forgotten those intimate moments earlier, and she did not want them repeated.

'Forgive me, monsieur, I am tired. Too much excitement, I think,' she said lamely, avoiding the challenge in his pale green eyes.

'Nonsense! You are concerned about me, and it does you credit, Alexandrine, but I insist you dance with Alain. To please me,' Luc said firmly, and she gave in with a faint smile and allowed herself to be led into the crowded ballroom.

'Why are you angry with me? I have tried hard not to offend you,' Alain murmured, keeping his voice too low to carry beyond her ears. He knew only too well how one word overheard could be misconstrued, misused or put to good use against someone who was momentarily in favour. And Alexandrine *was* in favour, he surmised. Whether the King's interest was genuine, or a ploy to keep the speculation away from his interest in Jeanne Poisson d'Etoiles, as had been the tactic of his great-grandfather with much success, it did not matter. Tonight she would be the most talked about woman at Versailles and everyone was waiting to see what happened from there. 'Your hands are cold, but your cheeks are flushed. With success, perhaps?'

'No, anger! And if you dare to insult me with one more word, I shall slap you again,' Alexandrine retorted, and someone close by tittered at the remark.

'Now that will really set the tongues wagging! So there is a temper beneath the docility. Good. But take care never to unleash it while you are here. It would destroy you,' Alain warned, at the same time wondering why he was so eager to give her advice. She was a woman and she would have her own way of dealing with any problems. What woman did not use the gifts with which God had endowed her? His wife was between them again! He had allowed her to enter his thoughts and give his tone a bite he had not intended. 'I do not agree with the King's description that Versailles is a fairytale kingdom. It is unreal, and far different from anything you have ever encountered or will encounter elsewhere. Most people when they come here become totally different from what they are in normal life.'

'Do you?' Alexandrine studied the handsome face frankly, wondering, if that was the case, what he was

like at home, surrounded by things he loved. Did the
cynic disappear and a man of compassion emerge,
capable of understanding human nature and not condemning it? A man who might have looked at her for the
first time and seen a shy, frightened girl from the country,
fresh from a convent, still sorrowing over the death of
her family and have offered sympathy and perhaps the
hand of friendship, instead of delivering insults about
her character and continuing in the days that followed
to cast her in the role of a harlot!

Tonight he was different and it made her suspicious,
but whereas Paul's deception was to deceive his father
and appease his anger, Alain Ratan had no reason to be
pleasant or to pretend he had changed his mind about
her. Perhaps he was genuinely sorry for the way he had
treated her—but she doubted it. He was a man of con-
viction. He did not like her, she was certain. He did not
trust her any more than he did other women—and yet
he was being agreeable. She had no doubt, had they
lingered outside, that he would have kissed her again,
and she knew deep in her heart, however hard she denied
it to herself, that she had enjoyed those kisses...

'I?' Alain's eyes rested amusedly on her face as they
came together again in the dance. 'Sometimes, perhaps,
when I am in pursuit of an elusive dream.'

'Of a woman, don't you mean?'

'I am not so old or ugly that I have to chase some
female who takes my fancy, madame.' The dark brows
knitted into a frown. 'Can we not dispense with these
formalities? May I be permitted to call you "Alexa"?'

'You may not,' she said quickly. 'We—We are not
sufficiently well acquainted for you to be so personal.'

No one had ever called her that before. It had always
been 'Alexandrine'. Even her brother and sister had never
been allowed to shorten her name. Luc called her 'child'
or 'my dear', very rarely Alexandrine. 'Alexa'. It had a
nice sound to it, but no! To allow him this small favour
might lead to others, and she could not risk that.

'What? Am I not the person who helped to select the
material for the captivating gown you are wearing—to

whom you turned for help when you needed a guest-list for your ball?' Alain declared.

'It would not be correct,' she insisted, and his mouth deepened into a smile which dared her to be adventurous and break the rules.

'Being correct, as you put it, can make life very dull. I shall call you "Alexa". That will be my special name for you. We shall be friends, but we are also adversaries in a game of chance.'

'Now you are being ridiculous!' Whatever did he mean?

'At Versailles, one can be what one wishes to be. Anything is possible,' he told her, as the music ended and he led her to the edge of the dance-floor. She saw the King looking in her direction and quickly turned away pretending not to notice the black eyes upon her. Perhaps, for others, anything was possible, but not for her. She had given Luc her solemn promise and she would not break her word nor betray his trust, not even with this man whose unfair assassination of her character had once brought her to tears, yet who attracted her as no other man she had ever met before. The men she had known she could count on the fingers of one hand. Her father and brother, the young man she was to have married, Luc, and a cousin with whom she had once been friendly, but not too close. Her mother had seen to that! 'Do the King's attentions bother you? Most women would find them flattering.'

'He is not very subtle, is he?'

'He is the King, why should he be so? He can have anything—and any woman he wishes—in this land.'

'Except me,' Alexandrine said firmly. 'Besides, I thought his interest lay elsewhere. With Madame d'Etoiles,' she added, discreetly lowering her voice. Jeanne was so certain that she would topple the present mistress from her position of power at the King's side and slip into it herself! Yet she still had not been invited to come to court.

'Like his great-grandfather, the King has an eye for beauty, but, as you say, he lacks the finesse all men should use when they woo a woman, especially an unwilling woman.'

'Are you speaking as an expert?' Alexandrine asked, wondering which of the women here tonight would interest him, if any. Did he have a mistress at court? What would he be like when he was with her? Cold and cynical, distrusting even, as they made love? Or gentle and considerate, shutting out the pain and bitterness which had made him such a misogynist?

'On the deceit and treachery of beautiful women who use their looks and bodies to obtain wealth and power, yes, I am,' Alain replied. The stinging comment was intended to wound, and he saw by the way she visibly flinched that he had succeeded. Yet the victory gave him no satisfaction and he instantly regretted ruining the pleasantness of their conversation.

In time she would show her hand. He could afford to be patient and, until then, enjoy her company, which he reluctantly accepted he did. What man in his right mind would not like to have her at his side? She was the object of admiring glances—and envious ones, too, he saw, his gaze alighting on a huddle of women not far away who continually peered over their fans and then put their heads together again to whisper and speculate. When it came to gossip at Versailles, the court ladies very often forgot their fine manners and became more like common fishwives, and the daily intrigue had ruined countless marriages. He himself had been the subject of comment for over six months after the death of his wife, but by then he was immune to it, and the last person who had been foolish enough to comment within his hearing on his wife's unfaithfulness had faced him across drawn swords in the cold grey light of morning and been despatched to the hereafter without a qualm.

'Come, I shall introduce you to some people,' he said, offering his arm. Still smarting from his words, Alexandrine hesitated before laying a ringed hand upon the grey silk. Light though her touch was, she felt the muscles beneath her fingers instantly tense. 'The people I named in my list are mostly here. The Duc and Duchesse de St Cyr are just passing. They have known Luc for years, and I know they will be pleased to attend your ball.' He exchanged a word with the middle-aged couple before moving on. 'Over there are the Duchesse de Metain and Madame Theodora. If you wish to be anyone in Paris, you must always have those two as guests. If they come, then you have been accepted. I sometimes think their opinion is as important as being noticed by the King. Not as lucrative, of course,' he added slyly.

Alexandrine's hand was kissed by marquises and comtes, her cheeks pecked by eagle-eyed dowager ladies weighed down with jewels. Her mind reeled with names and faces she was sure she would never remember. She found Alain's comments on people in the room both witty and amusing, and gradually she became aware of beginning to relax for the first time since her arrival at Versailles. She felt somehow safe at his side, yet knew he was the last man she could ever trust. A contradiction in terms: friends and yet adversaries. Perhaps he had not been so far from the truth, after all.

He appeared to know everyone, and by the different intonations in his tone, sometimes only very slight, but noticeable, she was able to determine his likes and dislikes. Most of the men he was acquainted with were only that, not friends. Apart from one other young man with whom he stopped to speak for several minutes and made an appointment to join him at the King's hunt the following afternoon, she suspected that only Luc was called 'friend'. She watched his lean mouth deepen into a sardonic smile as a group of richly apparelled men strolled past, their affected gait drawing little attention in the crowded room. If they had walked through Noyen, Alexandrine thought, barely able to contain a smile herself, they would have been laughed out of the village.

'Strutting peacocks,' Alain said derisively.

'More like hens in a farmyard!' she retorted, and the remark brought a deep chuckle from him.

'Yes, it is more appropriate, but do not be deceived by their pretty looks. Two of them are brothers, Marcel and Antoine Bièvre. Their speciality is consoling grieving widows and relieving them of their money, or alternately, offering sympathy to bored wives.'

'The main pastime of men at Versailles, so you have told me,' Alexandrine said. 'And the third? He looks harmless enough.'

The man was short and rather fat, his plump face quite sallow. As he laughed at something one of his companions had said, he revealed a perfect set of white teeth.

'That is Mario Collini, an Italian. He dabbles in the mystic, and I have heard it said that he has a cupboard full of poisons that kill rapidly and without trace. All for sale. Perhaps he has a little Borgia blood in him. Not a man to antagonise.'

'Enough,' Alexandrine said, turning back towards the main door. 'I am right in thinking that Versailles is not a nice place. Fairytale world indeed! It is a façade beneath which these men and women practise dangerous games.'

'Are you so naïve as to believe there is no evil in this world?' There was an incredulous note to Alain's voice that made her eyes spark with anger.

'I am well aware you think the worst of everyone, monsieur, but must I remind you that I was schooled in a convent? I have never mixed with such people before and I have little wish to do so again.'

'Madame d'Etoiles was also brought up in a convent, was she not?' came the dry answer, 'and she has visions of sitting beside the King of France as first lady of the land.'

No matter what she said, he would always retain his own misguided conception of women, she thought, abandoning the retort which leapt to her lips. Picking up her skirts, she began to make her way towards the exit with the intention of rejoining her husband. She longed to sit down, but no one sat in the presence of the King unless he specifically requested it, and that was rare. The stuffiness of the rooms was unbearable, and her feet, unaccustomed to the tight-fitting leather shoes with their high heels, were beginning to ache.

'Are you not dancing?' Paul stepped out in front of her, bringing her to an abrupt halt. Heads turned to see who had detained her, and perhaps more than one person was quick enough to catch the fleeting look of annoyance that passed across Alain's face as he caught up. 'I shall not allow you to refuse me.'

'I must, Paul. I am too hot to dance. Perhaps, after I have cooled myself with a glass of wine,' she protested, as a hand was laid upon hers. It was warm and wet with perspiration, so different from Alain's cool skin and the masculinity of his touch.

Paul was only twenty-five, yet already his way of life was beginning to take its toll, she noticed, taking care how she withdrew her hand so that he was not aware it had displeased her. The greyness beneath the eyes betrayed long nights gambling and drinking, despite his father's warning that he must control these excesses. Luc had even talked to her about buying a country estate for Paul to manage, which would take him away from the pleasures he pursued with such vigour and perhaps give him a new life. It was also a way of ridding the house of his presence, she had thought, but wisely had not mentioned this. Paul had openly ridiculed the suggestion, and his parting shot, as he left the room after another heated argument, was that his father could not last for ever... and upon his death he would inherit everything. Luc was so patient. She could not understand why. The bitter insults and then, fast on their heels, demands for money to pay his debts. Refusal brought more terrible rows. Compliance, more bills.

Paul's eyes flickered to the face of the man behind her, who shrugged indifferently. 'Then I shall leave you in Alain's capable hands—where so many beautiful young women have been before you.'

Alexandrine felt Alain's arm brush hers as he stepped forward, and instinctively her hand went out to restrain him. As Paul returned to his friends, she looked up into the hard, brown features and said quietly, 'Do not allow him to provoke you, please. He enjoys hurting people and he only will gain pleasure from it. Oh, the wretched man has made people stare at us again.'

'The gardens will be cooler and soon the lanterns will be lit. Perhaps, out there, you will find a little of the beauty lacking in here,' Alain said, tucking her arm firmly beneath his. Giving her no chance to protest, he escorted her out of the ballroom and along the corridor to one of the many open doors that led outside.

It was still just light enough for her to see the magnificent gardens and she realised she had barely seen anything from the carriage window. It would take hours to explore them fully and she knew she must not linger too long or Luc would begin to wonder where she was— and Alain Ratan might be tempted to think she liked his company more than she did. He must never suspect that she no longer found it as intolerable as she once had!

'Is that how Paul behaves at home? Luc gave me the impression when I saw him last that the situation had improved slightly.'

'I doubt if he will ever change,' Alexandrine answered, slowing her walk to gaze in awe at the display of flowers and trees and decorative fountains spread out before her. Here was perfection, created with care and love, and the results were breathtaking. 'He will never accept me as his father's wife. I'm sure he believes I...that I made Luc marry me. More, he considers his father a senile old man who did not know what he was doing, or is seeking to regain some of his lost youth by taking a young bride. Both are untrue. Luc knew what he was doing when he persuaded me to marry him. I was alone, without family or friends, in a large old house with no servants. At first I thought he proposed because he considered it his duty, because he had been a close friend of my father and mother, but later, after we had come to Paris, he told me...' She broke off and, even in the fading light, Alain could see the colour rising in her cheeks. She did not look at him as she continued shyly, 'That he cared for me very much.'

Cared, but had not mentioned love. Yet he had mentioned it to Alain that first evening. Had it been a lie, a deliberate attempt to conceal that all was not as it seemed? Alain wondered. Desire, not love, had prompted Luc into such impulsive action, else why go to such lengths when he could have done as Paul so cuttingly commented, and set her up in a fine house anywhere he chose? Instead of a free existence, for no man considered the demands of a mistress in any way binding upon his way of life, he had chosen the chains of wedlock. Alain supposed that no one would ever know the real reason why Alexandrine d'Albret had become the Marquise de Mezière.

Alexandrine allowed her gaze to return slowly to the main stone building with its flat roofs and imposing tall chimneys, which housed the royal apartments, state rooms, banquet hall and private chapel. Lights began to blaze from every window as the candles suspended in the huge silver chandeliers were lighted by servants. They threw a soft glow on to the courtyard beneath, where four long rows of mature orange trees stood, each in its own tub. The sweet smell of orange-blossom came wafting to her nostrils, carried by a pleasant evening breeze which instantly dispelled an unpleasant throbbing in her head.

'This is lovely,' she breathed. 'I suppose I should not blame Versailles for the people it attracts.'

'Wealth attracts more wealth. Beauty, more beauty. Greed, more greed. Not every man here comes seeking power—or another man's wife. Nor every woman a diversion. The nobility have certain positions to maintain here—very exacting positions, as you will discover. Like the old King, this one lives his entire life in the public eye . . . well, almost all,' he added with a wry smile. 'But he expects, nay demands, the highest degree of etiquette and dress. Many a family have become destitute trying to keep up the grand lifestyle demanded of them.'

'But I have no need to be here,' Alexandrine protested softly, most of her attention still centred on the cascading fountains that lined one entire path. Very little noise from the crowded rooms disturbed the tranquillity of the scene or masked the gentle sound of running water. Perhaps with a little thought and redesigning, she might be able to have a fountain built in her garden at home. There was room enough. She could line a room with mirrors, as she had seen tonight. With a soft laugh, she turned back to Alain apologetically. 'Forgive me, my thoughts are elsewhere.'

'You are saying that you have no need to be here. Before tonight that might have been the case, but not now that the King has seen you and asked that Luc bring you to Versailles again. It was not a request, Alexa, it was a royal order. And, if his health permits, Luc will have to attend more often now. What is wrong with him, by the way? I have not seen him look so ill for many a month.'

'I—I am not sure.' Alexandrine was ashamed to confess her ignorance and saw Alain's eyebrows rise. He, too, considered it strange, and hastened to add, 'I am sure it is nothing serious. Selim assures me that it is an illness Luc contracted many years ago during his travels. It is weakening and he has to rest. Nothing more serious than that.'

'I am glad you feel so confident.' There was an irony in his tone that she did not like. 'He will need the strength of a healthy man to survive the rigorous life here again. The nobility who reside permanently here at Versailles are jealous of their positions. Their one aim is to please the King at all times, in all things. They will lie, scheme and bribe anyone necessary in order to see that they do not fall from grace. Luc once told me he hated the frailty of their existences. I thought the description rather apt. If Luc is indeed in good health, this may very well be the medicine he truly needs to be back among the living with you at his side.'

'You sound like Paul: as though you would like to see him dead!' Alexandrine retorted. Lean fingers coupled her wrist, bruising it with a relentless pressure. Pale glittering eyes came close to her face.

'Luc is the only man I have ever called "friend" in many, many years. His is the father I never knew, for mine died fighting far from his home when I was a babe. He is a good man, and I will not allow anyone to hurt him. Not Paul—and not you.'

'Why, oh why, must you always be so distrustful, so cynical?' she cried angrily. 'Just once, could you not say something nice!'

Alain's eyes narrowed sharply. She caught her breath, her heart fluttering unsteadily at the way he looked at her. Pull free and run before it is too late, a warning voice in her head demanded, but her legs had no strength and she very much doubted if she could loose his hold on her.

'What do you want to hear, Alexa? That I think you are a lovely, desirable little creature? That I would like to make love to you? Both are true.'

'Oh, you are impossible!' she gasped, her face flooding with colour. Her legs had grown even weaker at his words. He thought her—lovely! Desirable! Was he seeing her as a woman or as another instrument of revenge?

'Why? Are my words not colourful enough? Did no good-looking farmhand in your village ever say them to you when he tumbled you in the hay?' The indignation and horror which rose in her cheeks only confirmed his suspicions that his assumption was correct. 'I could elaborate on that petal-soft skin, the way the fragrance in your hair reminds me of orange-blossom. How I find it difficult to be with you and not touch you in some way. And, of course, I must not omit the possibilities of that pert little mouth, lips that taste so sweet when they surrender. I want you, Alexa, but because you are Luc's wife I shall never have you, and I have just made clear that I will not hurt that man in any way.'

Not hurt Luc, yet he wounded her continually with his hateful remarks, mocked her intent to become a good and faithful wife. Watched her with what she now knew to be longing in his eyes, yet suppressed the need in him. She was shaken beyond belief. *He* desired her, despite all this!

'Am I meant to be flattered?' She tried to sound scornful, and instead was horrified to hear a tremor in her voice, betraying her agitation. 'I am not, monsieur. You insult me with such words. I know you do not mean them and I see no reason for such a pretence, except perhaps that you too have spent too long at Versailles.'

'Bravo, I have roused a little fire,' Alain murmured, drawing her closer. The arm encircling her waist was as imprisoning as the hold he maintained on her wrist. Crushed against his velvet coat, she could hardly breathe. She flung back her head and stared defiantly into the mocking features, terrified that for all his bold words about his friendship with Luc, if she showed him the least encouragement, he would whisk her off into the seclusion of the trees where they could not be seen and subject her to more devastating kisses, skilful caresses, against which she knew she had no defence. No schooling could ever have prepared her for a man like Alain Ratan!

A lackey passed them, pausing to light one of the hundreds of lanterns suspended from trees and trailing arbours. Without giving them even a cursory glance, he hurried on. Close on his heels came several couples who had slipped away from the overcrowded, abominably hot rooms, seeking air and privacy in the gardens. As they passed, Alain released her wrist and pressed her face against his chest, bending his head over hers so that neither of their faces could be seen, but she did not even realise what he was about and struggled to free herself.

'Be still, little idiot! Do you want everyone to know you are out here with me?'

'Why should you care? Will it upset your precious friendship with my husband? That will be no more when I tell him your true character,' Alexandrine taunted as she was allowed to raise her head again. 'You are a rogue! A dangerous rogue!'

'I have never been called a rogue before. Dangerous— there are some who consider me so. Why do you, Alexa? Is it because you fear Luc may believe a snippet of gossip about you, or because you fear to be here with me? Anywhere with me? I think that is the true reason, but, like most women, you have to find a feeble excuse to conceal the way you feel. I make you feel like a woman, and you enjoy it.'

'You make me ashamed to have trusted you this far!' she retorted. 'I shall not be so gullible in the future.'

'So far, I have been the perfect gentleman. Did I not save you from Paul's undesirable company? Have I not introduced you to the cream of Parisian society? You are too harsh in your condemnation, Alexa.'

'Don't call me that! I forbid it!'

'I think you like the sound of it. When you hear it, you will always think of me,' Alain mocked. He held her so tightly against him that he could feel the fierce thudding of her heart against his chest. Look but do not touch, he had promised himself that evening. Be with her, but do not offend her. Yet he could do neither, he had discovered. Her perfume enveloped him as he bent his head towards her, and try as she might, she could not avoid his determined mouth.

His lips lightly brushed hers, stirring her even with such a fleeting touch. She steeled herself for his kiss, praying that she would not weaken and answer him as she had done that day in her own sitting-room.

'Madame la Marquise, your presence is required at
once, if you please.' Selim's voice coming out of the
shadows to one side of them almost made her faint with
shock. Alain's arms fell away. She took an unsteady step
backwards,. and found the man a few feet from them.
'The Marquis has overtaxed his limited strength and is
returning home. He sent me to find you,' he added, as
if sensing that Alexandrine suspected him of spying on
her... which she most certainly did!

'I shall come at once.' She did not look at Alain as
she followed him back along the path and into the
banquet hall. There had been no accusing expression on
the Moor's face at finding her in the arms of another
man, but the contempt in the dark eyes had been more
eloquent than a thousand words. If she had been discovered in a thoroughly compromising position, she
could not have felt more ashamed and humiliated!

'Luc, forgive me, I was looking at the gardens,' she
said contritely.

'And I would not dream of dragging you away at such
an early hour,' Luc assured her, patting her hand apologetically. His face did have a drawn look about it, she
thought, and he needed the support of Selim's arm. 'I
have made my apologies to the King, and he has
graciously allowed me to leave. But you shall stay, my
dear. You are in good hands with Alain.'

'I will not hear of it!' She was aghast at the suggestion. To stay? In his care? 'I shall come home with
you.'

'No.' The firmness of Luc's reply took her aback. 'You
must stay. I have had my apartment here prepared for
you. Your maid awaits you there if you are too tired to
come back home. And I think you will be, young as you
are. My dear, you look quite radiant.' For a moment, a
thin hand touched one of Alexandrine's cheeks. 'Such
colour. I have never seen you look so well. Take care of
her for me, Alain, and see she is not bothered too much
by ardent young men.'

'Luc, I shall not allow you to go home alone!'
Alexandrine protested, growing desperate at the prospect
ahead. Alone, at Versailles? No, not alone—accom-

panied by Alain Ratan. Luc did not know what he was
doing!

'There is no more to be said,' her husband declared.
'Now, walk with me to the carriage and we shall say
goodnight. I shall see you in the morning, and I shall
expect a full account. You used to tell me everything
when you were a little girl, do you remember, seated on
my knee, pulling this old beard?'

In a confused silence, Alexandrine followed Luc and
Selim outside to where the carriage waited. Behind them,
Alain kept a respectful distance as she caught Luc's hand,
still hoping to change his mind. Of course all the guests
were expected to remain until the King and his party
retired, she had forgotten that... But who would miss
her?

Luc bent to kiss her flushed cheek, and said in a voice
too low to carry beyond them, 'Do you remember what
I once said to you, my dear? Many faces are worn abroad
in this city to hide a multitude of sins. Wear a special
face for Versailles and leave it behind when you return
to me. Enjoy yourself, but always remember who you
are...my wife!'

'How can I enjoy myself, when you leave me alone?'

'A smile can hide a thousand heartaches, deceive the
most probing eyes. Pretend, my child, and answer no
questions about me. It is not unusual for couples to go
their separate ways in this place. No one will consider
it strange that I am not with you. Only Selim and Alain
will know I have left Versailles, and the King. I wish it
to remain that way.'

'Very well. Of course I shall respect your wishes.'

She picked up her skirts and stepped back as the carriage moved off, concerned by the way Luc leaned back
in his seat and closed his eyes. It was as though what
little strength he had was draining from his body. Aware
of Alain beside her, she glanced up, and more of her
husband's words came into her mind, unbidden. You
will discover in time, that Alain is totally impervious to
womanly wiles...I know you will never encourage him.
He understands that my wife is out of reach. But did
he? He wanted her, and the knowledge frightened her.

'Shall we return to the dancing, Madame la Marquise?' The formality was for the servants about them and passers-by taking the night air. 'You will be safe enough in the ballroom.'

She would never be safe with him, Alexandrine knew, forcing her steps back towards the banquet hall and the sound of music from the adjoining room. Wear a special face for Versailles. What good advice! Her smile would mask the way she felt in this unreal world and, hopefully, protect her from gossip. And from Alain Ratan.

CHAPTER SIX

IT WAS well past midnight before the King began to indicate that he might be growing bored with the evening, but another whole hour had passed before he eventually quitted the room with his entourage.

Alexandrine heard the sighs of relief which ran through the guests. Some staggered wearily down the endless corridors to gloomy rooms set deep in the heart of the maze, for however small or unwelcoming their habitation, it was greatly treasured. To be afforded one tiny, windowless attic meant that person had succeeded in life—they had been accepted at Versailles.

Alexandrine found her way to the door and was immediately lost upon stepping out into the corridor. Which way to go? Left or right? She had no intention of remaining overnight at Versailles, only of finding Francine and returning home as quickly as possible. She had successfully managed to conceal her concern for Luc during the last few hours, but now he was uppermost in her mind. He would be asleep at this late hour, but in the morning she would beg him to tell her what was the matter with him. Selim's ministrations had obviously had little effect if he was still weak. They should consult other physicians; there were many in Paris of good reputation and, for Luc, money was of little importance. He could afford, and should have, the best. She would insist upon it. It was her right, her duty. And she must prevail upon her husband to allow her to nurse him. That would keep her away from Versailles and the prying gossips determined to invade her life. The King could not demand the presence of either of them if Luc was ill and needed her.

Declining the offers of men to escort her to her carriage, or to help her find her rooms—her lips tightened at the idea that she might be willing to slip away to seek a few stolen moments in the arms of a stranger—she hurried on. She was directed up more stairs, along longer corridors and was despairing of ever finding Luc's apartment when she saw Francine hurrying towards her carrying her cloak and gloves, and looking quite agitated.

'Madame, I never thought I would find you!' the girl gasped breathlessly. 'I have been searching this past half-hour, and been lost half a dozen times. This place has more hidden places than the Beggers' Quarter! The men are the same, too! Do you know I was accosted by some grinning stableboy who wanted me to... Well, you know!'

'It seems to be a popular pastime at Versailles,' Alexandrine answered with a grimace. 'Quickly, help me on with my cloak and let me find our way out of here.'

Her eyes alighted on a servant busy snuffing out some of the candles, and she sent the maid to fetch him to guide them back downstairs. Within minutes they had reached the courtyard, and without being pestered again. Not until then did Alexandrine realise that she had no carriage to take her home. Luc was not expecting her until the next morning.

'Madame, are you expecting to walk back to Paris, or will you accept the comfort of my carriage, and my company?'

Paul's head appeared at the window of one of the re- maining fiacres. He smiled as she looked about, sensing her reluctance to get in with him. Alexandrine did not like that look, it was too confident. He knew she must accept or indeed walk home, and that was unthinkable. Of course she could have returned inside and remained overnight, but that prospect was just as daunting as ac- companying him. With great reluctance she nodded, and was helped into the carriage, seating herself deliberately on the opposite side to him. She wanted no more thigh- pinching on the return journey! When Francine at- tempted to follow her, Paul fluttered his lace-trimmed handkerchief at the lackey and the door was slammed in her face, and she heard the girl being ordered to ride outside with the driver.

'It is too cold,' she protested in dismay. Francine's presence would have greatly comforted her; now she was beginning to grow uneasy. Paul was never nice to her without a reason.

'These peasant girls are hardy types. Rather like country wenches, I've found.' As the carriage moved off, Paul crossed one stockinged leg over the other and viewed her from beneath lowered lids.

Alexandrine turned her head away and stared out of the window, refusing to allow herself to be provoked, even at the comparison between herself and a country girl. She was not ashamed of her origins.

The night had become bitterly cold. How brilliant the stars are, she thought, leaning her head against the up-holstered back-rest. Was it really possible to tell the future from these twinkling jewels? As yet she had heard nothing from Solange, and it had been a week. Had she been expecting anything? The woman had forgotten or, more likely, was a charlatan. The future was in God's hands, and only His!

She was ashamed to think she had ever considered the woman's silly prophecy to be true and, what was worse and even more shameful, to think that Alain Ratan, Duc de Belaincourt, was one of the men mentioned. Her destiny, such as it was, lay with Luc. Nothing could change that, nor did she want it otherwise. She would not see him any more, and if he came to the house she would find some excuse to avoid him. That way, the id-iotic notion would soon leave her head. She had allowed herself to be swayed by his handsome looks and his worldliness, which, in its way, was so different from Luc's. It would never happen again! The silent resolve brought a soft sigh from her lips.

'It is little wonder you are exhausted,' Paul remarked, mistaking the sound for a stifled yawn. 'When I wanted to dance with you, you were hot and tired and needed to be refreshed. Yet, not long afterwards, you were ac-cepting invitations from any man who asked you and, by the look of it, enjoying every moment of the flattery pressed upon your unwilling ears.' His mockery stung her. With an effort she refrained from a sharp retort. She was too tired to argue, and he was correct. She had danced with anyone who asked her. Always upon her face was the same polite smile, masking what she felt when her hand was held too tightly, a suggestion whispered in her ear that made her shudder. Even the quite harmless, genuine compliments soon fell on deaf ears. She shut herself off from all of them. 'But, then, Alain had deserted you, had he not? Did you see the woman he was with? Isn't she a beauty? Madame Claudia de la Fontaine. Like you, she married a rich old man who soon died—she tired him out, didn't she?—and left her sickeningly rich. Alain prefers them like that, you know. Independent, with no clinging husband who might call him out. He'd kill anyone who did, of course. It wouldn't be the first time. No, he likes his women to enjoy the things in life that he does—and I don't mean horses.'

Paul broke off with a throaty laugh, and she quickly interposed, 'I have no interest in the Duc de Belaincourt. He was merely chaperoning me because your father had asked him.' She tried to make light of it, crushed beneath the weight of what he had told her. Claudia de la Fontaine was his mistress! But had she not expected him to have one? Why did she care? And he had dared to press his unwanted attentions upon her! The arrogance of the man! He had succeeded in his efforts more than he would ever know, but that was behind her now and she must forget it—and him!

'And he made no impression on you? I must remember to tell him how immune you are to his charms. You will be the first woman I can think of who has been...or perhaps you are not...' Paul leaned towards her and immediately the pungent Cologne he wore threatened to overpower her. 'Did he made advances towards you, dear stepmother? I wonder... He maintains you are too thin and countrified to arouse even one iota of interest in him. I didn't believe him, but now...' He chuckled again, enjoying some joke that was lost on Alexandrina.

In the darkness she grew hot with embarrassment to think she had been a subject of discussion for him and his friends...and Alain Ratan thought her too thin! Yet he still had kissed her, wanted to hold her and make love to her. It was a game with him, she decided. A horrible, cruel game meant to inflict the deepest, most searing wounds possible. As revenge, naturally, for the wanton creature who had betrayed his love. Poor Claudia de la Fontaine. Did she realise what a brute she had as a lover? His sweet words had meant nothing, despite the apparent sincerity behind them. They were intended to lure her into believing he might care, but he would not ruin the friendship he had with her husband by pursuing her further. He was a devil! Now she knew that evil could wear such a handsome face and be so seductive, she would be on her guard. Never again would she allow herself to fall victim to such a man.

'What the Duc may or not have said is of no interest to me,' she snapped coldly.

'Did you want him to make love to you? In comparison to my father, you must have thought him a delectable dish. Most women do, but Alain is so selective when it comes to a prospective bed-mate. I could tell you stories of the parties I have been to at Belaincourt. Never-to-be-forgotten nights when passion ruled and time was unimportant. My father was usually away on his travels, of course, and gave no thought to my education, so I took it upon myself to find others to teach me. I recall one plump, ripe little thing who...'

'I will hear no more,' Alexandrine cried.

'I am simply trying to show you that I am quite as capable as Alain, dear stepmother...more so in many ways. I think he deserted you for Claudia, and that peeved you, did it not? That is why you sought out every handsome man in the room to dance attendance on you?'

'I did not!' she protested. 'They came to me. I did but dance with them, nothing more. Stop this at once; you sound ridiculous.'

'Ridiculous, am I?' His tone changed, to a low, menacing note, quite unlike the usual affected voice she was accustomed to hearing. 'Then I must show you otherwise. As compensation for Alain's desertion.'

She caught her breath as he threw himself down on the seat beside her, his hands clawing at the front of her cloak, tearing it open with such violence that the silver and diamond studded clasp was ripped from it and fell to the floor. Alexandrine almost fainted as his hands, hot and wet as they had been in the ballroom, despite the coldness of the night, touched her bare skin.

'Come, madame, don't be shy with me. I shall satisfy you far better than that old fool you sleep with every night. Is it every night he comes to you? Or every week—or not that often? Are you starved for love? You shall have it . . . with me! Be still. You will enjoy it, I promise. I may act the fool, but no woman has ever had cause for complaint when I leave her.'

'Why do you hate me? What have I done to you?' Alexandrine cried.

'Done? Done, you stupid creature? He is lavishing on you money that rightfully belongs to me! To his son, not to some scatterbrained little fool who warms his bed! Why did he marry you? What have you given him? I'll never understand why he didn't set you up somewhere like any other mistress.'

'I am not his mistress.' Alexandrine fought against the hands squeezing her breasts, sick with fear. 'I am his wife, and you will do well to remember it! I am tired of your insults, the lies told behind my back to discredit me. You hurt your father deeply.'

'What do I care?' Her words had no effect on him. 'The sooner he dies—or I run you back to your little village cousins—the better. I'll crush you, and him, if he makes it necessary.'

His mouth on hers suffocated her screams. When she raked at his cheeks with her long nails, he cuffed her roughly on the side of the head and she fell back, her senses reeling, with his weight pressing her down against the seat.

'Struggle all you like, you little country bitch, it will make my victory all the sweeter!' he hissed, as she fought frantically to throw him off, to push away the fingers fumbling with the fastening of her bodice, pushing their way down between the hollow of her breasts. A great roaring in her ears threatened to pull her down into an abyss of darkness, but she struggled above it, knowing that, even if she were unconscious, it would not save her. He would have his way. He was enjoying her struggles, enjoying the feel of her body twisting beneath his in terror. In subjecting her to this sickening act, he was revenging himself upon his father for having married her and for lavishing upon her money that should have been his. He blamed all his ill-fortune at cards on her, his losses, the arguments with his father, the prospect of disinheritance—all her fault!

In the wake of the terror that momentarily numbed her mind and body came anger, flooding into her weak limbs, instilling fresh determination to free herself from the loathsome creature bent on subduing her. She pounded at Paul's face with clenched fists and, opening her mouth, screamed for the carriage to be stopped. So shrill was her tone that it quite startled him, and as he drew back his fist to silence her, she caught him by the hair and pushed him back against the window, with all her might. He uttered an oath as one side of his face hit it and the hand that touched his mouth came away covered in blood.

He swore at her, using the most vile language. As the carriage lurched to a halt and he tried to steady himself, Alexandrine fell to her knees on the floor and found something hard beneath one palm. Paul's expression was derisive as she swung at his head the ebony-tipped cane and then howled in pain as it struck his temple. Again and again she lashed out at his grinning face, his body, the hands that vainly tried to grab her again.

Somehow her free hand found the door-catch and she fell out into the road. The fall stunned her. She heard a scream, and then Francine was kneeling in the dirt beside her, trying to lift her, blenching as she saw the condition of her mistress's bodice. She knew instantly what had almost taken place and turned hate-filled eyes on the face of the man who stuck his head out of the open door. She had not been at the house for a week before the attentions of Paul Boussières had become unbearable. When he had forced her into his bed one night and subjected her to his brutal lovemaking, she had threatened to go to Alexandrine. He had laughed, and looked at her as she pulled her clothes over her bruised body, as he was looking at her mistress now—satisfied with the pain he had inflicted. And then he had told her the terrible things he—or someone—would do to her if she breathed a word, and she had known she could say nothing. Who would believe her? And she did not want to leave her new employment and a mistress who was kind to her to return to the draughty, sordid little house in the Beggars' Quarter. She was never going back there, to grow old before her time!

She had not told Alexandrine of that time, or of the second occasion it had happened. When the time was right, she would tell her sweetheart, Jules. He would take care of Monsieur Paul Boussières! Perhaps, one day, there would be another unrecognisable body found floating in the Seine. It was a comforting thought.

'You will regret this, madame,' Paul sneered. The blows he had been dealt had badly winded him and he was aware he did not now have the strength to subdue her totally. There would be another time and, in the meanwhile, she would pay for the insult to his pride. Slamming the door, he shouted up to the driver to continue.

'He cannot leave us here!' Francine cried, jumping to her feet, but the driver only whipped up the horses, ignoring her. It was not his business to become involved with what went on behind him.

'Let him! Do you think I would ride with him again?' Alexandrine asked, rubbing wrists and arms that were beginning to ache from the attack on her.

'These woods are full of scoundrels, madame. Our lives will be worthless if we are found alone and unprotected. Dear heaven, the fiacre is coming back.'

Alexandrine's senses almost left her again. Back? To finish what he had started!

'Help me, quickly. Into the trees...'

She tried to rise, but one heel caught in the hem of her gown and she pitched forward on to her knees. The noise of the carriage clattering over the uneven stones grew louder... She threw out her arms, and Francine hauled her unceremoniously to the side of the road as it passed by at a fast pace without making any attempt to stop. She glimpsed Paul's grinning features briefly at the window as she sank to the ground, overcome with relief. It was only a momentary respite, for almost instantly she knew that what the maid had said was probably true. There would be unscrupulous men in the surrounding countryside just waiting for the opportunity to rob some helpless traveller—and they were very helpless. She could not even protect her shivering body against the cold penetrating her gown, for her cloak had been left in the fiacre, and so many diamond studs had been torn from her bodice that it would not fasten again to give her some respectability.

'Someone will come along soon,' Francine assured her, slipping her own cloak about Alexandrine's shoulders in an attempt to warm her. 'There will be other guests returning to Paris. I shall stop the first carriage that comes along.'

'And perhaps subject us both to the advances of another madman?' Alexandrine asked through trembling lips. Her powdered wig lay some feet away, covered in dust. It looked somehow ridiculous, and she had no inclination to put it back on her head. One of her shoes was missing, and she could see no sign of it. She would not be able to walk half a mile, let alone twelve or more. How cold she was! Partly fear, partly reaction to what had happened, she told herself, bravely climbing to her feet, but no matter how she felt, they could not remain on this deserted road and await some fate which could well turn out to be far worse than what Paul had had in mind. Her legs trembled, the starry sky spun about her head, and she clung to Francine's arm with a groan.

'I cannot walk ... but I must! I must!'

She forced her legs to move. They could scarcely support her, and after only a few tottering steps, she swayed unsteadily, came to a halt, only to force herself on again.

She only just heard the approach of the carriage that came round the bend behind and was upon them before the driver had realised the two figures ahead were not shadows and pulled back savagely on the reins. But her dazed senses gradually became aware of voices clamouring in her ear. Francine's raised in consternation, begging help. And a man's, demanding why his journey had been interrupted.

A hand was laid on her shoulder. A finger beneath her chin tilted back her head, and an oath broke from Alain's lips as the moonlight fell upon her face.

'What devilry has taken place here? Have you been robbed?'

'Attacked,' Francine interrupted, staring daggers at the man who knelt beside her mistress. She had stolen downstairs to watch the dancing from one of the outside balconies and had seen them together. She had thought what a fine pair they looked, until she had overheard someone remarking on the new beauty the Duc de Belaincourt had found for himself, who would no doubt go the same way as all the rest of his women. He was no better than the animal that had abandoned them. If he laid one finger on her the wrong way!

'No, not you . . .' Alexandrine moaned as he lifted her, and the cloak fell away to reveal her state of undress. 'Cover me, I beg you.'

Alain swore again as he shifted his hold to cradle her against his chest and ordered a servant to help him to get her into his carriage. Francine was not riding outside this time, and sprang in beside her mistress without being asked.

'Don't touch her,' she hissed, as Alain reached for the cloak. 'Your kind have done enough to her this night.'

'Your concern for your mistress does you credit, girl, but utter one more word unbidden, and I'll throw you back into the road myself!' Grasping her by the wrist, he pulled her on to the seat opposite him, then took her place. 'Under the seat there you will find something to warm her.'

Francine glared at him, but his tone told her it was not an idle threat and she did as he bade her. The neat box she drew out, which most fashionable carriages carried in those days containing jewels or firearms to repel footpads and robbers, contained more earthly necessities—a decanter of brandy and four small glasses. She half-filled one and gave it to Alain.

Alexandrine choked and coughed as he trickled a little between her bruised lips, and pushed it away. Instantly he held the glass to her mouth and ordered firmly, 'Drink it. You are frozen.'

She had never tasted brandy before. The smell revolted her and the taste was almost as bad. It burned her throat, but he made her drink it all, and when the fire reached her stomach, she realised it was warming her and restoring her shattered senses.

She gave a soft cry as she felt the carriage beginning to move. 'Where are you taking me?'

'Home. Where else?' Alain replied, unwrapping Francine's cloak from her and tossing it across to the girl who sat shivering opposite, enveloping Alexandrine instead in his own of heavy velvet lined with fur. He tucked it firmly round her legs, and then, as he drew it across her shoulders, his fingers brushed her bare skin and she flinched, her eyes widening. In the dim light of the small lantern inside the carriage, she saw his face register instant anger. Derisively he commented, 'I am hardly likely to make love to you under the eyes of your maid, am I? I have more finesse than that. I am not Paul.'

'How—How did you know?' she gasped, ignoring the taunt that, had she been alone, he might have taken advantage of the situation. She felt too wretched to care what he said, besides, it was all part of the game he was playing with her. He would find it amusing to alternate between being nice and sarcastic, and he would try to steal the odd kiss, she was sure, but no more. Not when he had a mistress as lovely as Claudia de la Fontaine!

'His carriage passed me on the way back to Versailles as though the hounds of hell were after him. The young fool! There will be the devil to pay when Luc hears of this. He will disinherit him, for sure! You are going to tell Luc, aren't you?'

'I—I don't know... Yes, I suppose I should.'

'Suppose!' Alain exclaimed. 'He forced his attentions on you, didn't he?'

'As another has done,' she retorted, reminding him how *he* had blackmailed her into silence.

'I find the comparison insulting. Have I not always been honest with you? The fact that I believe you took advantage of Luc's concern and married him to gain the wealth and position you would otherwise never have had—has nothing to do with my wanting you.' The bluntness of his words robbed her of an answer. 'Luc's relationship with his son these past years has been a strange one, but then Luc himself is an odd fellow and one never knows what to expect from him. He is constantly in disagreement with Paul over his drinking and gambling and refuses to pay his debts, but in the end he always does. There are times when blood is thicker than water. Myself, I would have thrashed the young idiot long before this and sent him out into the world to fend for himself. Tonight, however, when he learns what Paul attempted... But then the house will be rid of him, and so will you. You will be able to live in peace and harmony and enjoy Luc's money all to yourself.'

He felt her shudder against him and looked down into an ashen face streaked with tears.

'You beast! You heartless brute! You have no heart!' The cry was torn from her trembling lips.

'No, Alexa, if for one instant I allowed myself to look too deeply into those lovely eyes, to believe instead of distrusting...' She was cradled against his chest, her cheek pillowed against a firm shoulder, and the words whispered against her hair were barely audible. 'I would be lost.'

She could not have heard aright. She was confused, or the brandy had addled her brain. She stifled her sobs, determined not to give way to more tears, tempting though it was as she lay within the comforting circle of his arms. His eyes were narrowed in thought as she deliberately pulled herself free, clutching the cloak tightly to her.

'If I am too thin for you, monsieur, why do you enjoy touching me?'

'Who the devil told you that?' Her words slammed into Alain like an iron fist. He remembered well the comment he had laughingly made last week while with friends. Paul had been among the group. He needed to look no further for the culprit.

'*He* told me...tonight. And much more.' Let him wonder about how many of his confidences had been revealed. It would be some recompense for the insults flung at her. 'Do not worry. I am relieved that it is only a game. I would find it repulsive to know that a man like you was sincerely interested in me!'

Alain had never heard such reproach in her voice before. It shocked him and made him draw back from her to the corner of the seat, where he sat considering her in silence. Unable to bear his gaze, Alexandrine turned her head away and did not speak to him again until the carriage halted in the Place des Vosges. How glad she was that there was no one about to witness her undignified return! Wrapped in a man's cloak and wearing only one shoe, her short hair all awry, and dirt on her cheeks and covering the white ball-gown.

Francine jumped down and turned to help her mistress, but as Alexandrine stretched out a hand, Alain leaned forward and caught it and pulled her so close to him again that she could feel his warm breath on her face.

'A game, you believe!' He gave a short laugh. 'Perhaps. Then you must beware when the game stops, Alexa, for when that happens, we shall cease to be adversaries. We shall become lovers!'

We shall become lovers! Lovers!

The words hammered at her brain and would not let her sleep. Barely had she climbed into the bed than light was stealing through the curtains to herald the approach of another day. She was stiff and bruised, and lack of sleep had dulled the usual brilliance of her eyes. When Francine came to tell her that the Marquis was waiting to take a late breakfast with her in her sitting-room, she could have cried...had she not shed all her tears into the pillow upon her return.

She was smiling, however, as she stepped out of the bedroom and crossed to the sofa where Luc sat and kissed him on both cheeks. She had put on a robe of rich blue taffeta, and Francine had vigorously wielded a brush upon her short curls. She had pinched her cheeks to bring some colour into them, remembering how the sharp eyes of her husband missed nothing.

'I hope you are feeling better this morning,' she said, as he drew her down beside him. 'Do you think you should be up?'

'Selim's potions have worked their usual magic on me,' Luc assured her. 'I slept the night through. This morning I feel twenty years younger—no, thirty—when I look at you. But you, I think, are a little tired.'

'I have never danced so much in all my life,' Alexandrine confessed. 'And it was so late before I came home.'

'You should have stayed overnight at Versailles. I told you that my apartments had been prepared for you. That is what they are there for. Was there some—special—reason why you made the long journey home?'

'Yes, I was worried about you,' she answered truthfully. 'My place is with you. I should not have allowed you to persuade me to stay.'

'It was unthinkable that I should drag you away. Did you enjoy yourself? I want to hear about everyone you met. Did the King speak to you again?'

'No, and I am glad he did not. It would be very embarrassing to have my name linked with his.'

'Most women would welcome it,' Luc murmured, patting her hand. He had taken to touching her far more than he used to, and she wondered if he were not regretting the kind of marriage he had chosen for himself.

'That is what the Duc de Belaincourt said, and I told him I am quite content to be the wife of Luc Boussières, Marquis de Mezière.'

'Alain stayed with you, then?' Luc was surprised at her lack of enthusiasm over the evening. What is she not telling me? he wondered. She should have been bubbling over with excitement, unable to contain herself. Most young girls of her age would have been. She was too composed. Had she met someone who had attracted her, and was afraid to tell him? Had she slipped away from the crowded rooms with a handsome stranger of her own years, not an ill old man who could make love to her only in his thoughts? No! She had promised, and he believed her. He must believe her, or suspicion would drive him mad!

'For a little while. He was with someone—a Madame Claudia de la Fontaine. She was very lovely.'

'Alain's eye for beauty is excelled only in his selection of fine Araby stallions. Do you like to ride, my dear? I don't expect you had very much time for that kind of thing in Noyen. We shall have to find you a gentle mare if we are to hunt with the King's party. I shall quite enjoy it again. It has been years since I hunted. I have spoken to Alain about it and he has promised to find me some suitable animals. Now, tell me all you did after I had left.'

He would not neglect her any longer, illness or not, Luc decided, as she began to reel off a list of the names she had encountered the night before, confessing that she had forgotten the faces that accompanied them, for there had been so many. If he took Selim's advice and rested more, allowed no excitement to invade his life, moderated his consumption of port that inflamed his condition, he would prolong his existence for months. Only months, not years. So little time...

He would not stagnate and wither. He would live, and depart this earth in a blaze of glory, regretting nothing. And then she would be free to do as she pleased, love whom she pleased. But, until then... Before he left her, he intended to ensure that she would never want for a single thing. She would have all his money and as much property as he could buy for her. She would have to go in search of a husband, but she would be rich in her own right, and by then he would have taught her never to trust on sight.

Now, at this perfect moment, she was his. How sweet her hair smelled. He had never known her to use the heady musk perfume he had brought back from the Orient, for she preferred lighter fragrances of apple or orange. He was struck by how young she looked this morning, remembering the dress she had worn the night before and how it had turned a child into a woman. And such a desirable woman... Her hair was growing quite fast, and the natural curls twisted about her ears and caressed her somewhat pale cheeks. She was still tired. He had awakened her too early, how thoughtless of him, but he had been anxious to hear how successful her evening had been, having no doubt in his mind about that. She was so unaware of her own potential. Doubtless, many others had seen it and wondered how best to use it!

He closed his mind to anything and anyone outside. Time was too precious to allow any intruders into his life. She was affecting him more than usual this morning. Perhaps Selim's powders had revived him too much, he

thought drily. Alexandrine's eyes widened in surprise as
Luc caught one hand and carried her fingers to his lips.
It was an unexpected gesture, but not so startling as when
one arm went around her waist and she was drawn close
against him. His closely-cropped beard tickled her cheek
as he laid his lips against her soft skin.

'I shall make you the most desirable woman in Paris,'
he whispered hoarsely, as he buried his lips against her
neck. His free hand slipped inside the blue taffeta robe,
and she quivered as he cupped a firm breast. Never had
he been so bold with her! 'You *are* the most desirable
woman in Paris. For me. Don't be afraid, little one, I
shall never hurt you.'

His kisses had a certain desperation in them which
sent a flicker of fear through her. He made her feel as
if he did not really want to touch her like this but could
not help himself. She found herself pressed down upon
the couch. The robe was pushed back from her shoulders
and breasts and then he drew back and sat looking at
her in silence, until she could stand it no longer and tried
to cover herself. Her hands were immediately slapped
aside.

'Don't be afraid,' he repeated, beginning to stroke her
bare skin again. She closed her eyes, not knowing what
to expect, and heard him swear at the rigidity of her
body. 'Is it too much to ask that I look at my own wife?'

'Have I ever refused you anything? It is you who have
decreed the strange way our marriage shall be,' she returned. 'Do you not think I have seen the way you look
at me? That I do not know that, when you touch me,
you would like...' She broke off in embarrassment. 'I
do not understand what you want of me, not now.'

'I ask that you do what pleases me, my dear. This
pleases me.' Luc's calloused fingers explored the smooth
curves of shoulders and young breasts. A year aboard
a merchant ship when he had scrubbed decks until his
fingers had bled, mended canvas sails and fought
Moorish pirates who boarded the vessel in search of
slaves, had not left him with the hands of a gentleman.
His kisses were stifling upon her mouth, his hands more
insistent upon her body. She closed her eyes again and
offered no further protest, accepting what was about to

happen. He was suddenly still. She sensed instinctively that something was wrong and opened her eyes on to a face that stared down at her with a terrible accusation masking it.

She cried out, 'What is it? Why do you look at me like that?'

'Where did you get these bruises?' His fingers bit into her wrists as he jerked them before her eyes. 'Who were you with last night? Answer me, or, as God is my witness, I'll take a whip to you!'

'No one! Luc, you are hurting me.' The change in him was horrifying: from a man intent on making love to her, to a fiery-eyed demon who shook her until her senses reeled.

'Tell me! A name, dammit! Give me his name, and he will die by my hand before the sun sets. You swore to me! You promised there would be no other until I die.'

'There has been no one, will be no one...' Alexandrine whispered. 'Please believe me. Not like that. There was a man, but he was drunk.' It was the nearest she dared come to the truth, but she saw that it in no way appeased Luc's anger.

'Am I interrupting something, Father? I did knock, but...' Paul stood on the threshold of the sitting-room. Behind him, Francine held Alexandrine's breakfast tray and a decanter of wine for Luc. Paul shut the door in her face, adding with an amused smile, 'We don't want the servants listening to our little squabbles, do we?'

'Where did you get that bruise?' Luc started up from the sofa, his eyes locked on his son's cheek. Alexandrine saw on it the mark of their heated struggle. The cheekbone was swollen and already beginning to purple. 'You! You and he! I'll kill you!'

'Before you lose all reason, Father, I think you had better listen. If you had not deserted your poor wife, none of this would have happened. You, if anyone, are to blame for the bruises on her—and on me.'

What lies is he about to tell now? Alexandrine wondered, hurriedly covering herself as Paul's eyes rested upon her half-naked form. It would not be the truth—he would not dare—and she would be forced to corrob-

orate anything he said or run the risk of Luc accusing
her of more horrible things. The change in her husband
had greatly frightened her. Even now, as he stood looking
at Paul, there was a suppressed anger in him—no more
than that, she acknowledged, looking into the twisted
features. Did he hate his son? At this moment, he looked
as if he did. And he had looked at her in the same way.
How could he believe she had betrayed him?

'You have not told my father, then?' Paul asked her.
How devious he was to throw the onus on to her! Mutely
she shook her head. She could only wait and see what
he said. 'Your silence has brought you great distress, I
can see that. And you thought it was for his own good.'
He shook his head as though himself greatly distressed
by what he had seen and heard. No play-actor who made
the art a living could have performed better! she thought
in disgust.

She had been subjected to his recriminations and his
lust! Now she was being forced to ally herself with him
in order to save herself from the wrath of her husband.
A totally unjustified wrath, but how could she explain?
The light flickering in Paul's eyes told her he would twist
her words if she attempted to discredit him, and they
would both be considered guilty. From the strange way
Luc was acting, she suspected, this would be the way of
it.

'What do I not know—that has been kept from me
for my own good?' Luc demanded sarcastically. He
dared not look at Alexandrine. One moment of madness
had almost brought him down. If he had not touched
her, he would not have seen those marks nor suspected
her treachery. Could she not have selected someone more
worthy than his son?

'Alexandrine, after you had left her, was lost—poor
thing!' What had happened to the term 'stepmother',
which he managed to deliver with great derisiveness,
Alexandrine wondered, as she sat up and stared at him
challengingly. Alain had been a late-comer upon the
scene, but he if necessary could substantiate her story.
But if she told Luc the truth, would he accuse her of
allowing Alain to make love to her, as he was suggesting

Paul had done? Why had he changed towards her in the space of a few minutes?

'So it is "Alexandrine" now, is it?' Luc said, also noting the alteration in his son's address.

'Father, how suspicious you have become! Do I have to remind you that little country girls should stay where they belong? You chose to bring her into this house. I do not want her here. I tolerate her presence because you insist on it. I shall be polite to her, when necessary. Last night... Well, I confess it is the first time I have ever gone to the aid of a lady—I use the term lightly—whom I did not like and whom I knew would certainly not thank me for it. As it happens, she was most gracious, and I do have her thanks.'

'For what? A tumble in the gardens? How many of your friends did you encourage to watch your little escapade? From the marks on her, I can only assume you were your usual clumsy self,' Luc snapped.

'And, as always, Father, you are your tactful self,' Paul returned. His calmness surprised Alexandrine. He was not usually so contained when his father riled him—or *vice versa*. 'Alexandrine, concerned for your welfare, I repeat—for you, because you had left early and she was anxious lest you were ill again—decided not to stay at Versailles, but to return home. I tried to persuade her otherwise. The roads are unsafe by day, let alone at night, but she insisted. I, too, decided to return to Paris in a hired fiacre. I had promised a certain lady that I would visit her... You understand, of course.'

'Please!' Alexandrine could stand the delay no longer. 'Just explain what happened.'

The look he threw her was full of triumph. She would support him. She could do no less.

'*En route*, perhaps four miles from Versailles, I came upon Alexandrine's carriage. Some drunken ruffian, from the village, I suppose, had waylaid it with the aid of two companions. They fled as my fiacre came upon the scene, but he was too engrossed in trying to overpower your wife, Father. He would have done so, had I not intervened. Heaven forbid that I should pass myself off as a hero... I am not! But no gentleman could stand by while that happened. And, for my pains, I am accused by the very man I sought to protect of... Really, Father! Does your contempt for me know no boundaries?' Paul turned away, dabbing his bruised cheek with a handkerchief, more to bring attention to his injury, supposedly sustained in helping her, Alexandrine mused, then because it truly hurt him.

'This is what happened?' Luc turned to her. His eyes, like pieces of jet, bored into her very soul. She was deathly pale and trembling. She could not help herself; her lips quivered; no words would come. She knew she should support Paul's story, but she could not. She had never told a deliberate lie in all her life, and until this moment she had always been proud of the fact. Now she wished she were an accomplished liar. She nodded, tears starting to her eyes. If Luc did not believe her, she would confess the truth and he must make up his own mind. Were the bruises on her not proof enough that she had fought her attacker, whoever he was? And the state of her when Alain Ratan's carriage had discovered her? What was she to do? Her mind reeled...

'This man who attacked you—he was from Versailles? A gentleman?' Luc demanded, seating himself at her side. Her head was forced back, making it impossible to avoid his searching gaze. 'Would you know him again?'

'A—A gentleman.' She was stuttering again. 'No—No, he was poorly dressed—and he smelled terrible! Of onions—or garlic...something like that. I was almost asleep when the fiacre was stopped. It was so late, and I was tired...'

'A peasant, obviously,' Paul declared, with a nonchalant shrug of his shoulders. He could see his father was weakening, fighting against the first impulse to believe the worst of the silly wench. He had her now! She had condoned his lies, so now he could make her do anything he wanted. Or else he would confess to his father how she had begged him to accompany her home, and on the way had told him how bored she was, how she needed *him*. The old man was ripe for it. A few careful hints here and there; the odd rumour carefully placed which would come back to him from a distant source, and, very soon, she would be discarded. And there was always the interest of Alain Ratan, who, despite his laughing comments about her unworthiness in his bed, stayed very close to her at all times. His father's best friend and his father's young empty-headed wife! How could he not succeed in his attempts to oust her from the house, from his father's life—and his!

He was the rightful son and heir, and he alone would succeed to the estate. She would be sent back to Noyen, or a convent—or, better still, meet with an accident—so that she could be unable to tell what she knew. She was dangerous. Better that she were silenced for ever!

Luc was silent for a long while. He stared at his son and then at Alexandrine. The expression on his face was pitiful to see and her heart went out to him, yet she dared not say a word lest he misconstrue her concern. He had to make up his own mind.

'Leave us.' Paul looked at Luc derisively, prompting him to add, 'I am grateful for your intervention. I shall not forget it.'

No, you will not, Paul thought, as he closed the door after him and the last sight of his father and Alexandrine were of them entwined in each other's arms. Luc's voice, a harsh whisper, came to him as he lingered in the corridor.

'Forgive me, my dearest wife. I am a foolish old man, and you are so beautiful.'

'I am your wife. I shall never belong to another man while I bear your name.'

Damn her for sounding so convincing! She was too dangerous to be allowed to live. First his father, then her. And that damned Moor Selim, who watched over them both like some avenging angel. And anyone else who stood in his way. Paul moved away from the door, allowing his imagination to run wild. There were so many ways to rid oneself of unwanted relatives. Poison, the Seine, the Bastille, where men and women lived out their lives in dark, damp dungeons, uncared for, unwanted, dead to the outside world. For him. Yes, for his father. For Alexandrine, there would be a time of repaying her for her scorn and her contempt. Then she could be disposed of. He wanted them both to suffer...

CHAPTER SEVEN

FOR THE week following the confrontation with his son, Luc Boussières was a different man. Alexandrine hardly knew the elegant, polite companion who sent her a gift every day, and awaited her downstairs each morning, after which he would suggest different places they could visit. Many invitations were arriving for them to attend balls and soirées, bals masqués for the Christmas period, which was rapidly approaching, and he handed them over to her, very often without even opening them. She had to choose where to go and which to accept.

Every decision was left to her. It was his way of apologising for his unfounded suspicions. She accepted it, relieved that the incident had been forgotten. He did not attempt to touch her again as he had that day, despite the new intimacy of their relationship. She was careful, whenever they went out together, never to allow her eyes to stray to another man, or to be alone with one. She could feel Luc's gaze on her the moment she left his side, following her round a room, noting whom she spoke to or walked with. He was jealous of her, possessive beyond reason, and she feared a repetition of the ugly accusations he had thrown at her that morning.

On most days they took a carriage-ride. Sometimes Alexandrine would stop to shop, with her husband following close behind. She asked his advice before purchasing anything, but he always agreed with her choice and often bought some small trifle for her himself. Once it was a pretty little bouquet of dried flowers, another day a delicate porcelain pomander in the shape of an elegant swan. She protested vigorously when he presented her with yet another piece of jewellery, this time a heavy gold bangle that twined about her slender arm like the coils of a snake. The eyes were two brilliant sapphires.

'Perhaps it should be I who wear this,' he joked quietly, as he placed it on her arm, 'but I think it looks better on you. Harem women in the East often are given these by their masters—to show to whom they belong. Would that I could command you!'

'I would not refuse you anything your heart desires,' Alexandrine answered, aware of his fingers lingering on her skin. He gave her a penetrating look before drawing back. 'Everything I have, you have given me. Sometimes your generosity makes me feel ashamed. I give you nothing.'

'I spoke to you once of desiring satisfaction; contentment. I have both now, my dear. That was what my heart desired and what you have given me. If I were to die tomorrow, I would have known what true happiness is. So many years I have searched in vain—and then, that day at Noyen, I knew my quest was over.'

'Don't speak of death!' she protested.

'It comes to us all, I'm afraid. But not yet, so don't worry,' Luc answered as he left her. If only she knew what it cost him to sustain this new healthy image he presented to her. Selim had warned him how it would be, but he had closed his ears and his mind to advice. He would not stagnate—he would not! When the end came, it would be swift... Oh God, let it be that way, he prayed.

One morning Francine brought Alexandrine a small package. She gave a soft cry as she opened it, to discover her fan and a letter with it in rather large script. She had not expected to hear from Solange again.

'Are you not going to read it, madame?' the maid asked in surprise as Alexandrine folded the paper without glancing at the contents and slipped the fan into a drawer.

'It is probably nonsense. No one can predict the future.'

'Solange can! She will have consulted the Tarot for you. Do not ignore it. Surely you must want to know about the men she spoke of...' She broke off as her mistress looked at her with a frown of disapproval.

'Of course I don't. She was implying that I shall have a lover, like most women do, but I won't! One man in my life is enough for me. Now go and lay out my clothes.

The Marquis and I are going to Madame Devereaux'
salon this afternoon.'

How could one be sufficient for such a lovely creature
when he did not even come to her bed? Francine wondered, as she went into the bedroom. Solange was never
wrong. She looked back, and a smile dimpled her thin
cheeks as she saw Alexandrine slowly open the letter and
begin to read:

> The signs for your future are favourable. But,
> before you find happiness, you will know sorrow
> and pain. Your life will be turbulent and not
> without danger, but, throughout, one man will
> stand by you, risk death for you—wish himself
> dead because of you.

Alexandrine caught her breath and the paper slipped
from her trembling fingers. What nonsense was this?
She forced her eyes back to the paper. She did not want
to read the rest of it, but she could not help herself.
What was it Solange had said to her in that drab kitchen?
'A disbeliever... Fate has not intervened to guide you,
or has it?' If she were to believe it had, that meant that
Luc's footsteps had been deliberately guided to her and
Noyen, that her parents and betrothed were meant to
die so that she would marry him and come to Paris.
Could God have been so cruel? But, then, was God the
same as Fate? Or were there other forces in the world
that few dared to recognise lest they find themselves tied
to the stake and burned for heresy—for aligning themselves with the devil?

How could Alain Ratan be part of her life? She did
not like him. It had been easy to convince herself of that
these past weeks when she had not seen him. Luc was
her world now, but the memory of Alain was still with
her. His kisses, his touch, the longing at night to have
his strong arms about her.

> There will be, as I told you, more than one man
> in your life. One has already made himself known
> to you. The second, also. Both are men of strength
> and character, but one will die, soon. You will
> need great courage to face what lies ahead for

you, madame, but the Tarot is never wrong. You
will emerge from your ordeal to find love and
acceptance once more. You will be happy. This I
promise. In times of doubt, always remember—
you will be happy!

She was happy now! She lived a perfect existence, so
what more could she want other than a husband who
cared for her, gave her all she wished for—a home, his
protection and affection, security. No woman could have
more than she. It was all nonsense, and she did not believe a word of it! If she accepted even a single word,
it would mean the end of the safe little world she had
come to know and accept was hers for life. It would
mean she accepted that Luc would die and that she would
take a lover—more than one, according to those silly
cards. How could they predict anything? Pictures, that
was all they were!

'Madame wishes me to take an answer to Solange?'
Francine asked, coming back into the room.

'No, but I expect she will be wanting payment for her
trouble. I still do not believe what she has written,'
Alexandrine declared firmly, as she wrapped a few coins
in a piece of paper, folded it and added her seal. 'There,
that should suffice. You can tell her what I said, if you
wish, Francine.'

'Why does madame not wait and see what happens?'
the girl asked.

'By tomorrow I shall have forgotten all about it,' came
the careless answer, which only served to deepen that
knowing smile.

Alexandrine told herself that she would forget, but
she did not. Throughout that afternoon her mind continually wandered from the music and discussions going
back and forth in the comfortable drawing-room of
Madame Devereaux' salon, which was frequented by
many men of intellectual backgrounds, writers, poets and
playwrights. Luc rose to the occasion by delivering a most
fascinating discourse on one of his trips to the East, but
even this failed to hold Alexandrine's interest. Her mind
seethed with questions, yet she knew of no one she could
turn to who might be able, or willing, to answer them

frankly. Most people would laugh at her, she suspected.
Towards the end of the afternoon she was delighted when
Jeanne d'Etoiles appeared, but she had little time to
speak to her, for she stayed only a few minutes and had
come to issue invitations to Madame Devereaux and
several of those present to spend the Christmas period
at her country home. She had already left an invitation
for Alexandrine and her husband at the Place des Vosges,
and hoped they would be able to come and stay until
the New Year, when everyone of importance usually returned to Paris for the celebrations of Le Jour des Rois.

Alexandrine barely had time to issue her own invitation to the ball she was about to give before her friend
left again. She was very silent on the way home and
through supper, which prompted to Luc to enquire if
she had not enjoyed herself.

'I did. Please, you must not think otherwise, but...'
How could she explain what tormented her? It was
impossible.

'You are perhaps in difficulties over...a certain surprise you are planning? Can I help at all?' her husband
said, smiling down the table to where she sat, seeking a
plausible excuse to allay his fears.

'Oh, Luc! Who has told you?'

'You did, my dear, if you recall, and from the activity
going on in the rooms that have been recently decorated
and the huge amounts of food I have noticed being
brought to the house lately, I suspect it is to be soon.'

'Yes, I had forgotten I had told you. How silly! I
wanted it to be a surprise. You are not angry that I have
not consulted you about it?'

'Of course not. It has been many years since anyone
has cared enough to go to the trouble you are taking to
please me. But it is a large undertaking and it is the first
time you have ever prepared for anything on such a grand
scale, is it not?'

'Yes, but I am managing. Pierre has been so helpful.
All the servants have, and I have invited only those
people you will find acceptable. I have their names from
a person whose advice I am sure you would trust,'
Alexandrine hastened to add. After all, had he not given

it concerning her, and Luc had been perfectly prepared to accept it then.

'Then I shall ask no more. You have sufficient money?'

'More than enough. I hope you will not be disappointed.'

'I shall not. Have you remembered to invite Madame d'Etoiles and her husband? I found her a most interesting young woman. It will be pleasant to talk with her again.'

'Yes, I have.' Alexandrine was secretly pleased that he had taken a liking to her friend. It would be nice to share confidences with another woman.

'Good. You may also write and accept her invitation for Christmas. I detest Paris at that time. At least, if we become snowbound at Etoiles, we shall have intelligent conversation about us.' Luc rose and came to where she sat and kissed her lightly on one cheek. Never, never with the intensity she had felt from him on that strange day. 'I shall take my leave of you, my dear. Selim has ordered me to bed early for the next two nights, if we are to hunt with the King's party the day after tomorrow. I hope we shall see Alain there. I would like to settle the matter of these horses before we go away. But I am forgetting. I shall see him soon, anyway. You haven't forgotten to include him, I hope? He is the only one who truly appreciates the contents of my cellar.'

'He is a close friend. How could I forget him?' Alexandrine forced a smile to her lips. She had not forgotten, she had deliberately excluded him. How foolish of her to think she could!

'I am assuming your—surprise—is to be soon?' He did not say 'ball', although he knew full well what he was to expect, despite her desire for secrecy among the servants. Selim's sharp ears missed nothing, no matter how low it was whispered, and it had been his keen eyes that had first seen the specialities being taken to the kitchen and pantry, discovered the kegs of wine and champagne carefully hidden in the cellars. He would not allow it, he had told Luc, who had shrugged aside the warning poured into his ear. He would not spoil Alexandrine's surprise or deprive her of the pleasure she was gaining from arranging it. And he *would* attend!

'This very weekend,' Alexandrine told him, her eyes lighting up as she dwelt on the preparations that had been made.

'Six days away! Then, after the hunt, I shall take to my bed until that evening,' he returned with a chuckle.

'Luc, your energy is limitless, these days. You put me to shame! My head barely touches the pillow before I am asleep.'

But the fire in me is beginning to die, Luc thought, patting her shoulder and quickly drawing back as he felt the warmth of her skin beneath his fingers. It will need to be replenished so that I can stand at your side as a man. Selim would not approve. Selim would point out the danger, the risk, of his folly, but he would agree in the end. One more time...

'Selim, a moment please. I wish to speak to you.'

Alexandrine had allowed Luc to precede her to the carriage which was to convey them to the Bois where the King was to hunt that afternoon. They had to start early so as to reach the place well ahead of Louis and his personal entourage, which would probably include his mistress and favourite courtiers. The Queen rarely accompanied him on such occasions. A wise decision, Alexandrine had mused, as she dressed by candlelight. It was so dull, the sky overcast with threatening clouds heralding rain, that she could not see to perfect her toilette without it.

'Madame.' The Moor turned to acknowledge her. He had gone back upstairs to fetch a heavy travelling-rug to tuck round his master. Just one, she noted, pursing her lips. He never thought of *her* needs. He still continued to act as though she did not exist. His huge frame dwarfed her and made her feel insignificant. She could never rid herself of the feeling that he hated her, yet Luc always spoke of him in glowing tones and, in his eyes, he could do no wrong.

'Thank you for that.' She nodded to what he held, at the last minute balking at asking what she had intended. 'I was about to suggest you brought along something warm for the Marquis. Do you also have his brandy-flask?'

'Of course. But that was not what you wished to ask me, was it?' The black eyes were always so challenging. The impassive features never altered. It was impossible to know what he was thinking.

'No, it was not.' Gathering her courage, she asked as casually as she was able, 'Do you believe in Fate, Selim?'

'*Inshal'lah*. If it is written, it will be.' The question did not surprise him at all. She had been right to assume that his background might provide some of the answers she desperately sought.

'But I can change it, surely?'

'Madame has been told something that disturbs her?'

'Yes . . . I mean, no! It was a silly thing—a gypsy predicted my future. I don't believe a word of it.'

'I think you do. Why else would you need to be reassured that it will not come true?' Selim replied quietly. 'No one can change what has been written for them in the book of Fate, madame. You must accept it—as we all must.'

It was not the answer she had hoped and prayed for. I shall never do that, Alexandrine thought, wrapping her cloak tightly round her as a chilling wind cut with the keenness of a knife-blade as she hurried to the coach. Never! Never! She would alter it, because she could not allow it to happen. It was as simple as that!

After waiting, together with a dozen other carriages of half frozen men and women for two hours, Luc and Alexandrine were to spend another four following the King's hunting party. He had arrived late, not in the best of tempers, and then a shower of rain had further delayed the start. Beaters waited amid the trees and bracken to drive out wild boar, pheasant, or whatever was taking refuge in the undergrowth, stamping their feet and hugging their hands beneath their armpits as they tried to get warm, and envying, sometimes even silently cursing, the food and drink that was consumed within the comparative warmth and comfort of the waiting carriages.

When they decided that the weather would not improve, the King deliberated for another half-hour before signalling for the hunt to begin. There were times when

Alexandrine felt as if her back would break or her legs drop off from the cold. She had chosen to wear the warmest apparel in her closets, a heavy velvet gown of saffron yellow with a matching jacket. The colour was pleasing to the eye on such a dull day. To ease the plainness of the jacket, which fitted snugly round her neck, she had added an intricate collar of gold lacework. Perched on the top of her fair curls was a hat of the same material, the wide brim turned back and fastened with a single yellow plume. She was neither warm nor comfortable, and began to grow anxious that Luc might also be experiencing extreme discomfort, but he seemed in the best of spirits the whole time and never once gave her any indication to the contrary.

Occasionally he would chat with Selim, who seemed as knowledgeable on the day's proceedings as he did, but mainly he concerned himself with pointing out to Alexandrine places of interest that they passed as the procession of carriages with their rapidly tiring, but determined, passengers wound their way after the King and his special party, or people he thought she should know.

As it began to grow dark, earlier than usual because of the gloominess of the day, word was passed back down the line, to the very last straggler still trying to keep pace, that Louis was returning to Versailles. As on that night of the ball, Alexandrine could sense the sighs of relief, their urgent commands to drivers to turn about, so that when their monarch returned to the *Appartement*, the gathering of the whole court which began at seven, he would be greeting by smiling, freshly-gowned ladies and gentlemen who were prepared to stand another four or five hours until he returned to the Queen or went to his mistress, hoping, mostly in vain, to be noticed.

Luc had warned her how it would be, and he had sent his valet ahead with a change of clothing to his rooms. She herself had wisely taken the precaution of wearing an outfit that, when the jacket was removed and a necklace replaced the embroidered collar, would suffice for the evening. Her only concession had been to change to shoes with low heels. She had not forgotten the agony of that last time!

'I hope you have not been too bored, my dear,' Luc said, as they waited for a convenient moment to turn round. The throng going past was quite chaotic and he had ordered their driver to wait.

'Not in the least. Was it a successful hunt? Has anything been caught, do you know?' The horns of the hunters had long since died away, and she noticed that none of the horsemen who rode past looked very ecstatic over the afternoon's chase. 'How lovely it must be to do this in the summer. I shall have my own horse by then, shall I not? Is it permissible to do so?'

'Others have chosen to do so before you...the old King's mistress Louise de la Vallière, for example. There was a beauty! Like a delicate flower, but she was so given to tears after the death of her last-born child that he grew bored with her. A pity, Versailles has never seen the like of her since, in my opinion. But then I have always been swayed first by a pretty face, and what lies behind it is of secondary importance.'

'Then someone like Madame d'Etoiles is fortunate to have both,' Alexandrine murmured.

'She is indeed. But do not underestimate your own abilities, child. Your father and mother were very proud of your aptitude for languages, the quick way you grasped new learning.' A thoughtful look crept into his eyes as he considered her galloping with the hunt astride some magnificent animal that he would purchase for her. She would master a horse with the same determination and confidence that she had tackled the preparations for the ball. An awesome task for one so young, yet he believed the evening would be a great success for her. His faith was well founded, his judgement of her strength of character, despite her tender years, faultless. 'Unfortunately, I shall miss the spectacle...' Unthinkingly the words slipped out, and immediately Alexandrine's eyes were wide with alarm. He could have bitten off his tongue for the blunder and sought to amend the damage. 'My dear Alexandrine, can you picture me astride one of Alain's hunters at my age? They are brutes! The one he rides himself cannot be handled by anyone else. I have told him he must find a docile mare for you, a gentle creature that will not toss you to the ground at the very first opportunity.'

He saw that his words dispersed her fears. She even managed to smile at the thought he conjured to mind. He glanced out of the window, about to order the carriage to move off, when he saw another parked under the trees a few yards away. It was an impressive sight, and it would surely contain a lady. No man would allow himself to be conveyed inside a carriage that was painted in pastel pink and decorated with fine goldwork on the doors and windows—although, at Versailles, the most outrageous things were apt to happen as men and women vied for one glance from the King or someone close to him who might whisper their names in his ear.

'Why, I think that is Madame d'Etoiles' carriage,' Alexandrine exclaimed, as the unusual colour also caught her eye. Then, as a familiar face appeared at the window, 'Yes, it is. May I speak to her? I shall be only a moment.'

'A brief word only. We must be at Versailles before the King reappears,' Luc answered, opening the door for her to alight.

She assured him she would only pass the time of day with her friend and return at once, but the moment she was within the confines of Jeanne's carriage, the young woman caught her by the hand and said in an anxious tone, 'Thank goodness I managed to catch you before you reached Versailles! Alexandrine, I have heard the most disgusting rumour. I don't know how to tell you. The Marquis's son, Paul...*Mon Dieu*, this is so difficult for me, but I know it is not true and you must know of it before someone else confronts you.'

'Jeanne, you begin to make me afraid. What have you heard? Tell me?' Alexandrine pleaded, her heart thudding unsteadily. Had she been seen in the gardens with Alain Ratan! Dear God, no! Not that, she prayed. Yet what else could have provoked comment that night? She had not been indiscreet when she had danced with other men. Every moment she had been aware of watchful eyes on her. Every step had been taken with care, every word meticulously considered before being uttered, and her smiles were for no one person in particular. 'Why do you mention Paul?'

'Something happened to you, on your way home from Versailles?' Jeanne asked, still hesitant to blurt out what she had heard. She had been stunned at first, then angry that such an innocent should have been so cruelly maligned. Alexandrine Boussières had become a special friend and she had defended her honour with vigour, but words would not be enough. Words could be twisted and misunderstood.

'Yes.' Alexandrine had grown very pale. The hand Jeanne clutched trembled as she came to understand. 'What have you heard?'

'That you were annoyed at being deserted by your husband and, when everyone left, you went off with the first handsome face that came along. Paul Boussières, concerned for your welfare, followed and discovered you in a most compromising situation with your companion. He ran the man off, not without sustaining some small injury to his face—and no doubt to his pride,' Jeanne added humourlessly. 'That one is proud of his looks.'

'It isn't true! It isn't! Luc had expected me to stay at Versailles, but I was concerned about him. He was not well. He should not have taken me, but he knew I had been looking forward to it,' Alexandrine cried. One story for his father to silence her. Another for his friends and the inquisitive ladies and gentlemen—she would hardly think of them as that any more—to spite her, wound her, make her an object of gossip. He knew it must in some way reach his father's ears. She grew cold as she remembered Luc's reaction to the bruises on her wrists. If he thought she would so much as look at another man... 'Francine, my maid, was with me. She will confirm that Paul offered to escort me home.'

'You were seen climbing into a fiacre, but no one saw the face of the man inside,' Jeanne told her, wishing she could offer something other than kind words to wipe the pain from her friend's face. 'I have been told—by friends, Alexandrine—that you were noticed by the King. He actually spoke to you on your first visit. That is a great honour, and that has surely made you many enemies.'

'It was only because my husband was known to his father and to him,' the other whispered brokenly. 'I cannot believe anyone would be so stupid as to think such a wicked thing of me. They do not know me.'

'But they know Paul. He is more popular than you might imagine. Some women, and men, from what I have gathered, think he has been badly treated by his father, who has taken a young wife and excluded his own son from his affections because of it. Others are pleasant to him and would side with him in a quarrel, I might add, because he owes them money.'

Alexandrine could only shake her head at the astounding news that had wreaked havoc on her day. She could not go to Versailles now!

'You must,' Jeanne told her, guessing the first thought that would pass through her stunned mind. 'You have to face them—and your husband. If you let them get away with this, there will be far worse in the future, I can assure you. My poor mother suffered from court gossip for many, many years. Because of it, I have not been invited there. One day I shall be, and when I do...' Her small mouth tightened. 'But we must do something to relieve you from this ridiculous and embarrassing position. Is there no one—apart from your maid, who would never be believed—to say that you did not go off with a stranger and, when you were rescued, repulsed the man who had helped you? Monsieur Boussières was heard to comment that he supposed it was because he was the son and not the father. That he had no fortune of his own and could not afford you, even though he did find you a most attractive wench.'

Alexandrine's cheeks flamed at the additional lie. Never had she imagined such hatred and malice to have dwelled inside him. And she had condoned his lies with her acceptance of the story he had told Luc. To try and alter it now would brand her in the eyes of her husband and everyone else. But what else could she do?

'It was Paul I was with that night.' Somehow she managed to calm the rising fear in her. 'He— He tried to make love to me. He had made Francine ride outside, and so she could not help me. We struggled, and I hit him—with his own cane.'

'Well done!' Jeanne exclaimed, clapping her dainty hands. 'Then what happened? The man could not have the effrontery to attack you and then return you home to your husband, surely? Whatever is the world coming to!'

'I jumped out of the carriage. Or, rather, I fell out, and he left me in the road and returned to Versailles. If it had not been for...' She broke off, aware of the sudden interest in her companion's eyes, but she could not contain the truth. Her reputation was at stake. Her marriage! 'Another carriage came along. The Duc de Belaincourt took me home.'

'Alain Ratan. I have heard of him. You danced a good deal together even before your husband left you, did you not?'

'Is there nothing you do not know?' Alexandrine was horrified to think how his company had been interpreted by those watching eyes. 'Yes, I did, because Luc had asked him to partner me. And afterwards he was merely being polite. If you know we were together, then you also know that his mistress was there, Madame de la Fontaine?'

'But he did not stay overnight with her, despite the time he spent with her that evening, did he? And Belaincourt, Alexandrine, is in the other direction to the one his carriage was taking. Where was he going?'

'Are you suggesting he was—following me?' Alexandrine whispered, a hand against her mouth. 'Oh, this is too ridiculous! We do not like each other. He is Luc's friend, not mine.'

'Men and women have been known to be attracted to each other by many different emotions, sometimes even by hate. They do not always become lovers because they have an overwhelming desire to be together for the rest of their lives. And the fact that he is a friend of your husband and, no doubt, has easy access to your home...' Jeanne paused to allow her words to penetrate Alexandrine's mind. 'I know very little personally about the Duc. He is rich, good-looking, available, but too sure of himself. I would not like that, not unless I wanted it. He will never marry again, you know. Poor Madame de la Fontaine thinks she may one day become la Duchesse de Belaincourt and live in that lovely old château of his, but she is wrong. He will not be caught again. And he detests scandal. You must accept that some people may decide he was your mysterious companion.'

For someone who professed not to know about Alain Ratan, she was very free with her comments, Alexandrine thought, searching her mind for some outlet from this devastating happening. If she confessed to Luc that it was not Paul who had brought her home, that it was he who had attacked her and had received the bruise on his face for his impudence, would Alain corroborate it? But for him, she might have arrived home in a far worse condition, if she had arrived at all!

'What are you going to do?' Jeanne asked sympathetically.

'I have no idea at the moment. I need to think. Perhaps Luc will not hear... But he will. Of course he will. We are to be at the *Appartement* this evening. He will be angry that I am keeping him waiting. I must go, Jeanne. Thank you for being my friend. I need one so badly.'

'When we see each other again, I hope this will have resolved itself,' Jeanne returned, embracing her. 'And if you need another friend—and he can be trusted— perhaps you do not have far to look,' she added, motioning a gloved hand towards the other carriage.

A horse stood beside it. A man had dismounted and was deep in conversation with Luc Boussières. Alexandrine's heart leapt at the sight of the leather-clad figure, so different from the other men who had ridden on the hunt that afternoon. But, as quickly as it had come, the pleasure died inside her. What were they discussing—her? If Alain Ratan was as averse to scandal as Jeanne suggested, he would not be above extracting himself from a possibly embarrassing situation by confessing to his old friend that it was he who had brought Alexandrine to the hotel.

He turned as he heard the swirl of her skirts and for a long moment allowed himself the pleasure of enjoying the sight that confronted him. Her outfit was so simple, yet effective.

'Madame la Marquise, you brighten this very dull afternoon,' Alain murmured, inclining his head towards her.

He did not look as if the afternoon had been boring for him, Alexandrine thought, noting the mud splattered on his trousers and boots, and the animal at his side looked as if he had been ridden hard. What a magnificent beast he was! His coat was as black as night and there was a pride about the way he held his head, a defiance hinting that he would know only one master and yet never be truly tamed. A suitable companion for Alain Ratan. Had he not confessed to her that he enjoyed a challenge?

His hand was firm about hers as he helped her into the carriage. As their eyes met, she found herself searching for some sign in those pale green depths that he had been discussing her with her husband, but there was none.

'No, it has not been a great success,' Luc agreed. 'I was hoping for a good afternoon's sport, as it was Alexandrine's first hunt.'

'Perhaps the *Appartement* will have more to offer us,' Alain laughed, stepping back and closing the door. 'Hello, what have we here? Perhaps it has not been so boring for some. Is that not the carriage of Madame d'Etoiles?'

Alexandrine peered out of the window at his words. A horseman had drawn rein beside Jeanne's carriage, but he stayed only a moment before riding on. She did not know him, but Alain did, and a broad smile across the tanned features.

'The King's equerry, de Briges, no doubt playing matchmaker again! I'll wager the King has sent madame some of the game bagged today—little though it was. That will keep the tongues busy tonight!'

'I am beginning to think it is men who start most of the ridiculous rumours,' she said, pursing her lips in annoyance. 'What harm is there in a perfectly harmless gesture such as that? It is an honour.'

'One which is bestowed only on the prettiest ladies at court. But she is not attending court, is she? Not yet.' His smile mocked her indignation. 'That will come soon. If the King has shown an interest in her, no one will be able to keep her away. Madame obviously has a great deal of her mother's blood in her.'

He bade goodbye to Luc and rode off, leaving Alexandrine smarting beneath the last taunt, and aware of Luc's curious gaze on her.

'I do wish you could manage to be a little more friendly to Alain, my dear. I have come to notice a certain sharpness in your tone whenever you speak to him. Yet you tell me he has given you no cause to be offended. What is it you dislike about the man?'

'His arrogance, I suppose. His assumption that every woman finds him attractive.'

'Well, he is, and most women do,' Luc returned, still watching her intently.

'I suppose I am being rather silly,' she replied, anxious to placate him, 'but I have taken your warning to heart. Friend or not, I prefer to keep him at a respectful distance. If I am over-cautious, what harm is there?'

'None at all. It is difficult to draw the line between beauty and evil once one steps over the threshold of Versailles. Both reside there, side by side. But be assured, if I trust Alain with you—and I do—you have no need to be apprehensive. He can be quite amusing when he wishes, and behind that arrogance you abhor lies a shrewd brain. It is little wonder he spends most of the year at Belaincourt. There are few like him at Versailles, which, I suppose, is why we get on so well together. The pursuit of a woman is not the sole topic of our conversations. Surprisingly enough, I found your Madame d'Etoiles most interesting, too.'

'She is one person I do consider a friend,' Alexandrine said without hesitation.

She was looking forward to spending Christmas in the country. She would have preferred to be in her own home in Noyen, but she knew she was not yet ready to return to the place where so many unhappy memories lingered. Jeanne's invitation would give her the time to allow the speculation abroad because of Paul's hint-dropping to fade naturally. When she returned, she doubted if anyone would even find her interesting. And it would take her away from the Duc de Belaincourt! That was the most important thing of all. She did not understand Luc's insistence that they become friends. One day he was jealous because he thought her unfaithful—the next he was throwing her at Alain Ratan.

As they had not rushed ahead like many of the other carriages, there was not the usual congestion when they arrived at Versailles, and they were able to make their way upstairs to Luc's rooms without the unpleasant jostling and pushing that nearly always prevailed in the crowded corridors.

The rooms allotted to the Marquis de Mezière and his wife were by no means large, but she knew it was a privilege to have them. Luc's valet Charles had laid out fresh apparel for his master in one room, where a single trestle-bed was set against one wall. Alexandrine's room adjoined it, with a tiny room on the other side of a curtained alcove to accommodate her maid. While he refreshed himself, she stretched out on her own bed, grateful to be able to relax for a while before returning downstairs to face the unknown.

There would be those who would think the worst of her because it gave them pleasure: friends of Paul who still considered she had trapped his father into marriage. But what harm could they really do her? So long as she had Luc's trust, she would bear any unpleasantness. When Paul came to understand that he could not drive a wedge between them, he might very well abandon his scheming to discredit her. Why, then, as she rose to allow Francine to brush her hair, did she feel such apprehension?

She stepped out into the other room as Selim was handing a small glass to her husband. Luc took it and tossed back the contents, grimacing as he thrust it back to the Moor.

'No more until tomorrow,' she heard Selim mutter before her presence was realised, and the man turned away, hurriedly pushing several phials of coloured liquid into a leather pouch.

'My dear, you look as fresh as when we set out this morning.' Luc turned to her, smiling, but his eyes were wary. What is he afraid I have seen? she wondered. What kind of remedy needed to be taken in such secrecy? 'I shall be a while yet. These old bones were colder than

I imagined. You go ahead in case the King arrives. We cannot both be absent.'

He did not want her to stay. Alexandrine knew that tone. Reluctantly she left him and fell in behind other ladies and gentlemen making their way downstairs. A head turned to one side of her. A fan fluttered and she quickened her pace, holding her head a little higher. She would give them no satisfaction with their malicious tittle-tattle!

'Good! Tomorrow, it will be the turn of someone else,' Alain murmured in her ear, as he fell into step beside her. 'What are you going to do about Paul? He's forcing your hand, you know.'

'Do? I don't know what you mean.' Alexandrine tried to ignore him, hoping he would go away, but as they drew nearer to the supper-room, the corridor was becoming more filled with people and it was impossible for their bodies not to touch as they waited to enter.

'Are you going to tell Luc the truth? Good heavens, Alexa, you must have heard the rumours by now. I suspect that is why you were closeted so long with Madame d'Etoiles this afternoon. Luc was growing quite impatient with you.' Alain remembered he had thought it strange, for he had always regarded his friend as a most tolerant man. Yet, while he had waited for his wife's return, he had become strangely agitated—and nervous. Alain had decided he was not as well as he pretended. It was an act for the court and for his wife.

He considered the short fair curls almost touching his shoulder, and then the jewelled necklace about her throat. Her pale skin enhanced the deep glow of the emeralds. They must have cost Luc a small fortune, he mused, as she lifted her head and her eyes challenged his scrutiny. Little wonder that Paul hated her! When he so desperately needed money to pay his gambling debts, he had to watch it being spent on items like this, to adorn the beautiful neck of his father's second wife.

'What if I choose to do nothing? As you say, this will soon pass.'

'Then there would be no danger to your marriage, if Luc did not hear of it. But if he does? I do not believe his health could stand the scandal. Are you prepared to take the risk?'

'I was prepared to be honest with him from the very beginning, if you remember, until you told me that Paul would probably be disinherited. To keep my good name, I must destroy Luc's flesh and blood. He loves him, I know. Why else would he be so understanding of his weaknesses?'

'Whose welfare do you have at heart?' Alain asked, his tone hardening. 'Luc's or that of his son.'

'How dare you imply...' She broke off, containing her anger. There were too many people watching them to allow the slightest sign of irritation or chagrin to touch her face. She smiled at a couple she knew, fluttering her fan before her face to scatter the overwhelming mixture of powder and Cologne invading her nostrils. 'I want him to stop pestering me, that's all. I don't care if he doesn't accept me, so long as he leaves me alone—and stops these horrible stories. It is unfair. I have done nothing to him.'

'Except deprive him of his father's wealth. Paul gave me the impression that he felt you were...interested in him.'

'He is mad! He disgusts me. In Noyen, he would be a laughing-stock.'

'This is Paris, but when it comes to gossip, it is little different from the smallest village. People will always want to know what others are doing. It is human nature.'

'You have overlooked one very important point, monsieur,' Alexandrine said, as she allowed him to usher her through the door into the supper-room. He stopped a passing lackey with a tray of full glasses and took two from him. The white wine was deliciously cool and bolstered her failing courage. 'If I tell Luc what really happened, I am forced to involve you.'

'I came to your assistance once. Do you not think I should do so again? Why are you so afraid to ask it of me, Alexa?'

'Have you not considered the implications for yourself? Paul told Luc that he came to my help when I was attacked, and that was how he obtained the bruise on his cheek. But, to others, his friends, he has told an

entirely different tale. That he saw me go off with another
man and, concerned for me—because I am his father's
wife, of course—he followed and discovered me in a
compromising situation with this—companion.' She
watched Alain's eyes narrow over the rim of his glass.
Her lips began to tremble and she could feel the colour
already mounting in her cheeks. He was considering the
talk that would be bandied about him! Jeanne had been
right about him. 'Perhaps no one has yet told you that
he is hinting that my mysterious companion—was you!'

'I am flattered, but those who know me will laugh at
such a story. I do not advertise my liaisons openly before
hundreds of people.'

'Do you not? What about Madame de la Fontaine?'
Alexandrine retorted.

'Claudia? She was the indiscreet one from the very
beginning, but it matters not to me because our relationship has nothing to do with anything so romantic as love,
or even caring. We fulfil in each other a mutual, selfish,
need,' Alain said bluntly. 'If there was a woman I cared
for, I would never allow her name to be linked with mine
in that way. I would protect her with any means at hand.
So you need have no fear about our names being linked.
Luc will probably find it exceedingly funny.'

'You—You will confirm what I tell him, then?'
Alexandrine felt faint with relief. She was not sure what
she had expected his answer to be, but certainly not this!
'Thank you.'

'If that is what you ask, of course. But I think it would
be better if he heard it from my lips. I shall tell him that
you were reluctant to tell the truth at the beginning because you did not wish to harm Paul, but that he has
now made it impossible for you to remain silent any
longer. I have a way with words when I wish, Alexa.
Leave it to me.'

'I am sure you have. But the truth is all that is necessary, monsieur.'

'And, as thanks, you will be sure to remember and
send me an invitation to your ball, will you not?' Alain
mocked softly. 'Luc asked me if I had been invited and
I said I had. You would not like to make me out a liar,
would you?'

'You shall have one first thing in the morning.'

'What shall he have? Really, madame, you astound me with your impudence.' Passing close by them, Paul had overheard her words and, seeing the attention centred on all three of them, sought to turn the moment to his advantage. His audience were ripe for some amusement, and this little country wench would provide it. If Alain were foolish enough to intervene before everyone, the suspicions about him would only grow. Instinctively, Alexandrine's fingers closed round Alain's arm, and his lips deepened into an ugly smile at the speculative glances passed to and fro. 'I shall suggest to my father that he keeps you on a tighter leash. When he is ill in bed you take yourself off to the back streets of Paris, where no decent woman would set foot, and with the daughter of a whore, too! Now I discover you trying to destroy a friendship of many years' standing, as you are destroying the bond between father and son. You are without shame!'

The words were thrown at her with such force that she recoiled from them and the hatred blazing in his face. She saw a woman nudge her companion and smile knowingly, and wished the ground could open and swallow her.

'I am prepared to accept an apology. You are drunk.' Alain's voice was like tempered steel. The pale eyes glittered dangerously as he surveyed the faces before him, daring the slightest comment to be uttered.

'My words were for her—not for you,' Paul said quickly. 'It is not your fault that you are as susceptible as I am to a pretty face.'

'Many men are. That is no crime, but few would attempt to violate the wife of his own father, as you did! You see, I found the Marquise where you had left her in the road with her maid. I took her home. If Luc hears this story of yours, I shall tell him the truth, and then I shall seek you out and kill you. I doubt if he will grieve long when he has such charming company to console him.'

'I am quite capable of defending my wife, Monsieur Ratan,' a cold voice declared from behind. Onlookers fell back as Luc shouldered his way to the forefront,

Selim a step behind him. 'However, I do not consider it necessary to soil my blade on this upstart I have fathered. It he who needs the tighter leash, and if I hear one more lie about my wife, in whose innocence I have no doubt, I shall tighten it about his scrawny neck until he chokes, and then pack him off to the Bastille. Come, my dear, I am sure you have had quite enough of his company for tonight. Will you join us, Alain? We shall find a hospitable inn that houses honest men, and take our supper there.'

'The King...' Alexandrine whispered, as she placed her arm on his. How silly her words sounded. How could she worry about protocol at a time like this? Some of the harshness faded from Luc's features, as he looked at her and sensed the inner distress she dared not reveal until they were far from Versailles.

'I am sure you will be able to find a plausible excuse for our absence, will you not?' he demanded, glaring at his son.

Paul was almost choking with rage. He could only nod before he turned away, crushed, humiliated, shutting his ears to the voices starting up around him. Barely had his father quitted the room with his companions than the King and the captain of the guard, who always escorted him on such evenings, entered the room by another door, making it impossible for him to escape.

He sought refuge among his friends, any one of whom he knew would desert him, did he not owe them money. They had to support him, for it was the only way they would ever be paid, and they never would be, if he found himself in the Bastille! 'Now do you believe me, gentlemen?' Once again he found himself absorbing this new crisis and seeking a solution from it with a deviousness that had often frightened him, but which of late had given him immense satisfaction. He was not beaten yet! The old man would pay for his insults. He would remember those who had turned from him at that dreaded name, and when he had the Boussières' wealth, he would use it against them. When Luc was dead, he would have so much power... 'I told you she was with a man that night...and it was the very same who has now defended her! What more proof do you all need?

My father is too old and senile to realise that he is being cuckolded by his best friend!'

His gaze alighted on a woman just sinking into a deep curtsy before the King, and he knew he had miraculously found the answer he needed. He beckoned to the nearest lackey. 'When the King reaches the other side of the room, ask Madame de la Fontaine to join me.'

CHAPTER EIGHT

'YOU ARE angry,' Luc remarked, looking at the silent figure reclining in a chair beside the fireplace. Not a word had Alain uttered since Luc returned to the room and informed him he had listened to Alexandrine's explanation of what had taken place that night and believed her to be innocent of the preposterous suspicions Paul had falsely spread. 'You have every right. Keeping my son out of trouble was a favour to me, but getting involved in the petty squabbles of my family, and being forced to protect my wife's reputation, is another thing.'

'I agree,' Alain returned bleakly, swallowing his hitherto untouched wine without appreciation for once of its age and bouquet. So Luc thinks her innocent, does he? And thinks I am the knight who came to her aid when in need. My God! If only the man knew half of what had been in his mind when he had held her in his arms that night. He had accepted then that they would become involved: how, he did not know, or when, but he knew it would be so.

'Alexandrine was fortunate that it was you who came along,' Luc added, wondering why Alain was so reluctant to tell his side of the story. They had not stopped at an inn for supper—his words had been meant for the occupants of the *Appartement* only—but had returned home immediately. Alexandrine had gone immediately to her room and Luc had followed and demanded the explanation due to him. She had supplied it without hesitation, her gaze frank and open, her lips sometimes trembling as she confirmed his worst fears. Paul! It had begun. The hatred was out of control now and would destroy them all unless he himself were the stronger of the two. For Alexandrine's sake, he would be!

'Why have you not asked me what happened that night?' Alain demanded, straightening in his chair. 'You overheard what took place tonight, so you know I brought her home. You knew, anyway, didn't you? How? Why have you said nothing?'

'Selim saw her return, and recognised the coat-of-arms on your carriage.'

'And he told you!' Alain's annoyance was mirrored on his dark features. An act of kindness had been misconstrued and enlarged out of all proportion by those who needed their lives to be enriched by the misfortunes of others. And he had allowed himself to be provoked tonight at Versailles. He could not believe, even now, that he was prepared to draw a weapon against a man to protect Alexandrine Boussières! Was he mad? What had prompted such an idiotic act? He was branded now, his name linked with hers, the very thing he had sworn would never happen. 'Does that black devil never sleep?'

'Be thankful he does not,' Luc returned. 'He saw the condition Alexandrine came home in—wearing your cloak, missing one shoe. He thought . . . Well, we shall not dwell on what he thought, for it was unjustified, but it kept him silent for some while, and during that time I was so unjust as to accuse my wife of . . .' He broke off, aware of the fierce frown on Alain's face.

'Of what, old friend? Speak out.'

'Alain, do not let this spoil a friendship of many years. I know Alexandrine is safe with you. Have you not proved it to me? She is a child still. She has to be cared for at all times.'

'Some children can be very dangerous,' Alain said quietly, remembering how soft her body had been against his in that darkened carriage. How his fingers had touched her breast and felt the warmth of her skin. Few women had roused him as she had done that night. She was forbidden fruit, yet he wanted her with a passion that was frightening. He had over-reacted to Paul's insults because of this longing. He prayed that he had not given himself away.

'Some men enjoy playing with fire and having their fingers burned, but that is not for you—not again,' Luc answered, refilling their empty glasses before seating himself on the other side of the hearth. 'Nor is Alexandrine that kind of a woman. You think me an old fool! It is in your eyes. Believe what you will, but I know her, Alain. I trust her. I hope to God she has forgiven me for my suspicions. When I saw the marks on her that Paul had inflicted, and thought... But then, I accept, I *was* a fool. And then the poor child confirmed his lies. She was trying to shield *me* from the truth, of course. The agony of mind she must have endured these past days—to be assaulted by my son and then have to lie so that she does not cause me pain! To be ogled and laughed at by those painted popinjays at Versailles! Tonight Selim told me what he had seen, and I knew I must act to stop this tirade of abuse against an innocent.'

'He certainly took his time,' Alain growled. 'He could have saved us all unpleasantness.'

'Selim has his ways. He, too, sought to protect me from the truth. I shall disinherit Paul at once. When I die, Alexandrine shall inherit everything I possess. Will you bear witness to what I shall write?'

'If that is what you want. He *is* your son, Luc, albeit an idiotic fool who gambles too much and allows himself to be used by those who do not hold you in too high esteem. But he is still your flesh and blood.'

'I do not need to be reminded of that!' There was a harshness in Luc's voice that deterred further comment. 'I knew that one day it would come to this. He shall have an allowance, that much I'll still grant him, for the blood we share. But nothing else. He can live here, if he wishes, but I shall make it clear I would prefer him to reside elsewhere. This is Alexandrine's home, too, and I will not allow her to be made to feel an outsider any longer.'

'And do you really believe this kind of destructive act will stop the tongues wagging?' Alain asked. 'They will say now that your wife has everything she wanted—your wealth, this house, a position in society—at the expense of your son. Paul will not allow it to rest.'

'A destructive act, you call it?' Luc stared at him, his eyes narrowing. 'My friend, you do not know the meaning of the word "destructive". If need be, I shall annihilate that young man to protect my wife. Do you understand that? I shall have the papers drawn up at once. They should be ready for your signature on the night of Alexandrine's ball. And, afterwards...' He paused, not speaking for several minutes. 'If anything should happen to me, I want you to take care of her. She is too trusting, too vulnerable, to be left alone in this world. Will you do this for me?'

'You will live for many years yet,' Alain said. He could not bring himself to think of her as trusting or vulnerable—only desirable. It was an impossible request, and he said so.

'I was not intimating that you walk two paces behind her every day of her life,' Luc replied with a strange smile. 'Only that she has someone to turn to in times of need. I ask no more than that, Alain. Do this for me? I have placed too heavy a burden on her young shoulders, but she will be free of it soon. Free like the little fledgling she is to try out the new wings I have given her. Guide her flight. Watch over her. For a friend.'

'Damn you, Luc! You know how important your friendship is to me. I haven't forgotten how it was when I needed someone to turn to...' Alain nodded abruptly. 'So be it. But say nothing to her. I shall observe from a distance, and intervene only if it is essential.'

To be close to her would be disastrous! To be with her and not possess her!

'That will be sufficient—for the moment. Drink up! We still have this bottle to finish and, while we do, we can discuss the horses you have for me.'

Alexandrine was on her way downstairs to go through a last-minute inspection of the table arrangements for the ball that evening with Pierre and the cook, when loud voices reached her, coming from the direction of Luc's rooms upstairs. Her steps faltered. She clutched at the banister, growing so pale that the major-domo looked at her in concern. Father and son had quarrelled every day since the hunt.

'Madame is not well?'

'I have forgotten something I need, Pierre. Go down and begin without me; I won't be a moment. And remember, there must be a lot of flowers—everywhere— even if they are artificial,' she added with a faint smile. November was departing the scene with a vengeance, blasting the countryside with bitterly cold winds and rain and today the first snow had fallen in the garden. Fires had been lit every day for weeks now, but for Alexandrine the snow flurries announced that winter had really come.

In Noyen, as a child, she would have wrapped herself in an old cloak and gone out with her friends to indulge in a game of snowballing, even skating on the village pond when the ice grew thick and safe enough. Christmas was the time when everyone came together and forgot their grievances, exchanged gifts and knelt in the tiny church in silent homage to the Saviour of the world.

But she was not in Noyen. Paul's furious voice brought her back to reality. Picking up her skirts she began to ascend to the upper floor, only to halt on mid-stair as Luc's door was flung open and Paul came storming out. The wildness of his expression made her draw back, a hand against her throat. He wheeled back towards the man who was coming after him, a heavy stick upraised to strike. Alexandrine cried out at the fury on his face also. Both men looked as if they were about to murder each other.

'Luc, no!' Even as the words tumbled from her lips, the huge frame of Selim dwarfed his master. The stick was plucked from his fingers and the hand that had held it coupled in an unrelenting grasp.

'You would have struck me!' Paul cried, experiencing a moment of triumph as servants came out below and gazed up at the scene. The more witnesses who heard his words, the better! 'Because I try to tell you the truth about her!' He flung a trembling hand out towards Alexandrine. 'She is a wanton, and you are blind to it. And to what is going on under your nose.'

'Out!' Luc thundered. 'Out of my house! Out of my life, or I will kill you.'

'My mother is turning in her grave at what you have done to her memory and are planning to do to me! I am your son, yet I am disinherited because I have only your best interests at heart. She is not worth this hatred between us.'

Luc laughed, struggling in vain to free himself from Selim's hold. Had he been able to do so, Alexandrine suspected, he would have thrown himself on his son, so incensed was he.

'There has always been hatred between us, never love. Not even affection. It is too late for anything else—for us both!'

'Calm yourself, Monsieur Luc. Do you want to bring on another attack, tonight of all nights?' the Moor demanded in a fierce whisper.

Alexandrine's eyes widened at the familiarity. Luc ignored it. Was he accustomed to being addressed so when they were alone?

'You allow your wife to give her favours to whomsoever she pleases and choose to do nothing about it, and now your servant addresses you as if he were part of our family,' Paul sneered. When his father's money was his and the old man was no longer troublesome, he would deal with Alexandrine! But he would not forget the Moor, whose contemptuous gaze made him quake in his shoes. That one was capable of anything.

'Selim is more of a son to me than you have ever been,' Luc flung back. His face had gone a sickly colour and he began to lean against the solid form beside him. Strength seemed to ebb from him, as he clutched desperately at the arm which went about his waist to support him.

'And I suppose Alexandrine is more like the daughter you never had! No wonder she seeks her pleasures elsewhere. You are not only old, but incapable of fulfilling your marriage vows. I should have realised it before. That is why her apartment is so far from yours. How convenient, too, for—late callers. But then Alain is a friend, and friends are to be trusted, aren't they, Father? Even with your wife?'

'Get out! Pierre! Selim! For the love of heaven, get him out of my sight!' Luc sagged in the arms which held him and seemed barely conscious as Alexandrine started up the stairs, pushing Paul aside to help the Moor to half carry, half drag, him back into his rooms.

'I shall take him now,' Selim said, as they reached the bedroom door. 'You have guests who will be arriving in a few hours, madame. No doubt you still have a great deal to do. Leave him to me.'

It was not a request, but a command, and she found
herself standing outside the door, alone. Behind her Paul
laughed, and the sound for some reason chilled her
blood. There was more than just enjoyment of what he
had seen—for that was written on his face as she turned
back to him, steeling herself to be strong, to hold her
own against him. Luc was ill again. It was up to her now
and she would not fail him. Paul would hurt him no
more. Why did she sense something evil radiating from
him? What harm could he do either of them now? He
was disinherited, banished from the house. At last she
and her husband could begin to live a normal life... or
as normal as Luc would permit.

'Your father has asked you to leave the house, Paul.
Please do so at once. If you do not, I shall be forced to
instruct Pierre to bring some men and have you removed. You may return to collect your personal belongings, of course, but do not attempt to see your
father. You will be prevented from doing that by any
means you provoke.'

'At last the true face of greed! The harlot has spoken.
So you think to deprive me of my father's love and devotion, do you?' Paul was playing to an audience, and
well he knew it—ears that were glued to doors and key-
holes, faces hidden in the shadows of the downstairs
rooms. He would give them something to talk about for
weeks. So tonight she thought to excel herself by giving
a ball, did she, to prove that the Marquise de Mezière
was well and truly established in the family home? She
was in for a shock! 'I shall leave, madame. It breaks my
heart to see what you have done to him. I cannot bear
it a moment longer. But I shall return. You will be
brought to account for what you are doing to that old
man. I swear his sickness is something you have insti-
gated. The anxiety you have caused him since you came
here has brought him to this low state. You have turned
his mind against me, but I shall prevail to win him back.
And I shall succeed. God forbid he should spend the rest
of his days in your care!'

It was an hour, however, before Paul eventually quitted
the house. He had sat at the bottom of the staircase while
servants hurried back and forth to the waiting fiacre,

loading into it clothes and personal items from his rooms. When he considered one of them too slow, he brought his cane down about their shoulders as an incentive to be quicker. The same cane she had used to strike him that night, Alexandrine realised, beginning to tremble again as the front door slammed behind his departing figure. She turned to find servants staring at her, and sent them scattering about their business with a sharpness of tongue she had never used before.

'Madame has brought new life to the old house, if I may say so,' Pierre remarked as they returned downstairs to inspect the dining-room arrangements.

She looked at him quizzingly. 'For the better, I hope, Pierre. I have not sought to change your master's house, merely to make it a home where his friends are welcome. Where he and I can live happily.'

'Madame has achieved what has not been possible before—with the Marquis forever out of the country. We all hope he will stay here now. That you will stay here, too, Madame la Marquise. None of us believes...' He broke off, and Alexandrine was amazed to see embarrassed colour stealing above the immaculate white of his stock. 'I have been asked to tell you that we—all the household—are happy that you have come to the Place des Vosges. The master is different since you came, and I—we are honoured to be in your service. We are loyal to you both, if you should ever have need of the observations of a humble servant.'

'Pierre, I am touched. Thank you. I know I am not what you had expected for your master, a girl from the country—and a very stupid one I think, to have allowed myself to be used as I have to satisfy the malice of a very unhappy young man. But I am not accustomed to the kind of intrigue and backbiting which prevails in Paris. I shall learn in time, I suppose, and perhaps even become like them.'

'No, madame, never like them. You have too gentle a nature, too kind a heart. Forgive me, I forget myself.' Pierre stepped to one side, and she moved past him into the dining-room and caught her breath in delight.

'This is exquisite! More than I had hoped for. It looks beautiful, Pierre.'

'Madame deserves the best. We all know she will be a great success tonight.' And, hopefully, put an end to the terrible things being said about her. Paul Boussières was a fiend, a sadistic animal who played on the weaknesses of others, used them for his own ends and then discarded them. More than one female in the household had become pregnant by him, more so during the absence of his father, when he held licentious orgies. He had tempered his ways within the house for a few months after the return of the Marquis, but now he was back to his old life-style and the poor young Marquise was caught up in the midst of his schemings to become the master, rich in his own right—at any cost.

Pierre considered him to be the spawn of the devil. He could never have been sired by Luc Boussières, a much-travelled man of learning and culture, who had once been a favourite at the court of the Sun King himself, whose mind was crammed full of the wonders of others worlds, other civilisations. Paul had no mind. His interests were basically crude and he was self-indulgent in everything—women, money, gambling, drinking. He shamed the proud name he bore and did so with relish, as if it was his heartfelt wish to bring down the house of Mezière. Thank God he had gone! There had not been one servant who had not sighed with relief as the door closed behind him, so how must the Marquis and Marquise feel about his departure? They were safe now, Pierre thought, enjoying a silent moment of satisfaction as he watched Alexandrine continue her inspection. And they would be protected against him in the future. Every member of the household had sworn an oath to it!

The kitchen was in turmoil, and became even more flustered at the sight of the mistress of the house tasting and inspecting the pastries and sweetmeats, adding more wine to the pheasant about to go into the oven, suggesting less garlic with the venison, asking about the desserts and the wines—a hundred and one things that most women take for granted every day—but this was the Marquise de Mezière, and she had servants to take care of such trivialities.

Alexandrine loved it—she felt like a child again watching as her mother baked the bread or sweet rolls for special occasions, or ground spices for a sauce. And as the cook and kitchen-maids saw the excitement rising in her face, they allowed her her way, and felt a sense of pride at her attention. Not every household could boast the personal attention of the mistress herself, and a capable one at that, who understood what was going on about her.

'When my guests have eaten well tonight, then so shall you all,' Alexandrine said as she turned to leave. 'Thank you.'

It was clear that she came from a humble background. No lady of breeding gave thanks to servants for merely performing their duties. But, said Cook as she continued with her pastry-making, had anyone present ever had such a kind mistress as the Marquise? Did she ever scold them or strike them? It was a pleasure to do her bidding and to see her so happy.

Happy was not the way Alexandrine considered herself as she went upstairs. Francine was busy laying out her clothes for that evening. She considered the three gowns, and could not decide which was the best out of the pale blue satin sewn with pink rosebuds, which reminded her of spring, a sombre black gown she had ordered from Madame Heloise for more formal occasions and which she considered made her look at least five years older, or a golden velvet embroidered with silver thread in the design of leaves, which made her think of the trees shedding their autumn glory upon the hard, baked earth. She sighed. She did not see anything these days except through the eyes of a country girl. The black would make her look sophisticated and elegant. The blue would bring out the touch of sapphire in her eyes, but the yellow— that would make her feel confident, and that was what she needed. To enhance the colour, she chose a simple necklace that looked like a golden rope. It matched the bracelet upon her arm. She would wear nothing in her hair, she decided. Tonight she would be herself.

'Madame is not going to rest?' Francine asked, as she made towards the door.

'In a while. The Marquis is not feeling well. I must go to him.'

As usual, Selim answered Luc's door. Before he could speak, Alexandrine said in a determined tone, 'I intend to come in, Selim. I wish to see my husband, and you will not prevent it this time.'

'Shall I not, madame?' The dark face twisted into a humourless smile. 'If I wished, I could break you as easily as I would a dry twig and think no more of it, but...' As she stood thunderstruck at his insolent words, he stepped back, motioning her to enter. 'It is time you saw what you have done and are doing to him. Come in and close the door.'

He was giving her orders! Alexandrine's temper rose as she stepped over the threshold. She would allow this to continue no longer. She would... Her footsteps faltered as her gaze fell on the figure crouched in a chair beside the window—the same chair she had found him in once before after days of being kept away. She hurried to him, faced him, and almost recoiled from the stranger who stared sightlessly in front of him.

'Does his appearance frighten you, madame? It should. You have brought him to this,' Selim said cruelly from behind Luc's chair, and she raised eyes brimming with tears to glare into the impassive face. Did nothing move him? Was he made of stone?

'How—How could you allow this to happen?' she whispered. 'You are his physician. It is your duty to take care of him.'

'Duty?' Selim caught hold of the lax head which until that moment had been folded against his chest, and raised it so that she could see the face of her husband clearly. The eyes were open, and she remembered how they had been before—glazed, as if unaware of what was happening about him. 'I love this man like a brother and you dare to speak to me of duty! For you he is killing himself! He will no longer let me help him—save for the potions I give him which will shorten his life... Allah forgive me for the love I bear him. I can refuse him nothing. My life is his, and he demands my obedience. For you, woman! For you!'

Alexandrine recoiled from the passion in the harsh tone. Never had she heard him raise his voice and it frightened her, but more than that, Luc's condition frightened her! His body was limp, his eyes wide as they stared at her. She knew he did not see her. Selim eased him back into the chair, arranging a cushion behind his head. He sat there like someone in a trance, or who had been drugged.

'What have you given him? I demand to know!'

'Do you indeed? I have given him a powerful drug. He will not know anyone for several hours. You will greet your guests alone tonight, Madame la Marquise. The triumph will be all yours. Make what excuse you will for his absence, it matters not to me,' came the brutal retort.

'Does it not? Well it does to me. Tonight was for him—for my husband. You have done this deliberately, to spite me! You hate me as much as Paul does. You both think Luc mad to have married me. Well, I shall prove you wrong. I shall find someone else to care for him—someone who will not make him look like—like this. It is you who are killing him!' she challenged.

'Me? If you were in my country now, woman, I would have your tongue cut out.' Selim came round the chair to face her, eyes blazing. 'I am Selim Mustapha Abdulla Bey. Once I had thousands at my command—and a hundred like you in my harem! I would have had your feet placed in boiling oil until you screamed for death to release you from the agony. I was all-powerful.'

'But now you are my husband's physician, his life-line to this world, and I tell you truly, Selim, if he does not improve, I shall make you answer to me!' Alexandrine cried, fists clenching into tight balls at her side. Why she was not afraid of him she did not know, but she was not. He was an awesome sight with his blazing eyes and black face which, for the first time since she had met him, now bore some semblance of an expression. But what did it convey? Hatred? Compassion? Contempt? He said he loved Luc, yet he admitted he was slowly killing him.

'What is wrong with my husband?' she demanded. 'I *will* know, even if I have to have you racked.'

A mirthless laugh broke from the man's lips. 'Do you think you could break me? Others have tried, better than you, and failed. I am his to command. I will do his bidding and no other's, even though my heart is heavy with the burden he places upon these broad shoulders. I do not fear death, madame. I am not a woman.'

'You demand respect from me, yet you offer nothing in return,' Alexandrine said, tempering her anger. He was sincere, there was no doubt of that. If she was to learn the truth from him, she would not do so by threats or force. 'I have asked nothing of him from the beginning, you know that. I have taken what he has offered with gratitude and love. Yes, love,' she added, as the wide mouth deepened into a distrusting smile. 'And, in return, I have tried to give, but he will not have me. You tell me you had a hundred women like me in your harem, Selim Mustapha Abdulla Bey. When you rejected one of them to favour another, did you know how she felt? Even the youngest, most innocent among them, did you know her innermost feelings or were you too intent on gratifying your own passions—as Paul does? Is that what your life consisted of? Then let me tell you this! I know what I am. I know my failings, but at least I have tried, and I think to some extent succeeded, in pleasing Luc since we have been married. He knows I will deny him nothing—my body or my bed. He refuses to accept either, and I know not why. Why do you blame me for this? He is ill, yet I am kept from him. I will not allow this to happen again. I swear, if you try, I shall have you taken from this house...'

'And your husband will surely die—and you will be in the greatest danger you have ever known, madame. For your sake as well as his, I suggest you are wiser in your actions.'

'Tell me why I should be? Explain this illness and let me try to understand how best I can help him,' Alexandrine pleaded, suddenly drained by the encounter of words.

'He is a tired old man, madame, seeking to keep alive the flame of youth he knows is dying inside him; seeking to revive his old body by surrounding himself with beauty such as your own and knowing, deep in his heart, how useless it is.' Selim told the lie without hesitation. It was what he had agreed with Luc to tell her if this moment ever arose. At all costs Luc insisted she be spared the truth—the full knowledge of the terrible sickness that plagued him, gnawing away not only at his weakened body, but at his mind. 'How best can you help him?' Selim repeated softly. 'Is it possible you will trust me? Will you listen to what I have to say, and believe it is in his best interests?'

'I will listen...' She was cautious of the change in him. The docility so different from a moment ago when he had glared at her with eyes of fire. 'I promise nothing.'

'How like a woman...'

'One more insult, and I swear...'

'Luc's life is in my hands, madame. I alone can keep him alive—and I shall, until such time as he wishes me to despatch him into Allah's keeping. He is not afraid of death, only the matter of his dying. We have already discussed it. It does not concern you—and that was not an insult. I have made him a promise, and I will keep it no matter what the consequences are to me personally.'

'Why do you say I am killing him? I ask nothing from him.'

'But he wants to give. His life has been unhappy, and he has found in you the salvation he has been seeking for many years. Not the right one... but a salvation he cannot refuse.'

'I don't understand! I give him nothing, and I see in your eyes the contempt you have for me because you know how our marriage is. I accept that he has no secrets from you. I am ashamed to be so...'

'Stripped of the outward mantle that most people wear in this life? Vulnerable to a stranger? Madame does me an injustice. I did not approve of his marriage to you, nor do I approve of his life-style these past months so that he may please you. He is not a young man, but old and tired and very sick. But, for you, he has donned the garments of youth and set out on a road which will lead all too soon to his death, unless...'

'Unless what? I will do *anything* to make him well!' Alexandrine cried, clutching at one of her husband's hands. They were cold and lifeless in her grasp and she drew back, barely able to suppress a look of revulsion.

'So much for your desire to help,' the Moor jeered, and for a moment he thought she might throw herself at him and rake his face with her nails, so furious did she look.

'This is not my husband! This is not the man I married!'

'The man who used to bounce you on his knee and you would pull his beard?' Selim mocked callously. 'But it is. Like this, he is an empty shell of a man, but when I give him my powders he is a flame, burning out too quickly because he wishes to please you in all things. You have given him pleasure, I admit. He has been happier these past months with you than I have ever seen him before, but . . .'

'Tell me what I must do to keep him alive, and I shall,' she begged.

'For a week—a few months or perhaps, no longer, and it will be no fault of yours when he departs this world. Not really. In some respects I am like his son. I need to place the blame upon the shoulders of someone else, and that is a sin for which I shall pay dearly.'

'What are you saying?' Alexandrine started towards him, wide-eyed. 'You say Luc will die? When? What are you trying to tell me? Does it give you pleasure to torture me so?'

'Once I would have gained great pleasure from the sight of a woman grovelling at the feet of her man,' Selim returned as she threw herself down at the side of the chair, catching hold of Luc's arm. There was no response, no flicker of recognition in the eyes that turned so slowly to look at her. 'Did I not tell you he would not know you? He is in my hands.'

'As you are in mine,' Alexandrine promised, climbing to her feet. 'If any harm befalls this gentle man, I shall have you killed!'

'Do you think you are capable of that, madame?' came the disquietening retort, and she looked at him steadily, no doubt in her mind.

'Oh, yes, Selim. Believe me. If Luc dies because of your lack of care, you will follow him to the grave within an hour.'

'Then I have nothing to worry about—and neither have you.'

'You say he will not be able to come down tonight?' Alexandrine grew pale at the thought of facing her guests alone. 'I wanted so much for him to be proud of me.'

'He will be when he hears how well you conduct yourself. It is too late to withdraw. You must do this alone.'

'Yes,' she acknowledged, 'I must.' It was a terrifying thought!

'Perhaps I should wear the black, after all,' Alexandrine said, speaking her thoughts aloud as she scrutinised her appearance in the wall-length mirror yet again. 'I need all the confidence I can get tonight.'

'Never wear black; you are too young,' Alain said from the bedroom door, and she spun round with a gasp. 'Your maid let me in. Why should you need confidence? From the display I glimpsed below, you have excelled yourself. Everyone will be talking about the Hôtel de Mezière for weeks! And that colour is perfect for you. Did I choose that excellent material, or did Luc?'

He knew very well it had been his choice, Alexandrine thought, as she saw the gleam which came into his eyes.

'I am glad it has met with your approval.' Her voice betrayed none of the excitement she felt rising inside her at the sight of him. How handsome he looked in a coat of rich burgundy, a white silk waistcoat beneath. His hair was unpowdered and so short about his neck that he did not need the usual ribbon to tie it back.

At the same time as her gaze dwelled on him, she was aware of his eyes inspecting her appearance, staring at the dark yellow leather shoes, rising slowly, scrutinisingly, over the full skirts of her gown to where the firm swell of her young breasts was exposed above the low curving neckline of her bodice, over the smooth shoulders and the exquisite line of her throat, the flawlessness of the features which were tinged slightly pink as her embarrassment grew. Finally to the fair curls, unadorned and natural. Her presence would grace the finest château in France, Alain mused, as he stepped back to allow her to precede him into the sitting-room.

'I did not invite you into my room, monsieur. I hope you have a explanation for this unwarranted intrusion.' She tried to sound annoyed.

'I have. Luc asked me to come early tonight. I have something for him, and now I am told by Pierre that he is indisposed and will not be attending his own ball. How can that be?'

'He quarrelled again with Paul. There has not been a day since the *Appartement* at Versailles that they have not exchanged heated words. Today was the worst! It does not matter what was said between them, I am sure you can well imagine it. Luc collapsed. He was beside himself with rage. I have never seen him so angry. He has sent Paul away—forbidden him the house.'

'And disinherited him. But you knew that, did you not?' Alain said, and she paled at the words.

'No, I did not!'

'He wishes me to witness the new will he has drawn up—of which you are the sole beneficiary. Did you not know that, either?' Alain was watching her carefully, but by the amazement which registered in her eyes he saw she had known nothing. Mutely she shook her head, too stunned to answer him. 'You say he has collapsed? Is the Moor tending him?'

'Yes. I have come to realise that Selim does have his best interests at heart. He is very, very fond of my husband.'

'And in sole control of him,' Alain remarked drily. 'Are not you also barred from seeing him when he is ill?' What was this sickness that plagued Luc Boussières? One moment a fit, healthy man, young for his years, and then little more than a cripple, helpless. He knew that some men, as they grew older, began taking certain powders and liquids bought from charlatans and quacks in the city, who swore that the things would revitalise their old bones, make them healthy and able to accommodate the youngest and most lively of mistresses. Was this what Luc had resorted to since his marriage? He tried to imagine Alexandrine in bed with him, and the

thought angered him beyond reason. His friend, and the
woman he coveted. It was an unbearable thought! He
had not been mistaken when he felt the response from
her lips. No man had yet satisfied her desires, her needs.

'Is your other business with Luc of a private nature?'
Alexandrine asked. 'Perhaps it is something I can deal
with, otherwise.'

'Perhaps you can. He was to come to Belaincourt
tomorrow. I have four horses for him to look at. He
wishes to choose two for you and himself, for future
hunts.'

'He did mention it to me. I am afraid I shall disgrace
him. I have not ridden in years, not since I was twelve,
and then the animal was one more accustomed to pulling
a plough than having me astride him,' Alexandrine confessed, her expression softening as she recalled the
occasion.

'Astride?' Alain queried, his eyebrows rising quizzingly. 'That I would like to have seen! I find it hard to
imagine you astride a work-horse. Did they teach you
nothing in that convent?'

'A great many things, and all of them dull,' she
flashed. 'Besides, that was before...'

He had to be mistaken, Alain thought, but he could
have sworn there was a wistful note in her voice as if to
indicate that she longed to see her old home again. Was
she not content with what she had, the proud name she
bore, or was Luc's continuing bad health beginning to
pall? Was she seeking some outlet from the confines of
marriage? He repressed the ugly thought.

She picked up her fan and said, 'I must go downstairs. The guests will be arriving soon.'

'I take it, then, I shall not be allowed to see Luc?'
Alain said, his voice hardening.

'Do you think I am confining him to his room against
his will?' she returned haughtily. 'You shall see him if
you wish. Come with me.'

She had no idea whether she would be admitted to
her husband's rooms. Selim opened the door before she
could even knock, and out scuttled Luc's valet Charles,
his face white, his whole body trembling, and almost
knocked her over in his haste to quit the room.

'The master has gone mad! God help us all! We are in the hands of a madman!' he cried in a quavering voice, and only just avoided the hand of the Moor which came after to strike him.

It was Alexandrine who did that. Her open palm caught the man a stinging blow across first one cheek and then the other. 'How dare you refer to the Marquis in such a manner! It is you who have taken leave of your senses. Control yourself! Do you hear me?'

'Madame la Marquise, forgive me, but he attacked me... He swore at me!'

'And had every right to do so, if you acted so before him,' she cried. 'Go away and control yourself.'

'He is mad... or being turned mad by those potions that the black heathen feeds him,' the man muttered as he backed away, well out of reach of them all. 'I have seen him. I shall never forget those eyes...'

Alain took a step forward, and he fled from their presence.

'Let me in, Selim,' Alexandrine ordered, and to her surprise her command was obeyed without comment.

Luc still sat in the chair by the window, as quiet and docile and as unaware of her presence as he had been during her last visit.

'Was the man raving? There is no change,' she exclaimed.

Not now, Selim thought, as he moved past them to stare at his patient. Thank Allah you did not show yourselves ten minutes ago! Then you would indeed have seen a different man. He would have to deal with the valet. He was a dangerous man now, possessing knowledge he must never divulge.

'The Marquis was sleeping. He awoke to find his valet going through his personal papers in the bureau behind him. Naturally he was furious, but he is too weak to do very much, and so his only attack was in words. He uses a very colourful rhetoric when he wishes, madame. It is best you do not have me repeat it for you. The man knew he would be dismissed for his act, and probably hoped to throw himself on your mercy.'

'He shall have none from me. He shall leave this house tonight!'

'That is no hardship. I am perfectly capable of attending to all the needs of the Marquis,' Selim replied, and Alain threw him a questioning look.

A plausible explanation, except that he believed the man had been genuinely terrified. Perhaps he *had* been discovered rifling his master's desk, but something had happened to turn him into a man out of his mind with fear. What could it have been? Luc seemed asleep, yet his eyes were open. Not looking at them, but past them. It was uncanny; even he felt uncomfortable. Selim's keen eyes did not miss his moment of discomfort.

'He needs only rest, Monsieur le Duc. In a few days he will be well again, I promise. But, as you can see, he cannot recognise anyone at this moment and is therefore incapable of signing anything. Which is why you are here, is it not?'

'Are you privy to every secret in this house?' Alexandrine asked, and a faint smile touched the black face at her indignation. He was beginning to accept that she was as innocent as Luc proclaimed her to be.

'Every one—and more, that have never even touched this house,' came the disquietening answer. 'Please leave now and allow him to rest.'

'I think Luc should be seen by another physician,' Alain said, as he accompanied Alexandrine downstairs.

'I thought so too at first, but now I am convinced he is in the best possible hands,' she assured him, and he frowned at her angrily.

'How can you say that? He did not know you! What is wrong with him, can you tell me? Or is it in your best interests not to bother with an old, sick man who will make you a very rich widow?'

At the foot of the stairs, Alexandrine swung round to face him, her eyes flashing with anger to match his. Two fierce spots of colour burned into her unrouged cheeks.

'You are Luc's friend, monsieur. I am his wife. I shall decide what is best for him. Please do not question my judgement again. Go and enjoy the wines from his cellar while you may, for, I tell you now, should anything happen to him, you will never again be made welcome in this house!'

'Perhaps you will not have a say in the matter,' Alain snapped. 'You forget that, as Luc's heir, Paul inherits everything when his father dies. Until a new document is drawn up with Luc's signature on it and mine as witness, you will be nothing more than a grieving widow. Think on that, madame, and enjoy your moment of power. It could be a short triumph. Very short indeed.'

Alexandrine blinked back hot, angry tears as he left her. What had possessed her to speak such thoughtless words. Fear of trusting him? Or fear of the mixed emotions he roused in her whenever they were together. When she had needed a staunch supporter, it had been he who had stood at her side and openly declared Paul to be a liar. He had been prepared to draw his sword in defence of her honour! Now, when she had been on the point of turning to him again, of considering him a friend, no longer an adversary, he had flung those hateful words at her.

Beware when the game stops, for when that happens, we shall cease to be adversaries. We shall become lovers. Again those words with their subtle threat invaded her thoughts. It was, to her mind, as if he deliberately sought to prolong the enmity between them, insulting her at every turn by comparing her to every woman he had ever known, his wife in particular, expecting her to act in the same way. Why? Because he truly disliked her, mistrusted her? Or was he afraid that the game they had played for all these months was almost at an end? And, when it ended, could he be as feared of that as she was? If Luc should die, she would be free, but alone and friendless in Paris. Paul would ensure that no one acknowledged her. At Versailles, if she were received there again, it would be to endure the backbiting and gossip she hated. There might only be one person who would offer his help, and that would be Alain Ratan— for a purely selfish reason: to prove to himself that she was like all the others. Would she accept or decline such an offer?

Across the room, Alain's eyes locked with hers. He had helped himself to a glass of wine and raised it towards her in a mocking salute. She ignored it and turned away to greet the first of her guests, Jeanne d'Etoiles, radiant in blue satin, sapphires glowing against her white skin, a small passionnée patch beneath one eye. Her large eyes were bright with excitement as she hugged Alexandrine and then kissed her on both cheeks with the affection she might have shown a sister.

'How elegant you look! And you have transformed this house! I remember my husband and I coming here, several years ago, to a dinner-party given by the Marquis, an informal affair. We sat in his study for most of the evening discussing poetry—or was it the philosophy of Descartes? I have never forgotten his library—all those dusty old books in foreign languages, but so many too that I found interesting. Ronsard and Balzac and Molière. My poor husband almost fell asleep with boredom.'

'He is not with you?' Alexandrine asked, leading her into the dining-room. Instantly they were offered champagne, ice cold in crystal-stemmed glasses that shone with muted colours in the candlelight. She had discovered many unused treasures Luc had brought back to France with him, and tonight had put many to good use.

'No, as usual he is away on business for his uncle, Monsieur le Tournehem, in Provence. But I am never bored; I do not have the time! I hope you will not be when you come to Etoiles. My guest-list is always very varied. But nothing I can do will excel this,' Jeanne exclaimed as she gazed in open admiration at the long tables laid out for the buffet.

On snow-white linen cloths was laid glistening glassware and silver. Heavy pewter tankards were set for the men who wished to partake of something other than wine and liquors, gleaming with that dull sheen that only that metal could produce. Porcelain plates waited to be filled with the variety of foods laid out and waiting for the guests: cold pheasant and hare, chickens by the score cooked in a variety of ways, wild boar, roasted over a

spit and basted in its own juices, cheeses and delicacies
to delight the palate, pastries and sugared biscuits soaked
in brandy, brandied peaches at least two years old, served
with a thick cream made that morning. To drink, there
was an abundance of wines from all over France, champagne and brandy.

Beside the tables lackeys waited, while others remained by the door, holding trays of champagne or wines
for people when they entered. She had placed another
two on either side of the front door, too, to offer something warming when guests first arrived.

'Where is the Marquis?' Jeanne asked, noting the absence of her host for the first time and looking enquiringly at her friend. 'Oh dear! He is not indisposed?'

'Why do you say that? As a matter of fact, he is. He
will not be able to attend tonight, but he was taken ill
only this morning. How could you know?'

'News travels fast in Paris, my dear, especially when
it is spread with such malice by Paul Boussières. I was
with a friend, Madame Celestine, this morning and not
an hour before she had overheard that unpleasant young
man bewailing his misfortunes to friends. How his father
had been turned against him and, when he had attempted to defend himself against the lies which had
blackened his character, you had struck him and accused him of the most vile things. At every turn his help
had been misconstrued, used by you to oust him from
the house and from his father's side. I think he has taken
leave of his senses! His need for money has addled what
little brains he possesses. Forget him.' Jeanne squeezed
her arm affectionately. 'Tonight shall be the triumph you
deserve. Tomorrow Paul Boussières will be the nobody
he really is. There will be enough people here tonight to
see for themselves what you are really like and to counter
these outrageous statements he makes. By the way, who
has been invited? I am dying with curiosity. Apart from
the Duc de Belaincourt,' she added with a soft laugh.
Then, as voices sounded behind them, 'But I think I
shall find out for myself. Your guests have begun to

arrive. Good luck, Alexandrine. I shall go and avail myself of the Duc's very pleasant company. He is too handsome to be left all alone.'

CHAPTER NINE

'MADAME, I THINK we should bring more wine from the cellar. It seems to be going at an alarming rate.' Pierre had been waiting patiently at Alexandrine's side while she tried to extract herself from the company of a gushing but very affable woman who had introduced herself as Madame Reynard, the wife of Hugo, Comte Danzin, one of the Gentlemen of the King's Bedchamber. Alexandrine remembered hearing of her at one of the salons, a lonely middle-aged person with a pompous husband who spent very little time with her. To while away long hours alone she had taken to doing charity work for the poor of Paris. To be included on one of Madame Reynard's charities was considered a privilege. Alexandrine had promised she would help in any way, remembering the deplorable surroundings from which Francine had come to her. But the woman wanted more than just a promise, and in order to get away from her she had agreed to provide not only clothing and food, but money.

This night was going to cost her far more than she had envisaged! She had told Luc she could manage, but already her funds had been depleted. She would need to ask him for more to pay off all the merchants and vendors who supplied the household. And now they needed more wine. Thank goodness Luc's cellars were well stocked! She went into the sitting-room to the desk where she knew the keys were kept and gave it to the major-domo, instructing him to bring back whatever he considered necessary for the remainder of the evening.

'Madame is a great success.' Pierre smiled with pride. Her success was also success for the family, and the household who had made such elaborate preparations for tonight. Not one thing had gone wrong. Only the absence of the Marquis marred what was otherwise a perfect evening, but, even so, the Marquise had carried the occasion well all by herself. She had great poise and far more confidence than she realised. Everyone was enchanted with her and he had not heard one word said against her. To the contrary, it was Paul Boussières who now would find himself on the wrong end of many tongues. Good riddance! the man thought as he turned away. The old house was at peace for the first time since the first Marquise had died. Years of estrangement from society, from the outside world were ended.

'Where do you get your energy from?' Jeanne demanded, cornering Alexandrine before she could return to the dining-room. 'I have not seen you stop talking since I arrived. To think you were once afraid to meet people!'

'I am actually enjoying myself,' Alexandrine confessed. 'I just wish Luc could be here beside me. This was all for him. I think it will be safe enough to slip away in a while and see him. I am so worried, Jeanne. He looks so strange after one of these attacks.'

'And you say Paul arguing with him this morning brought it on?'

'Yes. Luc was quite violent, Paul too. I admit quite frankly that to watch them was frightening. And then...' Her voice dropped to a whisper as she related how Charles the valet had left his master's rooms, quaking with fear.

'I think the sooner you have your husband examined by another doctor, the better,' Jeanne told her. 'These seizures are obviously due to his age ... and perhaps the amount of wine you have told me he consumes daily, but nevertheless it will ease your mind to know it is nothing more serious. I shall pray that your visit to Etoiles will restore his health. You both deserve to be happy, and with that dreadful son of his out of the way, perhaps that is now possible. But do find another doctor. I can give you several names.'

'Please do. I shall give them to Selim. I trust his judgement, Jeanne, but perhaps you are right. He cannot know everything, even though he has been with Luc for many years and nursed him through these attacks before.'

The words froze on Alexandrine's lips as she looked across the crowded room and saw two people coming towards them. One was Alain Ratan, and at his side was a striking woman in a crimson gown, the bodice cut so low across her full breasts that it was a wonder it ever stayed up, she thought, her lips tightening. Claudia de la Fontaine! Her name had not been on the guest-list he had given her. How dared he bring his mistress to her ball! It was the height of rudeness, but even as a reproach rose in her throat, she caught Jeanne's warning eye and realised what a mistake it would be not to make the woman welcome. It should not matter to her how many women Alain Ratan partnered, here or anywhere else. To comment on it would arouse a suspicion that she was jealous.

Jealous? But she was! Dear heaven, she had never felt this way before.

'Madame la Marquise, may I introduce Madame de la Fontaine, an old friend of mine,' Alain said cordially, acknowledging Jeanne's presence with a smile. They had talked for some time while the first guests were arriving and he had been pleasantly surprised by her intelligence. She was nowhere near as stupid as she looked, nor as fragile. Many would underestimate her true worth.

Alexandrine stared into the other's frosty features, refusing to allow herself to be intimidated by the flashing eyes that inspected her appearance. 'Had I known you were a friend of the Duc de Belaincourt, madame, I would certainly have included your name on my guest-list for tonight. I have him to thank for correcting my mistake. I do hope you will enjoy yourself.'

'Madame la Marquise...' As she turned away, Alain excused himself from Claudia's side and hurried after Alexandrine. She saw Jeanne engage the woman in conversation, drawing her back into the dining-room when she looked as if she wanted to linger to hear what was being said. 'I should explain about Claudia's presence.'

'There is nothing to explain.' Alexandrine's voice was as cold as her expression. 'You omitted to include her name, that is all. And now you have rectified that. Is it supposed to be important?'

'It should be, if you consider the implications behind what I did. Good Lord, you speak as if it was deliberately intended to annoy you.' Alain's lips tightened at her attitude. 'Why I don't leave you to fend for yourself is beyond me! I am sure you are capable of it.'

'Neither do I,'' she flashed. 'And, yes, I am capable. More so now than I ever realised. And glad of it.'

'Damn it, you will listen!' Alain exclaimed, and his fingers closed around her wrist like an iron band. Opening the door nearest to them, he glanced quickly back over his shoulder to ensure that they were not being observed, and pushed her into the room.

'Don't tell me you will scream—we've been through all that before,' he said mockingly, closing the door and standing with his back against it. She stepped away from him, rubbing her wrist, and he frowned as if not realising how his hold had hurt her. 'You will listen to what I have to say and then you will apologise for the nasty suspicions you have about me. Every time I try to be pleasant—to help you, I am made to feel a fool, if not a rogue!'

'Help me?' she echoed, quickly regaining her composure. 'We are both well aware why you are—pleasant, as you put it. It is the game you play, isn't it? With me and every other woman. To make us accept you as a friend, a feeling human being, when in reality you are cold and inhuman, drained of all decent feelings. You are arrogant and selfish and the only difference between you and Paul is that you are more subtle. Where he would use force, you use words. No, don't you dare to touch me!'

'Dare!' Her scornful words brought Alain away from the door. Pale eyes glittering, he took her by the shoulders and shook her. Had she been wearing a wig, it would have tumbled from her head at the force he used. She gasped as she was thrust backwards on to a sofa. He threw himself down beside her, his hands once again on her shoulders, restraining her when she tried to move. 'You will be still and listen to me. Do you not think me capable of using force? Believe me, I am, but you would not be worth the effort.' It was a lie. He had never used his strength to have a woman and would not

and could not have done so with her, even though she
roused his temper more than any woman he could remember since his wife died. And more than most men,
too. She was becoming a constant thorn in his side, yet
for some inexplicable reason, he welcomed the pain. She
had brought him back to life after years of being dead.
He hated her for it—despised himself for allowing it—
and yet yearned more each day to possess her. Her eyes
were wide with apprehension as she stared into his hard
face. He had intended to frighten her, and he had succeeded. He could feel her body trembling against his.
He had no way of knowing it was not fear that he might
hurt her—but fear of her own so far unfulfilled desires
and dreams. Alexandrine d'Albret, the little country girl,
had money and position now, but little else to offer a
man. What did she know? How could she compete with
women like Claudia de la Fontaine?

Misunderstanding, Alain slightly relaxed his hold but
did not let her go. He was lost for a moment as he considered the soft mouth, felt the fierce thudding of her
heart against his chest. She did not seem to notice that
one hand slid behind her shoulder and down to the small
of her back or that his body was relaxing slowly against
hers, pinning her back against the cushions far more effectively than before.

'Claudia's coming here tonight, with me, may help to
still some of the stupid rumours. Don't you understand
that? Everyone knows we have a certain—relationship.'

'They might say you are using her as a shield to hide
what is between *us*.' Alexandrine's voice was hardly
audible. He *had* been trying to help her and she had
misunderstood! Or was he more clever than she assumed? Why, oh why could she not trust him?

'If she believed there was anything between *us*, my
dear Alexa, she would claw out your eyes—and in front
of all your guests! Claudia has a very jealous nature.
And so have you. Why else are you so annoyed that she
is here?' Alain murmured, sudden bright mockery
gleaming in his eyes.

'Jealous? I? Of whom, may I ask?' Her cheeks flamed
at the insinuation. 'You have a high opinion of yourself,
monsieur.'

'So we are to play the game to the bitter end, are we?'

If she pretended what was between them was indeed a game, perhaps she could prolong these moments—steal a few more kisses... Oh, the madness of her thoughts! She felt his fingers slide over the firm curve of one breast and laughed shakily. 'Of course. Is that not what you expect of me?'

An expletive broke from his lips and she knew immediately that it had been the wrong thing to say. A wicked smile crossed the dark features as he bent his head towards hers—and she found there was no way to escape the lips determined to claim her own.

'Then I shall not disappoint you, Alexa.'

Let him kiss her, if that was what he wanted! Alexandrine was adamant she would not answer him. Yet scarcely had his lips touched hers than her own flared to life with an eagerness that shocked her. It had not been like this when Luc had held her in his arms and tried to make love to her—and he had more right than this man! Yet, of the two, she knew that, had she been free, she would give not only her heart but her body to Alain Ratan. If this strange sensation within her was love, she was doomed, for she had no willpower with which to fight him. Or was it merely need—a desperation brought about by the loneliness of her existence? Of all the people she had met over the past months, only Jeanne d'Etoiles could she truly call a friend.

Her marriage was a farce, her husband little more than an invalid who wanted to look at her, but not make her his wife. She had promised never to take a lover while he was alive and had done so honestly believing she could never be tempted by another man. Alain Ratan tempted her as if he was the devil himself. Perhaps he was. The Sisters had told her evil came in many forms, many disguises.

She felt Alain's hand become more insistent on her breast, tried to shut her ears against the soft endearments whispered in her ear, against her hair, the smooth hollow of her throat. She felt as if she was being lifted and borne away on a huge cloud. Nothing was real but this moment, lying in the arms of this dangerous man. She felt anger in the rough kisses that bruised her mouth as though he, too, despised what happened every time they came together, yet was as incapable of fighting it as she.

And then it was suddenly different. There was only tenderness in the mouth that plied her own with gentle, yet insistent, soul-searching kisses. Her senses clamoured for more even though her heart cried out against such foolishness. It was more than need she was experiencing, more than just a hunger—a moment stolen and then forgotten. It was love she had discovered at last, and she found it more frightening than anything she had ever known in her young life! It made her totally helpless, a puppet responding to the man who manipulated her. That was all he was doing, she knew, but it no longer mattered. The material of her gown was eased away from one shoulder and then Alain's lips, as light as gossamer, touched her bare skin. They did not stop there, but continued down over the rise of her breast. Alexandrine fought and lost the battle raging inside her and slipped her arms about his neck, ran her fingers through the crisp, black hair, as the fire he had kindled raged out of control. Even when his tingling kisses lightly brushed a pink rosebud nipple, she offered no resistance—she could not!

An embarrassed cough from the direction of the doorway brought them apart. Alexandrine, panic-stricken, hastily rearranged her bodice as Alain turned to face the servant behind them, effectively blocking her from view.

'Pardon me, Monsieur le Duc, but Monsieur Paul has arrived and is demanding to have access to his father,' Pierre said. 'I think madame should speak to him. I rather fear he has been drinking.'

'Paul? Here?' Alexandrine gasped, leaping to her feet. 'Luc has forbidden him the house! I shall not admit him.'

'And have him cause a fuss before all your guests?' Alain answered. He did not show his annoyance at the interruption, which—when he thought on it later—he came to consider a blessed intervention before he had committed himself totally to the moment. It would have been so easy. She had been so willing. 'Let me speak to him. You go upstairs and see how Luc is. Perhaps he will receive him if he is well enough...for a moment only,' he added.

Alexandrine nodded, eager to snatch the suggestion as a way of escaping from the awkwardness of her situation. She could not look at him. She allowed him a moment after leaving the room before she followed, and found herself confronted by Claudia de la Fontaine.

'So he was with you! He lied to me when he said you meant nothing to him,' she said in a fierce whisper. 'You shall not have him, do you hear me? He is mine.'

'Yes, madame.' Alexandrine paled at the venom in the sibilant tone, but managed to keep her self-control Upstairs, away from the watching eyes, she would be able to regain her composure before going to her husband's rooms. 'He is yours and you are welcome to him,' adding with an infuriatingly confident smile, 'If you can hold him.'

Picking up the skirts of her gown, she ascended the stairs. Alone in one of the empty, darkened corridors she leaned weakly against a wall, a trembling hand held against her wildly beating heart. What would have happened if Pierre had not interrupted them? She was badly shaken by the tumult which still engulfed her. In the darkness she could still feel Alain's lips brushing hers, his fingers caressing her bare skin. Her cheeks were still burning when she knocked on Luc's door.

No answer. No sound from within. Her expression became puzzled. Even if her husband were sleeping, Selim would be awake and as watchful of his patient as ever, she thought, and knocked again, more insistently.

She tried the door, and to her amazement it yielded to her touch. Usually it was locked. Some inner instinct told her something was terribly wrong and she pushed it open, calling Selim by name as she did so. The sitting-room· was dark. No candles burned anywhere in the room. Beyond, a flicker of light came from the bedroom. She started across the door, which was wide open, and the next moment cried out as she stumbled over something lying in her path and fell heavily on the Persian carpet. Her groping fingers encountered not a piece of furniture, as she thought, but cold skin...a face! A scream rose, and died in her throat as she thought of all the people below. Luc! Was it her husband prostrate on the ground before her? A candle. Where were the candles?

It was several minutes before she located one and managed to light it. The sight that met her eyes made her reel back against a table in horror. The room had been ransacked, drawers pulled from the desk and the sideboard, papers strewn across the floor. Curtains had been ripped apart as if someone had been searching with great thoroughness through every item of furniture, every piece of clothing. Beyond, the bedroom screamed of the same chaos. And, at her feet, sprawled Selim!

Forcing herself to step round his motionless body, she entered the other room. The bed was empty, the sheets crumpled and trailing almost to the door. More papers and personal items littered chairs and floor. Of Luc Boussières there was no sign! For a moment her senses almost left her, and she was forced to cling to the bedpost for support as her legs turned to water. What terrible thing had taken place? Where was her husband? Only Selim would know that—if he were not dead. She ran back to where he lay and threw herself down beside him, searching for some sign of life. A heartbeat. Thank God! He groaned as she lifted his head, and her hand came away with blood on it. She fetched water and lifted him again, holding the glass against his lips until his eyes opened and recognition sprang to them.

'Luc!' The name was a hoarse cry upon his lips.

'Gone. What has happened? Where is he?'

'Do you not know?' Accusing eyes stared at her, then he shook his head and winced as the movement caused him pain. 'Help me to a chair—I must think.'

'What is there to think about?' She was beside herself with concern as she complied. 'He must have wandered off while you were asleep—he cannot have gone far. Perhaps he is somewhere upstairs.'

'And, before he took this stroll, he ransacked these rooms?' The Moor snapped. 'He has been taken. I know not by whom, but I can guess. But where?' He lifted his shoulders in a shrug of despair. 'I have no idea.'

'Taken?' Alexandrine froze on her knees beside him. 'You are not making sense. He is ill. Why should anyone want to—to abduct him? Selim, you thought that I...'

'For a moment only. You are the person who would profit most by his disappearance and his death. At least you would have been if the second will had been signed...as it is there is only one heir.'

'Paul,' she breathed, still not understanding any of it. Luc abducted? With the house full of people?

'Is someone taking my name in vain yet again?' Paul declared from the doorway. She had not closed it when she entered. 'What on earth is happening up here? Have you taken to indulging in orgies in my father's rooms?' Without waiting for an answer, he sauntered past them and into the bedroom. When he came out again, there was a derisive look on his face. 'Pray, what have you done with my father, madame? I wish to make my peace with him.'

The words almost made Alexandrine break into hysterical laughter, for she knew that was the last thing that had brought him to the house. How opportune that he had arrived at this precise moment... She started to her feet, staring at him coldly.

'He—He has been abducted.' How stupid her words sounded.

'Abducted!' Paul's laughter echoed around the desolate room. Hardly the reaction of a concerned son, she thought, wishing she could put some sense of order to what was happening. 'While you are entertaining a hundred or more people below? And who, may I ask, has spirited him out of the house? And how?'

'It would not be difficult. There are stairs that the servants use, which lead directly to the street,' Selim broke in, a hand held against his throbbing head. Whoever had struck him had used considerable force. He should have been dead! It was a mistake to have left him alive, as someone would find out to their cost.

He was behind it, he thought, as he stared at Paul Boussières. He would not have thought he had it in him—and yet he was his father's son. It was not only possible, but seemed a certainty that he had hired men to abduct his own father. To what ends? To gain money, of course.

Luc had first refused to pay his debts, and now had disinherited him in favour of his wife. The disgrace when that was known would be nothing to what would happen to him at the hands of people to whom he owed money! Not only friends and gambling partners, but moneylenders too, Selim surmised, men who would have few scruples about obtaining it from him by any means at their disposal.

'How convenient.' The drunken pose he had adopted when he entered the house and spoke to Alain—or rather was lectured to by the man—now dropped from him like a cloak. Gone was the slur in his voice which rolled his words into one. Gone was the swaying gait. Alexandrine watched with growing apprehension as he straightened and fixed both of them with a cold look. 'I suggest you lower your voice, stepmother, unless you wish the whole house to hear what I am about to say... and that would be very dangerous for me, and most unfortunate for you. The same mishap that has befallen my father may well happen to you—and to you!' He spun round on Selim, throwing up a hand to ward off the Moor who had sprung to his feet at the threatening words. 'Touch me, and Luc will die. I have left word that if I do not make contact within two hours, he is to be disposed of.'

'Do you know what you are saying?' Alexandrine whispered. 'You have taken your own father from his house by force! To what ends?'

'To have what is due to me, madame. His money. His property. All that he possesses. You shall have none of it. Do you think I don't know about that other will? He was going to leave me without a sou—and the old fool thought I would stand for it. Never!'

'It was never signed,' she cried, and could have bitten off her tongue as Selim swore in his own tongue. She could think only of having Luc safely back home. Money was of no importance to her, or her clothes, or the jewels he had lavished on her. 'Take all I have. Sell my jewels... anything... but have him brought back to me. You do not realise how sick he is.'

'He is old, and it is time he died,' Paul returned callously.

He had known he would enjoy this moment of victory, but he had never anticipated such enjoyment at the sight of Alexandrine's distraught features and the tears that streamed unchecked over her ashen cheeks. He would never have admitted it to anyone, but he secretly found her desirable, so much so that he now decided she would be allowed to stay here once he was master. Or perhaps he would buy a place in the country and have her taken there. Who would miss her? She was a nobody. And when he had finished with her, his triumph would be complete when he cast her out to fend for herself with only the clothes she wore on her back. No money—no friends—nothing, but her body to use in order to stay alive—as she would have to use it to satisfy him to keep her worthless life. Soon, very soon, he would have everything he had ever wanted. No one would ever look down their noses at him again. He would demand and receive their respect. The name of Paul Boussières would be remembered!

And the Moor, Selim. He would be sold to some rich widow who enjoyed the avid attentions of such servants. How that would bring him to heel! How delightful this evening was turning out to be.

Alexandrine's unexpected disclosure had heightened his pleasure. He had thought the will disinheriting him had been signed several days before, and he had Alain Ratan to thank for the fact it had not. If only he had called here sooner. His men had searched high and low for it without success, but now it did not matter. Without signatures, it was not valid. *She* inherited nothing. He was still the only legitimate heir!

'You want your father dead?' Alexandrine said in disbelief. 'I know you are not the best of friends, but what you say is terrible. Paul, please have him brought back home. If I ask, he will forgive you this—this silly, reckless escapade.' She was desperate to reach him. 'I—I might even be able to persuade him to pay your debts, or increase your allowance.'

'How generous, but I have no need of your help. My father will remain where he is until he dies. A month or two at the most, I have been told by the man I got to examine him this evening. Then I shall assume my natural

position as master of this house, the next Marquis de
Mezière—and you, stepmother, will do as I say or find
yourself in the street where you belong.'

He made the term sound almost obscene, Alexandrine
thought, fighting to keep a hold on her reasoning. The
whole thing was so bizarre, like a nightmare.

'I think it is time I informed the authorities that your
father is missing and that you claim responsibility for
moving him from this house—and deliberately causing
his death,' she threw the words at him defiantly.

'Call the watch if you wish. Who is there to bear out
your words but this servant of my father's? Now, in my
case, I shall soon have statements from five—I repeat
five—witnesses, who this morning overheard my father
disinherit me because you had asked him. They were
also witnesses to the way he lost control of himself and
launched himself at me with a stick. Had they not prevented it, I should have been beaten severely—or even
killed. They will testify to his lack of judgement in the
simplest matters and will provide me with the where-
withal to have him confined.'

'If only that had been true,' Selim growled, and Paul
sneered at him, 'I wish he had killed you!'

'Walk with care, Moor. Your days are numbered, as
are hers, although she has more to offer than you. I may
be generous.'

'How—How can you have witnesses? There was no
one here this morning save the three of us and Luc?'

'And Charles, the valet,' Selim reminded her stonily.
'I always knew there was something wrong about that
man.'

'As you say—Charles. He has been in my service for
the past two years. A most able spy. I pay him well and
have promised him much. He would murder his own
mother for money no matter how small the amount. Shall
I tell you where my father is going to end his days and
why there is nothing you can do about it?' Paul asked,
laughing softly. 'He is going to the Bastille, where he
thought to put me, and he will stay there because my
five excellent witnesses will swear that he is senile—out
of his head—bewitched by this child-woman he has
married, who consorts with thieves and beggars across

the Pont-Neuf, even with fortune-tellers, who also have the habit of dabbling in the black arts—who can supply potions for every need. As you no doubt can, Moor. I shall say the two of you consorted together to poison my father so that she would inherit his money and share it with you.'

'No one will believe you,' Alexandrine cried. Selim started out of his chair, but fell back with a groan, too weak to launch himself at the man he detested, who taunted and threatened them—and wished to see dead the only friend he had in the world. 'I shall tell them the truth.'

'Truth? What a little fool you are! Who will believe you? Who believed you the last time? I was very convincing about the way you had begged me for a lift in my carriage and then attempted to seduce me—offering me half my father's money if I would help you to get rid of him. And using your body as an inducement. My adjectives about you were so colourful that I surprised even myself. Only Alain spoiled it for me, didn't he? Were you thanking him when Pierre found you together in the salon?'

Claudia, Alexandrine thought, swaying unsteadily. She had seen more than she thought, and probably invented a great deal more in order to blacken the character of her supposed rival.

The Bastille! That dreaded place. Luc had sired a monster. Paul was right: there was nothing she could do about it. His witnesses would lie to protect the investment they had in him. Once he assumed the title of marquis, they would be paid, and he would be rich for the rest of his life. And Luc would be dead! No, she would not allow it to happen. She would think of some way to have him released.

'There is no way out save that which I shall give you,' Paul taunted. 'The Governor is also a man who likes money, and he will be well bribed to ensure that my father is allowed no visitors. He will be all alone in a dark, damp cell. He was raging like an idiot when I told him, but that will soon cease. The Bastille is a big place, you know. Sometimes the gaolers forget to feed the inmates. How sad. He could go without food for days. Of course

I could have sent my father to a madhouse, but I think the Bastille a more fitting place for him, don't you? Every day he is there, he will wonder what I am doing and what you are doing, my dear. He will in time, I suspect, go as mad as I proclaim him to be now... but it will be a very slow process. His brain will decay through lack of use. No books, no one to talk to. No visitors. He will pray for death to take him every day. I don't want that to happen too soon. Perhaps I shall visit him from time to time, to let him know he is always in my thoughts. Oh, yes, the Bastille will be a far better place for him to end his days, and only you and I will know that he is not the old fool I say he is.'

'I will kill you for this,' Selim threatened. 'By Allah, I swear it!'

'Selim, be quiet! He is capable of anything, even of killing you,' Alexandrine said, forcing herself to concentrate on how best to placate the evil in their midst. She could turn to no one for help lest Paul kept his threat and had Luc murdered in cold blood. Who would there be to say that he had not died a natural death? A pillow over the face while he slept! Poison in his food! And then Paul would be the Marquis de Mezière! 'And just how do you propose to account for your father's absence?'

'Has he left the hotel? He is ill, is he not? Confined to his rooms with the Moor tending him as always? And you, madame, will confirm that. Also the fact that tonight father and son have been reconciled. He has forgiven me my bad ways and even agreed to pay some of my debts. You have jewellery. I want it. It will go some way to providing what I need for the moment. Later...' He gave her an ugly smile, aware she was totally in his power, 'I shall have no need, shall I? We shall go downstairs together. Not only have I been reconciled with my beloved father, but you and I have settled our differences too. You will be pleasant to me in front of everyone. You will tell them how wrong you have been about me. Will you not?'

'I will do anything to save Luc's life,' Alexandrine breathed. 'Let me send him clothes or food?'

'No, not yet. First, I want to see how obedient you are, both of you.'

'I shall go—go to the King!' Alexandrine declared, sudden hope dawning in her face. 'I shall make him listen to me. He will free your father.'

'Will he? Do you think the monarch of France is interested in our petty squabbles? He might be interested in you, though. What would you be prepared to give in return for his generosity? No, madame, there is no help for you. When my father dies, the Moor will testify that it was a natural death. He will be buried with all due pomp and ceremony—and promptly forgotten. Then you and I shall come to some—arrangement. It would be a pity to waste the gifts with which you have been endowed, few that they are. But I have friends who would pay you to entertain them.'

Alexandrine turned away, nausea rising in her stomach at his lack of subtlety. She was aware of Selim's gaze, but the hatred in those black eyes was not for her. For the first time she felt a sense of togetherness with this man. Together, perhaps, they could thwart Paul's insane plans and have Luc returned safely home. They must! To allow him to be taken to the Bastille, alone and friendless, without anyone doing anything to help him, was unthinkable.

Alain Ratan! He would help. He was Luc's devoted friend. Yet what could she tell him? To disclose what had happened could bring about her husband's death. She was trapped! She could do nothing but go along with Paul at this moment and pray that somehow a miracle would happen.

'You are considering alternatives. There are none,' Paul continued. 'You will do as I say, or my father will meet his maker far quicker than he thinks. Your obedience to my wishes will keep him alive—for the moment.'

'Yes. Yes, anything,' Alexandrine said. 'I will do what you want, but, in return, I need to know that he is alive. Let Selim go to see him, to take him some small comfort. He is sick. As you say, he will soon die, but at least allow him to do so with dignity.'

'Would you be grateful for that?' Paul asked, his gaze raking her. She felt as if she had been touched by the hand of death, but she nodded.

'So long as I know he is alive, I shall do whatever you ask. If he dies, Paul, I shall have you killed too. I am only a village girl, if you remember, a coarse peasant girl. I shall take my revenge upon you if you take your father's life. Now...if we could come to some arrangement.'

'Arrangement?' He laughed at her ploy. 'I need nothing from you. I have everything I need in the Bastille. Keep your favours for the Duc de Belaincourt, madame. He will enjoy them only for a short while now.'

She had gambled and lost! Even Selim's eyes were suddenly sympathetic, knowing what she had been prepared to offer.

'Shall we rejoin *our* guests, madame?' he asked. 'And remember what I have said. One wrong look, one whisper to anyone, and Luc will die before dawn. And that would be a pity because I want him to die slowly—very slowly, regretting every minute of his life that he was not pleasant to me, his own son! To remember it was I who put him where he is. To wonder what is happening to his little wife...'

'I think I am going mad,' Alexandrine whispered in horror.

'Of all of us, you are the only sane one, believe me,' Selim muttered. She could see he was in pain and would have gone to him, but Paul caught her roughly by the arm and pulled her back.

'He is a physician—let him heal himself. You will remain in my father's rooms, Moor.'

Selim nodded, the look in his eyes proclaiming what he dared not put into words. At the top of the staircase, Alexandrine's steps faltered as she looked down into the crowded rooms. How could she go through with this? Someone must surely help her! Paul offered his arm with a smile that could have charmed angels and, as if in a dream, she took it and began to descend. Alain Ratan, Claudia de la Fontaine at his side, came out of the dining-room to look up at them, his handsome features hardening as he saw at whose side she walked.

'Do not even consider it,' Paul whispered, guessing her train of thought. 'I have only to lift my hand, and Luc will be dead.'

'You intend him to die anyway.'

'But you can prolong his life. I might even be generous and allow one of my men to take him a few things in a day or so. Wouldn't you like that?'

Alexandrine looked into the smiling face and nodded, conceding defeat.

Before dawn the following morning, at last succeeding in getting her mistress to sleep, Francine slipped out of the house and made her way to her old home across the Pont-Neuf. She had no reason to think she had been seen, and therefore was unaware of the furtive figure who followed her from the house, noted where she went and with whom she spoke, and kept a discreet distance behind on the return journey. And then went directly to the rooms of Paul Boussières to make his report.

'You must eat,' Francine protested, as Alexandrine pushed away the tray on her lap. 'At least a little fruit. You will need all your strength to fight that monster.'

'Fight him? I dare not! He will kill his own father if I do. Don't you think I want to? I thought of a thousand ways last night while he was parading me round the room telling everyone we had resolved our differences.' Alexandrine buried her face in her hands. Would the memory of Alain's contemptuous gaze never leave her thoughts? His eyes had followed her wherever she went, there was no escaping them, or the ugly suspicions she knew lurked in his mind. How could he think otherwise when she was being so pleasant and friendly to the man who had publicly abused and humiliated her? 'It's no use. I can keep Luc alive only if I do as he says. I need time. Dear God! I pray for a miracle.'

'I went to see Solange,' the maid confessed. 'I hoped she could help you. She knows everything that goes on in Paris.'

'Paul obviously hired men. If only we could find them and make them talk.'

'She knew nothing, madame. She will make enquiries for me,' Francine added, dashing her hopes.

'It was a kind thought, Francine, and I am grateful. We can do nothing but wait, and time is not on our side. The Marquis is so ill.'

'Solange sent you a message. Something she saw in the Tarot. She was most insistent that you know about it.'

'Another prediction?' Alexandrine was about to dismiss the message unheard when she thought how right the woman had been so far. 'What nonsense does she send me this time?' She did not want to believe, but she was finding it difficult to remain the sceptic she had been before.

'I am to warn you to take care. Her exact words were, "Beware the hunter when coloured lights fill the sky." Yes, that was it.'

The hunter? Coloured lights? Alexandrine shook her head in bewilderment and flung aside the bedclothes. She had more important things to do than try to puzzle out another riddle. She sat before the dressing-table while the maid brushed her hair, racking her brains for some solution to her terrible problem, but two hours later, when Selim came, she had found no answer. To keep Luc alive, she would have to do whatever Paul demanded.

'I think I have found a way, madame. May we speak in the bedroom, where we cannot be overheard—and alone?'

'I have no fear that Francine would relate our conversation to anyone,' Alexandrine told him. 'I trust her completely.'

'Torture can break the strongest man, let alone a young girl,' the Moor answered, ushering the maid out. Satisfying himself that she had left the sitting-room, he closed the door behind him and turned to face Alexandrine. He could see by the puffiness beneath her eyes that she had cried herself to sleep. They would only be the first of many tears shed before all this was over, he thought grimly. From his pocket, he took a rolled piece of paper and held it out. 'If you are willing, this will be the key to free the Marquis.'

Alexandrine sank slowly into a chair as she read the contents and saw the signature at the bottom. 'But this is the new will Luc had drawn up! I don't understand. I thought he had not signed it.'

'He did not. I did. It is not the first time I have forged his signature when the need arose. But, as you can see, it has not been witnessed by the Duc de Belaincourt. I suggest we take this to him and tell him the truth. Ask him to put his signature below that of the Marquis.'

'But what will that accomplish? How will it free Luc from the Bastille?' she cried tremulously.

'Lie to the Marquis. Tell him Luc signed it the morning Paul left—before their argument. Use your charm, madame. I have noticed he is not immune to you.'

'After last night, I doubt if he will receive me. He wanted to see Luc again. He did not believe he and Paul had buried their hatred for each other. I lied to him then, and told him I had been present when father and son embraced each other and swore never to argue again. I do not think he believed me. Selim, I don't think you understand what you ask.'

'I understand more than you think, madame. I am not blind, but I do not think it too much to ask, that you do anything asked of you to free your husband, to give him a few more months of life. In that place, in the conditions he will be forced to endure, he will not last four weeks. It is the truth, I tell you. And he will die in great agony without me there to ease his pain.'

'If—If the Marquis should sign this, Selim, what then?'

'You will say you found it at the bottom of your jewel-box, that you believe Luc put it there for safety, knowing that if Paul discovered it he would destroy it. Once it has been witnessed, it becomes a legal document. The Marquis's lawyer is a very accommodating man—and ambitious. For a price, he will backdate the notarisation by at least two days. Don't you see? With this in your possession, Paul would be a fool to harm his father. What good would it do him? You are the legitimate heir, the sole heir, now. Everything will belong to you when your husband dies. How will Paul pay off his debtors without his father's help? Or yours? It is a risk, but we have to take it.'

'Yes. Yes, I will do what you say,' Alexandrine agreed. 'Have my carriage prepared immediately. I shall go to Belaincourt.'

'We may have some trouble leaving the house. Monsieur Paul has men outside the front door. The servants have been told that you are not to go out and, if you do, they will all be sent packing. They will be too frightened to disobey.'

'Some, perhaps, but not Pierre or Francine,' Alexandrine said, bristling at the thought of being a prisoner in her own house. 'And did you not say there was a staircase which leads down the back of the house? We can use that and perhaps not be noticed. Paul never rises before noon. I shall not take long to get ready. Do you think you should hire a fiacre rather than use the carriage? Its absence may prompt him into doing something drastic. Oh, I pray we are not seen!'

'If we are, I shall deal in any way I have to with whoever has the effrontery to try to stop us,' Selim replied gravely. He opened his coat and showed her the curved dagger in the wide belt about his waist. He would use it whether or not she sanctioned it—and she hardened her heart against the thought of his taking a life. She could not afford weakness at this time. Paul was fully prepared to take his father's life. Therefore she must be prepared to be equally ruthless to save it! 'To free him, I shall kill, madame.'

It was a bitterly cold day. Even enveloped in a heavy cloak, Alexandrine still shivered as the hired fiacre carried them towards Belaincourt. She knew it was not totally the atrocious weather which chilled her so. It was the thought of facing Alain Ratan and lying to him. His château lay to the west of Versailles, on the edge of the dense woods where the King's hunt had taken place. It was enclosed by trees, which gave way just before the house to a dozen or more outbuildings. Alexandrine glimpsed a forge, where a smith was busy, several barns well stocked with provisions and winter feed for the animals on the estate, a granary and a wine store. Everything and everybody was well organised on this estate, she thought, as the fiacre drew to a halt.

As Selim helped her to alight, a man came out of the stables and stood watching them, hands on his hips. There was a fine sleet falling, but even so Alexandrine was sure Alain recognised her, yet he made no move in her direction. Despite the cold, he wore no top coat and the sleeves of his shirt were rolled back above the elbows.

'We are not welcome here,' she said quietly, as Selim's gaze followed hers.

'That is of no importance.'

'You are right. Let us get this done and leave as quickly as possible.'

When she entered the long, low stable area, shaking the snow from her cloak, Alain was kneeling at the side of one of the horses—a pregnant mare, she saw. He was stroking the glossy brown neck, talking softly to soothe her at the entrance of strangers. Without looking up, he said ungraciously, 'If you have come to see your horses, you have chosen the wrong time. I have my hands full with this mare. She's overdue to foal.'

His rudeness brought her to an abrupt halt. A stable-boy working at the far end discreetly picked up a pail and went outside. Alexandrine pushed back the hood covering her pale features as she moved closer, steeling herself against the contempt in his tone, and in the eyes that were suddenly lifted to look at her.

'Did you not understand? I have no time to waste with you.' The mare moved restlessly, in obvious pain, and instantly she once more had all his attention. 'Gently, my beauty. It won't be long now.'

'Monsieur Ratan, I beg you to listen to me. I need your help desperately!'

'Then I suggest you turn to your new friend and companion—Paul,' he snapped, climbing slowly to his feet. She needed his help? His angry features swam suddenly out of focus, and Alexandrine raised a trembling hand to her forehead. She was shivering, yet she felt terribly hot. She saw him frown, and from a great distance heard him say cuttingly, 'Are you ill? Or is it just the after-effects of too much champagne?'

'Please listen!' She was not aware of falling, only of strong arms closing about her, then nothing.

As swiftly as Selim moved to catch her, it was Alain who swung her up into his arms and hurried with her into the house. He called for a servant and ordered wine to be heated and liberally spiced to revive her. When her senses returned, Alexandrine found she had been deposited in a high-backed chair before a large hearth where a cheerful fire blazed. Two large mastiffs were stretched before the flames, unperturbed by her arrival. Selim stood to one side. Alain was leaning back against a carved desk strewn with papers, watching her with narrowed gaze, his eyes as unfriendly as before. He allowed her several minutes to compose herself and sip the wine that she had been brought.

'Thank you. I am feeling better now,' she said, lifting her head from the cushions someone had placed behind it. 'Will you listen to me, please? You are the only one I can turn to. I know you don't like me, let alone trust me, and I cannot stop you thinking the worst of me. But you are his friend. It is Luc... He is in great danger.'

'Go on.' Alain's body had grown rigid at her words, his pale eyes flickering more than once to the stony face of the Moor, but he could read nothing there. Alexandrine's cheeks were ashen, her eyes brimming with unshed tears. Something or someone had frightened her badly! She certainly had not dressed to impress him, he thought, looking at the plain woollen gown visible beneath her cloak and remembering the shimmering little figure he had been with the night before. His lips tightened as he recalled who else she had been with, who now resided at the Place des Vosges, reconciled not only with his father—but with her!

'Luc is not at home. Last night, while we were all downstairs, men came and took him away. They abducted him! Paul was behind it. He told me so, and then threatened to kill Luc if I did not go downstairs with him and pretend that all was well. I had to, don't you see?'

'Are you seriously expecting me to believe that Paul would have his own father forcibly taken from his own house and detained somewhere else?' Alain demanded incredulously. 'The man is a fool, but he's not going to run the risk of the Bastille for that! What is his reason?'

'He knew Luc had made another will that disinherited him completely. The valet, Charles, has been Paul's spy for two years. Nothing could happen at home without Paul knowing,' Alexandrine explained. Strength was draining from her like quicksilver. It was plain that he did not believe her. Tears would not sway him, or anger. She lifted her shoulders in a helpless shrug. 'I didn't know what to do. So long as I obeyed Paul, he promised to keep Luc alive, to see he was well cared for in that— awful place.'

Alain was beginning to have an uneasy suspicion that she was telling the truth. Why else had she been so pleasant to that little upstart after all he had done to her, clinging to his arm for most of the evening, laughing at his smug jokes, as if they were old—and close— friends? 'So last night's little charade was for the benefit of your guests? And now, you say, he is back at home?' he asked, straightening.

'Yes. Until this morning I had no idea what to do. I was afraid to tell anyone, and you left early.'

Because it had made me furious to see her at Paul's side! Alain thought. He had been in a black mood by the time he arrived at Belaincourt, and Claudia had sought to turn it to her advantage. She had been un- usually sympathetic, taking care not to antagonise him further by mentioning the disastrous evening to him again. He had drunk too much and allowed her to stay, a decision he deeply regretted in the light of day. He had made it a rule never to bring his women to Belaincourt. His life at the château was private and he would con- tinue to keep it so, despite this one lapse.

He went to the fire and threw another log on the flames. One of the dogs stirred and rose to its feet and sniffed at the hem of Alexandrine's cloak. It was an ugly brute, with a scarred face and eyes that stared at her with the same unfriendliness as those of his master. Before Alain could warn her not to touch him, she had lifted a hand and slowly stroked his head, and could only watch in amazement as the dog licked the fingers which had just touched him. Like the horses he owned, his dogs only knew one master and were not always too friendly with strangers, yet here was this creature settling himself beside her chair as if he belonged there! It was the chair Alain used on most evenings, but the occupant was not the same.

'I had a dog once,' Alexandrine said, smiling faintly as the animal yawned and went back to sleep. 'He was very old, and died while I was in the convent. I missed him very much. He was ugly, too, like this one, always fighting, and he had the most awful yellow coat. But he was my dog, and I loved him. To me he was the most beautiful animal in the world.'

'What is it you want?' Alain returned to the desk and threw himself down into the leather chair behind it, angry at her childish reminiscences. 'What place do you speak of? I can't understand that, after taking all the trouble to spirit Luc out of the house, he would tell you where he has him hidden. All you have to do is to hire men and go and get him.'

'From the Bastille?' she asked through trembling lips, and heard him swear beneath his breath. 'He has men who are prepared to lie and swear out statements that Luc is senile, unable to manage his own affairs, and that they consider I am a bad influence on him. That I married him solely to gain his money and knew how incapable he really was. Paul is going to imprison him once he has these, and leave Luc there until he dies and the title become his—and the wealth he covets.'

'And, in the meantime, Madame la Marquise will be in fear of her life. More,' Selim added meaningfully. 'She has already been threatened, as I have. But there is a way out—if you are willing to take it—to help an old friend.'

Intimating that if he did offer assistance, it would be for Luc and not his wife, Alain thought. The man's insolence provoked his temper, but he controlled it.

'The Marquis is also my friend,' Selim added. 'Are you prepared to risk your life to save him? I am.'

'I'm damned if I'm going to let him rot in the Bastille!' Alain flung back. 'Well, speak up. What is this great plan?'

There was a slight smile on Selim's lips as he produced the new will and handed it over. Patience, it told

Alexandrine. He will do it. She was not so sure. She thought he had shown very little concern.

'I—I found it this morning, hidden at the bottom of my jewel-box. Luc must have put it there for safety. Paul had his father's apartment ransacked last night—searching for it, I suppose. Luc made no secret of the fact that he was going to disinherit his son.'

'And when did Luc put his signature to this document?' Alain lifted suspicious eyes to her face, challenging her words. He had no reason to suspect it was not Luc's handwriting, he knew it well enough, but he could not understand why he had found it necessary for such haste and not waited for Alain's arrival. It had been all arranged. Had he realised that the quarrel with Paul would bring on another attack and been forced into a desperate move to protect his estate? It seemed the only explanation.

'Madame knew nothing about it, naturally, as she is now the sole beneficiary,' Selim broke in, saving her the necessity of yet another lie. 'The Marquis signed it yesterday morning. He was expecting you, was he not, to act as a witness? He gave me the impression you were to have come early—before mid-day.'

'Did he? How strange, when we arranged to take care of the matter during the evening,' Alain returned sarcastically. 'I well understand why I am required to sign this. Your reasoning is excellent. However, I do not trust you. At this moment, Paul stands to gain by his father's death. Once this is notarised, his wife will be in that position. And Luc could still rot in a stinking cell.'

'He may be dead already!' Alexandrine cried in a trembling voice. Did he really believe her capable of such callousness? How could she love such an unfeeling monster? 'Paul has set men to watch me. If I am missed, he will send someone to kill Luc. Take me home, Selim. I was a fool to come here and beg from this man with no heart! I shall keep Luc alive, Monsieur Ratan, at any cost. I happen to love him very much!'

She was almost at the door when Selim's hand on her arm halted her. She looked up at him and saw him indicate towards the desk, and turned to see Alain sign his name on the parchment and affix his seal.

'Take it. It is as far as I shall go for you ever again, madame. Now you have all Luc ever wanted you to have,' he said harshly. He rose to his feet, resting his fists on the polished oak surface as he stared across the room at her, his eyes piercing her like daggered flints. 'Be warned! If you have used me, and anything happens to him . . .'

'Alain, why have you deserted me so early? Is that wretched horse not better yet?' a petulant voice declared from the doorway. Claudia de la Fontaine stood there, regarding the three of them with an amused smile. She heard Alexandrine's sharp intake of breath at the flimsy night-garments she still wore, and experienced a moment of triumph. Now she knew whom Alain Ratan belonged to! She had not understand the conversation she had overheard, but the way Alexandrine clutched a piece of paper tightly against her breast as she pushed past her told her that Paul would be very much interested in it.

'Go and put on some clothes,' Alain snapped. 'And market your wares somewhere else! I never want you to come here again. My carriage will take you home or back to Versailles. I don't give a damn where you go.'

Claudia's lovely face blenched visibly. She had thought she had won him over for ever because he had allowed her to stay the night. Now she found him closeted with the Marquise de Mezière. And angry that he had been interrupted! His words shattered her. She knew he meant them—that she would never again set foot inside Belaincourt.

'When shall I see you again? Tonight, at Versailles?' Her tone became pleading. She knew she had gone too far in making her unannounced arrival, but she had been incensed at the sight of him carrying Alexandrine into the house.

'I don't know. Perhaps.' The offhand way he answered told her that she would never more share his bed.

'Were you making love to me last night—or to her? She flung the words at him, unable to conceal her feelings any longer. 'Where are you going?' She tried to detain him as he strode past her, but he shrugged off her hands. 'Back to your horses?'

'I prefer them to people, Claudia. I thought you knew that,' came the unflattering reply as the door slammed behind him.

'Jules, come in. I have a job for you.' Alain looked up into the thin face of the man who entered the room. He had simply appeared at the door some three months before to seek work, and although Alain was not in need of any extra men, he had been impressed by his knowledge of horseflesh and his desire to keep his private life just that. Alain had learned little about him since that day, apart from what his intuition told him—that the man was a product of the alleys of Paris, probably from across the river, where he would have rubbed shoulders with beggars, pickpockets, thieves and murderers, all safe in the haven known as the Beggars' Quarter.

He was no stranger to that part of the city. Many men and women from his circle of friends and acquaintances often frequented those dark streets which teemed with the dregs of human existence, suitably masked so that their identities would remain secret. He did not go there for their reasons—to flirt with danger, gamble, drink until the early hours or carry on an affair with a girl who would be well paid to remain silent in the morning. He found he possessed a talent for shedding the cloak of respectability and good breeding, the need for perfect manners which were always prevalent at Versailles and in the company of his own immediate circle, and this allowed him to wander unchallenged in places where a strange face courted danger.

Jules had the look of many of the men he had encountered in those places, solitary figures whose quick, darting eyes missed nothing. But because he was a good worker and gave no cause for complaint from the other servants, Alain was content to allow him to remain at Belaincourt. He could be trusted with the animals. Alain asked no more of him.

'I was looking for you earlier, monsieur. The Moor, the one who was with the Marquise, he left me a remedy to be taken to the apothecary. I can't understand what he's written.' (Alain knew he could not read.) He held

out a piece of paper. 'He said if I get all these powders
and mix them with a little water, your mare will recover
and foal within the next twenty-four hours, with no more
trouble. Can you believe that?'

Selim doing him a favour! Payment for his signature,
Alain thought. There stirred within him a reluctant
gratitude. He dared not refuse to try it. The mare was
tired, and he would lose her if something were not done
quickly to relieve the strain weakening her. He had tried
everything he knew.

'Get one of the other servants to fetch this at once. I
have something else for you to do. You know the
Marquise's maid, do you not? Don't lie—I have seen
you together.'

'What if I do? She's nothing to me—just a girl I know,'
Jules answered sullenly. What had he done wrong? He
had been so careful, not that it was difficult working at
Belaincourt. The food was good, the other servants were
not unpleasant to him—he suspected most of them were
afraid of him—and he had a roof over his head. Pickings
were slim, these days, but he was forcing himself to be
cautious—and patient. When he was rich, Francine
would soon change her mind!

'I have seen you together in the market.'

'She's just a girl,' Jules replied with a shrug. And when
he was rich, Francine would marry him. He had so many
plans. He eyed Alain warily. What was this all about?
Had he worked for a whole year, only to be sacked? The
opportunities he would miss—all those fine houses—the
jewels . . .

'I am glad to know your loyalty will not be called into
question,' Alain replied drily. 'I want you to hire men,
and I am sure you will know where to find them when
I tell you what they are required to do. You are to watch
the house of the Marquis de Mezière in the Place des
Vosges. If anyone leaves, you will follow, find out where
they go, and leave men—four at least—to watch while
you report back to me. The life of the Marquis could
depend on your not being seen.'

'Anyone?' Jules questioned.

'Those are my orders.' Alain stepped back from him, hardening his heart against the weakness threatening to undermine his judgement—whispering to him to trust her. He would trust no one until Luc was safely at home, not even her!

CHAPTER TEN

ALEXANDRINE HAD been confined to the house for two days, unable to leave even her rooms without feeling someone's eyes on her, watching her every move. It was not the fault of the servants. She could not blame them in the light of the threats held over their heads, but how she prayed for some miracle which would enable her to slip away for just one hour so that she might be sure of the safety of the new will in the hands of Luc's lawyer.

He had not been in his office that day she had visited Belaincourt. The stunning news that he would not be in Paris for at least three days or more ended her hopes of having her husband released quickly from his imprisonment. She had returned home in despair, not daring to leave the important document with anyone else and, once in the privacy of her sitting-room, had secreted it in the lining of a glove, allowing only Selim to know its whereabouts. Two short days, for she wished them to pass quickly and be done with. No matter what the cost, she would somehow leave the house tomorrow. For Luc—she paused in the midst of arranging some artificial flowers in a porcelain vase upon the dining-room table—they must seem like eternity.

Paul had said nothing more of moving him to the Bastille, and she bore his continued insults and leering looks in silence. She was totally in his power until the will could be notarised. Then, how different things would be! She comforted herself with the thought of telling him of its existence, of having the lawyer confirm its contents. Of watching Paul's face as he realised that his efforts had been in vain. No matter what happened to his father, he would not inherit one single sou!

Was Luc still alive? Paul would tell her nothing, enjoying the agony she went through each time he dwelled on the subject of his captivity. Somewhere near, but not close enough to be easily discovered, he had taunted. And not too comfortable, so that his father could grow accustomed to hardship and privation, ensuring that the Bastille would not be foreign ground to him. He was fed water, never wine, and slops of food suitable for swine rather than a human being. And at night he slept on a stinking palliasse filled with vermin of all kinds. His words had revolted her. She had wanted to throw herself at him and strike that grinning face, wipe the satisfied smile from it once and for all, but she was silent. Not one word escaped her lips.

'I am glad to see you are making yourself useful, madame,' Paul sneered when he found her some time later going through the next day's menus with Pierre. 'You—get out and don't listen at the door!'

The man left the room without a word, his eyes burning with loathing. How much longer could the household be goaded like this? Alexandrine wondered. Pierre had more difficulty in controlling himself each day and the cook had threatened only yesterday to cut Paul's throat with a knife while he slept ... fortunately out of his hearing. The other servants considered their positions too important to be jeopardised by the quarrel he was having with the mistress of the house. What did it matter who controlled the purse-strings, so long as they received their wages?

'I thought perhaps you might care to put a few things together for your husband,' he continued, considering her with a look that brought a blush of colour to her pale cheeks. She had not slept a full night through since Luc's abduction, and it was beginning to show. 'You look terrible,' he added sourly. 'I shall expect an improvement before you entertain my guests tonight.'

'Entertain?' She quashed the fear which rose inside her. What was expected of her now? Things for Luc? He was all-important not she. 'I may take him some clothes, and food?'

'You ... No, of course not!' Paul snapped. 'Pack a valise for him. It is cold and damp where he is going.

One of my men will see that he has it for his journey tomorrow. Yes, madame, tomorrow my father will be admitted to the Bastille. I have my sworn statements—everything I need, including your continued silence, for you know I am quite capable of keeping my word and having him killed at any time. After tomorrow, he will become a number. His name will cease to exist, unless I change my mind and sign the paper to have him released. There is no chance of that, I can assure you.'

He wandered around the table and perused the menus she had been studying, and then pointed to one. 'That one for tonight. I am entertaining some friends—a dozen or so. I wish to thank those who have so generously aided me, and to encourage their continued support. You will join us for supper, and afterwards, you will be pleasant and obliging to them. Do you understand?'

'Perfectly.' Her answer was hardly audible, and he laughed at her horror.

'Your maid Francine is an amusing little thing. Perhaps we can make use of her her too. I've always found her most . . . er, responsive.'

'You . . . have . . . ?' She choked over the words. The girl had said nothing to her. 'I will not have her used!'

'You will do as you are told, madame. Remember the consequences if you do not. Get upstairs and pack my father some clothes. Nothing more. I would not have him, or you, think I am relenting in this matter. He will learn to adapt to his surroundings soon enough. If he does not . . .' His shrug brought a cry to her lips.

'Is he well? Can I not send medicines? Have you no sense of decency? He is your father!'

'An unfortunate mistake which will soon be rectified. You have little time—do it now.'

Inwardly seething, Alexandrine went upstairs. She found Selim in Luc's bedroom, selecting warm clothing for her to approve. She gasped in alarm at the black face turned towards her and she saw that one eye was badly swollen, his mouth cut, and he moved stiffly as if his whole body was in pain.

'What has happened to you?' she whispered. 'Surely Paul has not dared...?'

'He is heady with victory. At the moment, he would dare anything. I tried to leave the house to find the Marquis, and his men caught me. Do not concern yourself, it is Allah's punishment for the pain I have inflicted on others in the past,' came the humourless answer.

'Have you been that wicked, Selim? I think not. It is you who have cared so diligently for my husband these past months, and for many more that I do not know about. Let me bathe those bruises.'

'No.' For a moment his expression was almost kind. 'But I thank you for the offer. The pain will pass. I have put out the warmest clothing I can find. Luc will need every garment. Who knows what he is suffering even now? He was taken in only his nightshirt. My past wickedness may come in useful, madame, when we have him safely home again. It will give me great pleasure to take his son somewhere equally as unpleasant as the place where his father now dwells and teach him the meaning of pain—slow, unendurable pain. I want to hear him scream in agony, beg me for mercy.'

'Selim—no!' Alexandrine cried. 'Do not think like that. Once Luc is back with us, there will be other ways of dealing with Paul. Disinherited, he will find himself in desperate straits and we shall make sure that no one allows him ever again to borrow money or to bribe people to help him. He will suffer, but it will be because of his own doing, not of ours. Luc would not want that. I do not understand the strange bond between them, except that they share the same blood, and a son is always very important to a man, is he not? I have been wishing these past days that I could have a child—another son for him. But that will never happen, will it?'

She challenged Selim with her words, but it was as though he had not heard them. Bundling the clothes into a valise, he closed it and put it beside the door.

'I am expected to go downstairs tonight and entertain some of Paul's friends. He has made it quite clear what is expected.'

'And I am to wait on them like a common servant!' She heard repressed fury in his voice. 'But I will. It will be one more score to even, and you will not stop me, madame. When the time comes...'

Paul was treating them both as less than the lowest servant in the house, Alexandrine realised. And Francine, too, was to be subjected to his sadistic treatment. Tomorrow—that was all she must thing about, not tonight. Tomorrow she would leave the house by some means and reach the lawyer, and then let Paul try to dictate to her! She would have him thrown into the Bastille, into the very same cell that he intended for his father—and he would never leave it if anything happened to Luc.

'Perhaps you are right, Selim. I do not know. Although you are my husband's friend and confidant, you have never been mine. I do not understand your dislike of me, for you know it was not my wish to marry Luc, but his. And I have done my best to make him proud of me, yet still you look at me with contempt in your eyes. I have done nothing to deserve it. No matter. This is not the time to discuss it.' She paused by the door and looked back at him. 'Can we not work together, just this once, to free my husband?'

'I thought that was what we were doing, Madame la Marquise,' the Moor replied. 'May the grace of Allah protect you from the evil which surrounds us all.'

Alexandrine had closed the door behind her before she realised he had touched his forehead and lips, in the traditional way he always did with Luc. Had she been accepted at last by this puzzling man?

She took her time with her toilette that evening, dreading the evening meal. Three times Paul sent for her, his demands for her presence growing more threatening each time until at last she accepted that she could delay no longer.

'Lock the door behind me, Francine, and do not come out for anyone,' she ordered. 'No matter who comes to fetch you.'

'But, madame, I am expected downstairs too,' the maid protested.

'You will do as you are told. I will not have you used by that—that *canaille* downstairs. How long have you been subjected to Monsieur Paul's advances? Don't lie to me. He told me himself.'

'Since a week after I came here,' Francine said, lowering her eyes with shame. 'I wanted to tell you, but he—he threatened me. I was so afraid you would think badly of me and send me away...'

'That I shall never do!' Alexandrine took the girl in her arms and hugged her. 'We shall win against him, I promise. But it may take time, and I am afraid the Marquis has little of that. And we must tread carefully, Francine. He must think we are totally cowed, frightened to go against him. If he thinks for one moment we would try to thwart his plans...' She could not suppress a shudder. 'I did not know there was such wickedness in the world.' She stood back and turned slowly before the maid, a tight smile on her face. 'Do you think my appearance will satisfy him?'

'It will anger him, madame. Why have you chosen black?' Francine asked, in awe as she realised how sombre her mistress looked.

'I am in mourning for my husband. I am not sure whether he is alive or dead. Until he is safely back in this house, I shall not wear anything but black,' Alexandrine declared bravely. 'Let him try and make me!'

'This is the place?' Alain asked in a low fierce whisper, unable to hide the anger in his voice or his expression as he stared across the badly lighted cobbled road towards a row of ancient warehouses.

'What better place to hide someone?' Jules replied with a shrug. 'The place backs on to the river. Either he could be smuggled out before a rescue could be accomplished, or his body would be weighted down and thrown into the water. It's the kind of place I would hide someone I didn't want found.'

'I shall remember that if we ever fall out! Where are your men?'

'Two round the back. Two each side of the street. No one can get in or out without them being seen. They know what they are doing, monsieur.'

Which is why I wanted your help in this, Alain thought, as he pondered the best approach to be made. Rush Luc's prison and risk his being killed—or spirited away to some other unknown place before he could reach him—or be patient—make each move slowly and with great care until he was within touching distance of the man he had come to rescue—then and only then to release the cold fury seething inside him?

'We await your orders, monsieur,' Jules said, his low tone matching Alain's.

Both were in dark clothes and merged well into the shadowy background. Jules did not feel uneasy beside the Duc, sensing that he was a man who would not risk life or limb unnecessarily—but when it came to a fight, he would be a formidable opponent and as deadly as any to be found in his own old haunts. He had seen the skill with which he wielded the sword at his side. There was a knife at his waist and another he knew was pushed into the top of Alain's leather boots. He might be numbered among the aristocracy that Jules and his kind despised, but he was not like all the rest. This man was a fighter—he would risk his life to serve those he cared for, as he was doing now. There was little difference between them. Jules had no hesitation about taking his orders and had warned his men of the dire consequences should any of them turn coward and run, or hesitate to act when ordered to do so. As he stared into the shadowy features, he found himself wondering if it was really Luc Boussières that the Duc was trying to help, or someone far prettier—far younger—whose gratitude would prove far more rewarding than that of the old man?

'You are sure the Marquis is held prisoner inside?' Alain asked again.

'Quite sure. I set a man to watch the house, as you instructed, and this afternoon he followed a man who left carrying a valise—to this place. One-Eye is a cousin on my mother's side. His ability to scale walls and roofs like a cat is somewhat of a compensation for the loss of half his sight, and he managed to get on to one of the most reasonable roofs and looked through into the pigsty below. The Marquis is not being treated as one would expect, monsieur. What use will he be to ransom if he is dead? He lies on a stinking palliasse of paper and rags—my cousin said he could smell the stench even from where he was—and there was no food to be seen, even though his captors, four of them near by, were stuffing themselves with the best of fare. They have been well paid, and the wine was plentiful, monsieur.'

'Maybe they will have drunk themselves into a stupor by now,' Alain said, measuring the distance to the main doors. No, not through there, he reasoned. From above and behind—a diversion before he appeared. He would have only one chance to get to Luc. Jules' words told him they did not intend to keep Luc alive for long. How convenient for Paul if his intervention brought about his father's death!

'One, maybe—perhaps two, but they come from my side of the river. I am not sure, but I think I recognised several faces. They will not be easy to take.'

'Then this is what we shall do.' Alain spoke rapidly to him for several minutes, grateful that the man did not interrupt.

'Monsieur has the mind of a soldier,' Jules murmured, finding no fault with the plan. 'I could not have decided better myself.'

A compliment, if ever there was one, from someone raised on violence and mayhem! Alain mused as they separated.

They went in quietly, swiftly, descending on the occupants of the warehouse without warning, in two waves, as if on the battlefield. The first would engage the enemy, the second would come up from behind and overwhelm. One man dropped from the roof into the four men splayed in a circle below him, gambling. Another came through a back door, which, although barred, gave under the weight of a hefty shoulder. Jules slid noiselessly through a front entrance and threw himself whole-heartedly into the mêlée.

Barely had the fight begun than the remainder of Jules' men launched themselves forward in the same manner. Alain was greeted by violent oaths, candlelight flashing on naked steel and the sight of a dead man sprawled on the floor as he entered and looked quickly for Luc. Another of the kidnappers, throwing off his assailant, managed to reach the door where Alain was, but the expression on the features of the tall man who barred his way warned there would be no quarter given. He turned, desperately seeking an avenue of escape, but Alain was before him, sidestepping the wicked-looking knife that flashed towards his throat. His fingers reached down for his own weapon, and it came free of his boot and upward into the man's chest before he was even aware of the danger. Alain stepped over him and continued across the uneven wooden floor towards the man who had raised himself painfully on one elbow and was staring disbelievingly at the approaching figure. One trembling hand stretched out in desperate appeal...

'Luc! *Mon Dieu!* They will pay with their lives for this!' Alain was appalled at the condition of his friend. In two days, Luc had been given neither decent food nor washing facilities. His hair was matted and clinging to a face gaunt with pain and fear. He was a brave man, but he could not hide the terror that must have haunted him these past days, Alain saw, his fury intensifying. 'Rest easy, old friend, while we deal with this rabble. Then I shall take you home.' And deal with the one responsible for it all—your son Paul—he added silently to himself.

'I knew you would be the one to find me.' Luc's words were barely audible.

Alain felt a shock of surprise, even uneasiness. 'Then you knew more than I.' He passed them over lightly, gently settling the old man back on the makeshift bed.

'Be still a moment longer—it is almost over. Then you shall have a warm bed, food to fill your stomach and Alexandrine to hold your hand.'

He wheeled away as some sixth sense warned him of danger, and barely escaped a murderous blow from an upraised knife. He had left one weapon in the chest of the man by the door and did not reach for the one at his belt. In a murderous rage, he attacked his assailant with bare fists until he lay senseless at his feet.

'Well, done, monsieur! We shall remember how well you can use your fists. Such men are rare indeed—among your class,' Jules remarked with a grin, and Alain was too pleased with the success of the undertaking to reprimand him for his forwardness. A dry smile touched his lips as he examined a raw knuckle, but his thoughts were his own and no one uttered further comment.

'Clear away this mess so that no trace remains of what has taken place here,' he ordered, nodding briefly in the direction of the watching men. 'You have done well. Jules will settle what is coming to you. If you are interested, I may have use for you in the future. Now, Jules, let us take the Marquis home.'

Paul had scowled at Alexandrine when she had entered the dining-room and commented most unpleasantly on her appearance, but she had stubbornly stood her ground, ignored his comments and seated herself at the table. He reclined in a chair at the far end facing her— Luc's place, she thought, her temper rising. She would never survive this evening! He was doing everything in his power to provoke her—and succeeding. The sight of Selim being forced to bring in the wine for the supper brought fierce recriminations to her lips, but a look from those jet eyes kept her silent. To protest would only bring down more humiliation upon their heads. Patience, she told herself. Patience. Tomorrow, it would be different!

She would enlist the help of Francine and Pierre. They were all in danger from Paul, and both were loyal, she knew, and would not balk at disobeying him. About the other servants she was not so sure, and dared not risk her attempt to escape from the house being disclosed.

Once the will was with the lawyer, let Paul do his worst! He would not dare to harm his father, for she would immediately inform the authorities and have him arrested for murder. There would be many witnesses willing to testify as to his complicity in the affair, and those who had helped him now, she thought, looking down the oak table, would retire into the background and remain silent. She would ensure their silence by paying Paul's outstanding debts. Selim had forged her husband's name many times and would do so again if it became necessary. Paul would find himself alone and friendless, a victim of his own greed. How that thought comforted her!

'Why do you dress in black, Madame Boussières?' a man on her left asked as the meal was almost over. She had talked like a wooden doll, the smile on her face frozen there throughout the last two hours. She looked at him, her eyes a frosty haze of sapphire and topaz lights. 'Are you in mourning? Paul said nothing to us, or we would not have imposed ourselves upon you in this way.'

His name was Raymond Moussiènes, she recalled, a banker of some high repute in the city. A family friend, she had thought, until he had appeared tonight. He had always advised Luc on his investments and knew very well how wealthy his client had become from his travels over the years.

'Mourning? Yes, I am, monsieur. For my husband, who has been taken from me.' There was laughter from a few who sat at the table, but others, she noticed, viewed her not without some sympathy. They were businessmen, she reasoned, who sided with Paul because he owed them money, and although she hated what they were doing, she could not blame them for wanting to be paid in full. She had felt a chill of fear as she recognised two faces alongside Paul—Alain Ratan had pointed them out to her that first night at Versailles. The two brothers, Marcel and Antoine Bièvre, whose speciality was consoling grieving widows. The way they looked at her...! And that other—fat, with his red face even redder after much wine, who laughed and portrayed those gleaming white teeth. The Italian, Mario Collini. What was it she had been told? 'He dabbles in the mystic...and has a cupboard full of poisons that kill rapidly and without trace.'

Paul's gaze met hers, and a smile touched his full mouth. It was a warning! One wrong move, one word to upset his friends and his plans, and Luc would die by this man's hand!

'Madame is greatly disturbed by my father's condition,' Paul murmured. 'Such a loving wife, do you not agree, Raymond? To deck herself in that ghastly colour before he has even left this earth? Or perhaps, like me, she anticipates each day and just wishes to be prepared for it.'

'You are without honour,' the man said in disgust, but his remark only brought laughter from the far end of the table.

'Are you any better than me? You are here, waiting for your money like all the rest. And you will be paid soon, I have promised that. Be nice to me, Raymond. The longer he stays alive, the longer you will have to wait for your money...'

'We did not talk of murder,' Raymond Moussiènes snapped, growing quite pale.

'What a harsh word! I am a dutiful, loving son who has only his father's best interests at heart,' Paul chuckled. 'I want him to have peace, to rest in his last days without mundane things invading his life. And so I have taken it upon myself to provide him with the quiet he deserves, the solitude, that he may reflect upon his life before he meets his maker.'

Behind Paul's chair, Selim stiffened visibly, and for a moment Alexandrine held her breath. She could almost feel the urge of his hands to close round the man's throat and choke the lying words from him. She marvelled at his composure, at the meekness with which he obeyed a command to refill empty glasses. Paul had ordered him to be clad in the Boussières livery of blue and gold. He looked rather magnificent, she thought, so proud of the way he conducted himself. It was an example to her not to give way to her own emotions. She smiled as he bent to refill her glass, and thanked him.

Paul sneered, 'You see what a gentle-hearted creature she really is, gentlemen? She has even made friends with the heathen my father has kept around as a pet dog all these years. She has him eating out of her hand, just as she did my father. It is well I had him removed from her presence. She had bewitched him with her smiles.'

'If anyone at this table believes that, they are as foolish as you,' Alexandrine retorted, drinking slowly. Her nerves were at breaking-point. She needed the stimulant of the wine to revive them and give her courage to go on but she dared not. How much longer was she to be paraded in this way? She had begun to grow used to Luc's little idiosyncrasies, but with Paul it was horribly different!

'You forget yourself, madame!'

'I do not forget who I am. The Marquise de Mezière, the wife of Luc Boussières, your father. I do not forget that you have schemed and bribed your way back into this house against his wishes. I do not forget that you plan to kill him. That these men you have brought here tonight are a party to what you intend to do. I shall mark them well—all of them! Their day of reckoning will come, as will yours.'

'But it is what we both want, my dear stepmother. What we both talked of when you first came to this house,' Paul said, leaning on the table, his eyes gleaming as he stared at her and challenged this momentary show of rebellion. 'My father was never capable of satisfying you, was he? That is why you turned to me, even though you have pretended otherwise. Am I not doing this for you? To give you what you want—your freedom? Gentleman, hear how she maligns me!'

I think I am going mad! Alexandrine lifted a trembling hand to her warm cheeks as all eyes turned in her direction. If she repudiated the statement, she put Luc's life in danger. To remain silent, condemned her!

'Are you not enjoying yourself in the company of my friends?' Paul's smile became malicious as he saw she had barely touched the full glass of wine. 'Drink up, madame. You are beginning to annoy me with that holier-than-thou attitude. You can dispense with the farcical pretence now, as my father is not here to see it any more, is he?' When she gazed at him icily, he added, 'Gentlemen, I think we shall have to assist the lady to grow more comfortable in our presence. Martin, will you be so kind...?'

One of the men rose and came to where Alexandrine sat. Raymond Moussiènes glared at him as he was asked for his chair, but he complied. Obviously he knew the man sufficiently well not to argue with him, she thought, as the other lowered himself into it and pushed her glass closer to her.

'Monsieur Paul wishes you to drink with us, madame. Come now, do not be difficult.'

'I am not thirsty,' she replied with a firmness of tone that belied the rising apprehension in her heart. Paul was going to try to make her get drunk—and then...

'I'm afraid she is not the kind of companion we are used to, Paul,' Martin chuckled. 'No matter, let us see if we cannot make her a little more accommodating.'

Alexandrine saw the look that passed between him and the man beside him, but before she could move, he had leapt to his feet and was by her chair. Her arms were pinioned to her sides and then Martin was holding the glass against her lips, forcing the red wine down her throat. She gasped and choked and twisted her head away. The liquid spilled down over her chin and neck, trickling between the hollow of her breasts.

'Allow me.' Paul's grinning face appeared over hers. He wiped his napkin over her shoulders, pushing back the velvet gown until the bodice was in danger of slipping down completely, and down into the front of it, where the wine had trickled. 'More, I think, Martin.'

She heard a roar of rage as another full glass was pressed to her lips, and this time her head was held by someone from behind so that she was forced to swallow it all, and gagged on the raw wine. Paul, no connoisseur like his father, had brought up a cask from the cellars which was not yet ready for consumption.

She heard a struggle and the sound of glass smashing, but she could see nothing, for her vision was blocked by the men who surrounded her, intent on enjoying her torment: the sight of the untouchable Marquise de Mezière being reduced to the same level as the other women they associated with. She heard Selim cry out in his own language, then silence, and knew with a terrible finality that he had been prevented from coming to her assistance. No one could help her now—she was completely at the mercy of these animals. This could not be happening! How could she ever look Luc in the eyes again if these men touched her—shamed her? She opened her mouth to scream, even though she knew how useless it would be with the servants all under Paul's thumb, and instantly regretted it as Martin tipped more wine into it. She spat it out, full into his face. He cursed her in street language and slapped her across one cheek.

'Gently, Martin. We do not want her insensible, just co-operative,' Paul reproved. 'The wine will be more effective than force.'

Alexandrine's strength was gone. She had no more fight in her. Tears poured down her cheeks, and at the sight of them, Paul smiled and nodded for Martin to give her more wine. He had promised himself that he would beat her—and he had! Soon she would beg; he was looking forward to that. She would grovel before him as his father would also, and he would deny them both his favour. He was master now!

With one final, desperate effort, Alexandrine kicked out and sent the man reeling back, overturning a chair as he did so, but it was of little use. As Martin bent over her again, she compressed her lips as tightly as possible, determined to resist, but he gripped her jaw in fingers that bit painfully into her skin, prising her lips apart. Through fading senses she faintly heard more noise— voices which were little more than a blur. Had Selim

freed himself or Pierre come to her rescue? Poor little
man, what could he do against these men?

The grip on her arms was released without warning.
Behind, she heard a howl of pain, and saw the man who
had held her stagger back against the wall, blood
streaming from one arm. Martin turned, the glass falling
from his hand, and received the full thrust of Alain's
sword in his chest. He died without comprehending who
had killed him, so swiftly had the attack come.

Alain Ratan—here in the house! And looking as if
this was not the first fight he had been in this evening,
Alexandrine thought in bewilderment as she sank back
in her chair, her hands against her mouth to stop the cry
of relief which leapt her her bruised lips as she looked
up into the dark features. A miracle *had* taken place!

He was dressed little differently from the last time she
had seen him. A dark-coloured shirt, streaked with dirt
in places and hide breeches and muddy boots that came
up to his knees. He looked more a countryman than a
member of the élite of Versailles and one of the noblest
families in France. Tonight there was a touch of the alleys
of Paris in the narrowed eyes which raked over her, in
the tightness which showed about his mouth. He looked
deadly—dangerously so—and she realised that she was
seeing yet another facet of the character of this highly
unpredictable man.

Selim pushed his way to her, wiping blood from one
cheek. He had just begun to recover consciousness when
the door had burst open and all Hades had been let loose.
Outside in the hall were armed men. Paul's friends and
the servants loyal to him, including Charles, had been
disarmed and had been brought downstairs. 'The
Marquis?' the Moor asked hoarsely.

'Safe. Outside in my carriage. He will have need of
you,' Alain said bleakly. His gaze returned to
Alexandrine, and immediately she became conscious of
her state of undress and fumbled to rearrange her bodice.
'You are . . . all right?'

'Yes. But I—I do not think I shall ever take wine
again!' She tried to make a brave show if it, and failed,

for huge tears crept into her eyes again. She wanted to fling her arms round his neck and thank him. She knew not how, but he had found Luc and brought him safely back to her.

Beneath the powder and rouge, Paul's face paled as he stared at the man who not only challenged his authority and the success of his plans, but looked at him as if he would like to send him after Martin. How could he possibly have discovered where he had hidden his father? Yet he had, and was now revelling in returning the senile excuse for a human being to his own house, and to the loving arms of his wife! Paul saw the faces of those he had lied to, coerced and bluffed. He cowered from Alain Ratan and from the man who stood in the doorway, two loaded pistols aimed at them. He could bluff them again, he suspected, in time, but it would be for a short while only. Damn the man! Had it been for Luc, or for Alexandrine?

He had thought the liaison impossible, knowing of Alain's contempt of women, but now as he looked at them both and tried to control the fear in him, he understood. They had joined forces against him, and the Moor was part of it too! They would all have to be destroyed along with his father. The next time, he would not hesitate to kill first and worry about explanations afterwards!

'I am tired of your games, Paul.' Alain's dangerously low tone was a warning of the immense anger raging inside him. His free hand gently touched Alexandrine's cheek where she had been struck. How did he know? she wondered, as his fingers, lighter than a breath of wind, rested momentarily on the bruised place. Someone was foolish enough to make a whispered comment on his interest in the wife of Luc Boussières and received a blow on the jaw from Selim, which laid him unconscious on the carpet. 'Well done, my friend! Take warning, all of you. I would not have been so gentle with him—nor shall I be with any of you—if I hear ever again that you have set foot in this house or uttered one word against its or its occupants. Paul Boussières is an outcast by his own choice. He will be completely for-

bidden this house and contact with his father and the
Marquise. That is his father's express wish, and I shall
ensure that it is carried out. If the Marquis's health de-
teriorates because of what has happened to him, I shall
seek out each one of you—remember that! There will
be no hole into which you can crawl, and no one powerful enough to stop me from killing you.'

'And who will it be for?' Paul sneered, silently cursing
the weaklings he had called friends, who did nothing to
help him. 'My illustrious father, whom you call friend—
or his wife? I have a name for her too...'

Alain moved so quickly that the movement of his
sword was a blur before Alexandrine's eyes. Paul cried
out as the tip slashed the front of his new coat from
shoulder to hem, and threw up his arms to protect his
face. Candlelight gleamed on the blade, which hovered
before his agonised vision, and then, with a short laugh,
Alain lowered it again with the cutting remark, 'I shall
not soil my hands with your blood! Others will do that
for me soon enough when it is discovered that you cannot
keep your promises. You are no longer a part of his
house. Get out—and, this time, do not come back. If I
hear that you have set foot over the threshold again, I'll
kill you.' Alain turned slowly and regarded the men
present. 'I, too, shall remember who is here tonight. It
is my heartfelt wish that one day every single one of you
will find yourselves in a place similar to that in which
the Marquis de Mezière has been forced to dwell these
past days. I pray you will all suffer as he has suffered.
An old man, sick and feeble, confined in conditions not
fit for the lowest of animals!'

The terrible strain he had been forced to endure had
momentarily unhinged his mind, Alain thought, making
it impossible for him to distinguish between friend and
foe. He thought Luc had recognised him and realised he
was safe, but as Alain had been carrying him to the carriage, he had turned on the man who had just effected
his rescue, his hands closing so tightly about Alain's
throat that he could scarcely breathe. They had both
fallen, wrestling to the ground. The strength of the older

man had stunned him. One moment half dead, the next a gibbering idiot with the strength of a dozen men! To free himself, he had been forced to knock Luc unconscious and he had not recovered his senses by the time they reached home.

He had left two men outside in the carriage with him while he and Jules entered the house and took command. The others had followed, and gone through the house to deal with any opposition.

'We—I knew nothing of this,' Raymond Moussiènes protested, mopping his brow with a handkerchief. 'Madame la Marquise, Monsieur le Duc, please believe me. I came here, as we all did, hoping to be paid.'

'And willing to remain silent, no matter what you saw and heard?' Alain asked derisively. 'You disgust me. All of you. You are all as guilty as Paul Boussières himself.'

'He told me the old man would not pay any more of his debts,' another protested. 'What else could we do but go along with him? I've been waiting over six months...'

'And to pass the time more amicably, you had no qualms about forcing your unwanted attentions on the Marquise. And you call yourselves men? Attacking a defenceless woman! Conspiring against an old man who has never harmed any one of you! You *were* all conspiracy to a plan to murder the Marquis, gentlemen, I am sure you realise that.'

'At least we'd have been paid!'

'No, you would not. You see, the Marquis had a new will drawn up the very morning he was taken ill—the very same day he was dragged from this house and imprisoned on the orders of his son.' Alain flung the words at them, a faint smile touching the corners of his lean mouth. Paul gaped in disbelief, remembering Alexandrine's denial. They had planned it—together! He floundered for words, and could find none. 'Paul will inherit nothing, not a sou, when his father dies. It will all become the property of his wife—the woman you have abused here tonight. I suspect it will be a very long time before you are paid, if at all. I assure you that I speak the truth. I myself witnessed the document that morning and countersigned it. It is now safely with the Marquis's lawyer. The Marquise knew nothing of this, of course, until this moment.'

He lies so easily! Alexandrine thought, dazed by what was taking place. None of it seemed real.

'It's a lie,' Paul shouted, finding his voice at last. 'I had the place searched, days before. I would have known if he had planned this.'

'From your spy Charles?' she asked coldly. Slowly, carefully, she rose to her feet and, as she swayed, Alain's hand steadied her. She smiled at him gratefully, not refusing the offer of his support and not caring whose eyes watched her. She was safe...Luc was safe...Luc—what was she thinking of?

'My husband...I must go to him,' she said, at the same time wishing the room were empty so that she could try to tell Alain of her gratitude.

As she turned towards the door, Paul gave a strangled cry and launched himself at Alain, in his upraised hand a knife he had just snatched from the table. The next moment, his neck was in a vice-like hold, and his eyes began to bulge from his head as Selim tightened it slowly and deliberately.

'No, Selim,' Alexandrine said, not caring if Paul lived or died, only that this man did not dishonour himself by such an act. 'He is not worth it. Would you lower yourself to his level? Let him live. Perhaps, without money or friends, he may find some worthwhile purpose in life.'

'I *have* purpose!' Paul's face was red from lack of air. He reeled back from them, holding his hands against his windpipe. 'I shall spend the rest of my life wishing you dead—you and he and Monsieur le Duc de Belaincourt! One day, you will be...'

He turned to run, but found his way blocked by Jules. For the first time Alexandrine realised that the face was familiar. She had been too dazed before to recognise him. Francine's sweetheart, who had left the Beggars' Quarter to better himself. With Alain? How had such a combi-

nation come about? And the men she could see beyond
in the hall—roughly clad, surly faced, all armed and not
to be argued with. Where had Alain been to hire such
men? None of them worked at Belaincourt.

'Let him go,' Alain ordered, and the man stepped
back. Suddenly everyone was trying to get through the
door at the same time. 'Look at them! Rats deserting a
sinking ship! Don't worry,' he added, as he turned and
saw the apprehension mirrored on Alexandrine's face.
'You will not be bothered by the likes of them again.'

'You seem very sure, but...' She shivered, remembering how they had looked at her, how Paul had
squeezed her breast and pinched her, exactly as he had
done in the carriage. She would never lose her fear of
him.

'There will be men watching the house until Luc is
well again—and afterwards, if he wishes it.'

'Why... How did you know where to find him?'

'Later.' Abruptly Alain turned away, issuing orders
for Jules to have Luc brought into the house and taken
upstairs now that it was safe for him once more beneath
his own roof. If he lingered with her, to tell her what he
had felt when he saw her struggling against those men
while Paul watched with that terrible grin on his face,
he would place himself in a far worse predicament than
that which his lies might bring about. No one could prove
he had not been at the house that morning, but there
would always be someone, somewhere, to notice that his
interest in her was no longer as casual as it had been in
the past. He was a danger to himself while he was with
her! 'Go to your husband, madame.'

'It might be better for me to examine him alone first,'
Selim advised, hurrying out into the hall as Luc's inert
form was carried in by two men. 'Take him upstairs.
Pierre, show him the way. I shall come directly.'

The major-domo did not argue, even though he had
never been given orders by the Moor before and did not
even know if he was right to obey them, but he did. The
master was home again, and that was all that mattered.

'No, Selim, I am quite recovered. We shall see Luc through this crisis together,' Alexandrine declared, pretending she had not noticed Alain's curtness with her. 'Your help will not be forgotten, Monsieur Ratan. I hope you will visit us as soon as Luc is well enough to see you.'

She followed her husband upstairs without a backward glance. As if she really did care for him, Alain thought, as he stared after her. Sheathing his weapon, he spun on his heel towards the door, his features suddenly taut with anger again. It was a look Selim did not miss. Moments later, he joined Alexandrine in Luc's bedroom and informed her that two armed men had been left inside the hotel and another two were watching the street outside. Alain had left, taking Jules with him.

'We must think of some way to thank Monsieur Ratan,' she said absent-mindedly as she and Pierre undressed Luc, now feebly but incoherently mumbling at them from the bed.

Selim's penetrating stare pierced the thin shell of her armour. He knows! she thought, quickly averting her eyes from his. He had realised that what she felt for Alain Ratan was far more deadly than friendship. It could destroy her marriage. Her life, even.

For two weeks she rarely stirred from Luc's bedside. She slept, when she was unable to stay awake, on the daybed beside the window. Selim remained awake at those times and took her place as she kept vigil. There were times when Luc was lucid and knew them, others when he mumbled and cursed them both, accused them of betraying him—and her in particular of breaking her vow to him. The first time it happened, she sat in a shocked silence, unable to believe the words which poured from his mouth. He did believe she had betrayed him! It was all in her mind, so how had she given herself away? She was sure she had not. She would do nothing to bring pain to the man who had married her and cared for her since her parents' death. The kind of love they shared was not exciting, but it was love, and she did not want it to end. She would not see Alain Ratan again, she told herself night after night as she bathed Luc's forehead and whispered to him in the semi-darkness. She would be true to her husband in body and mind. She would not allow her thoughts to dwell on what could never happen. And if she allowed it to—heaven forbid that she should be so wanton, so weak—she would have shamed herself, for Alain wanted her only as another conquest! She meant nothing to him except perhaps a few minutes' pleasure, which would be forgotten the instant they parted. Perhaps he wanted her only because he knew of the promise she had made. Perhaps he enjoyed watching her waver on the brink of indecision whenever they were together. No, he was not Paul. He had every right to feel bitter because of his wife's betrayal, but he was no sadistic monster.

The long days took their toll of her strength. She grew visibly thinner, and so pale that Selim insisted on her retiring to her rooms for a whole day and a night, and she slept the clock round. She did not want to, but the moment she fell upon the bed, too weary even to allow Francine to undress her, she fell into a deep sleep.

Jeanne d'Etoiles arrived the following morning as she was trying to pinch some colour into her cheeks. She looked terrible; pale and dull eyed. What a picture for Luc to see when he is himself again! she thought, as she went downstairs to greet her friend. Naturally Jeanne was seething with her usual curiosity and Alexandrine took her into the Blue Salon and told her everything that had happened since the night of the ball.

'And your husband is well now? Well enough to travel?'

'In a few days, perhaps. He was sleeping peacefully when I left him last night . . . the first time since he came home.' She gave a shaky laugh. 'I mean the night before last. I have lost a day. I have been asleep, too.'

'And in sore need of it,' Jeanne murmured, noting the dark shadows beneath Alexandrine's eyes. 'You have been neglecting yourself.'

'Nothing seemed important while Luc was so ill. Selim thinks that within a few months he will be strong again.'

'Then he shall not leave Etoiles until he is well. I am leaving for the country at the end of this week; earlier than I intended. I came to ask if you could both join me. It is what he needs, Alexandrine. Peace and quiet. Bring that Moor if you are satisfied with his ministerings, or I shall find you another physician, if you wish.'

'No, Selim is the best there is. At least I believe so. Oh, Jeanne, you tempt me with your offer.' To take Luc into the country, away from Paris and Paul, to an atmosphere where he could grow well again in comfort, without harassment. And, for her, a chance to get away from the lingering presence of Alain Ratan. He had been to the house several times and had spoken to Pierre or Selim, never asking for her. She had watched him ride up on several occasions and waited to be advised of his visit, but he always left again without wishing to speak to her. 'I shall speak to Selim. The end of the week, you say? If it is possible, yes, we shall come.'

'The remainder of my guests will not arrive until the end of the month, so you will have plenty of time to yourselves,' Jeanne added, causing Alexandrine to wonder if her curiosity was not yet fully satisfied.

'I have not seen the Duc de Belaincourt since that night. Is that what you wanted to know?'

'Nor has anyone else. It would seem that Alain has suddenly become a recluse. He has shut himself up at Belaincourt. Even the delightful Madame de la Fontaine is deprived of his company. She has found a new friend, however, to console her—Paul Boussières. She is quite wealthy in her own right, you know. Perhaps she finds it amusing to keep him.'

'I care not what he does or where he is,' Alexandrine said, paling at the news. Paul and Claudia! Both, in different respects, rejected. No good would come of the liaison. It boded ill that, of all people, they had come together.

Three days later, Selim pronounced Luc well enough to travel. Since their own carriage was not big enough to accommodate four people in comfort, not to mention

an abundance of luggage and other servants, it was decided that Alexandrine would follow in that, while Selim
took Luc ahead in a carriage provided by Jeanne. Preparations were made to leave that Friday morning before
the Christmas festivities began everywhere. The remainder of the household who were not going to Etoiles
were delighted when they were given leave to spend a
month with their families, returning to the house late in
the month of January to prepare it for the return of the
Marquis and Marquise.

As Alexandrine was about to take her leave of Luc
that evening, with Selim waiting at the bedside to ad-
minister a sleeping-draught, he caught her by the hand
and held it tightly. He was thinner than she was, despite
the great care everyone took with his food and his personal toilette. His eyes were sunk into a gaunt face that
at times was almost like a skeleton. Only that uncanny
strength remained with him, to startle Alexandrine every
time he touched her. 'My dear, are you looking forward
to this little trip?'

'Yes, Luc, I am. Why do you ask?'

'You should be at Versailles at this festive time.
December is a month for celebrations there, fireworks,
grand ceremonies, boats on the river.'

'I have no wish to freeze to death!' She laughed softly.
'I know you like Jeanne as much as I do, and we shall
enjoy her hospitality at Etoiles. What has happened will
soon be nothing more than a nightmare that will fade
and vanish from your memory.'

He threw her an odd look. They had not talked of
Paul or what he had tried to do, for Selim had advised
against it.

'Alain—have you see him?'

'Why, no. At least, not to speak to. But you saw him
a few days ago, did you not?'

'Did I? Oh, yes, how silly of me to forget. He said he
would come back. I was so sleepy that day. I haven't
thanked him, you know. I tried, but ... I seem muddled
these days.'

'It will pass,' she assured him. She had noticed it too—more so as the days passed.

'Will you thank him for me? Belaincourt is on the way to Etoiles and it will take only a moment. Do this for me, my dear. That young man is most important to me, and he did risk his life.' He uttered an expletive that made her wince, for she rarely heard him swear. 'Where is that son of mine—that cur who would have me dead? Is he in chains? I shall have him thrown into the very cell at the Bastille that he intended for me.'

'Luc, calm yourself,' Selim urged, moving forward, not liking the sudden excitement in his voice. 'Agree, madame, and then he will sleep in peace.'

'Yes. Yes, of course I shall go to see him. Rest now, Luc, you have a long journey ahead.'

She bent to kiss the leathered brow as he relaxed back amid the pillows. What had she done!

'Monsieur le Duc has just returned, madame. He will be with you in a few moments.' Gaston, whom Alexandrine discovered ran the house with the help of a very small staff, was most apologetic when she arrived just after two o'clock. The Duc de Belaincourt had been away for the past day and a half and had been expected back that morning, but so far he had not returned. Would she care to wait? He could not be very much longer. He was always so punctual.

What to do? Wait, or return home? She had spent more time than she had intended that morning buying last-minute presents and settling the most pressing household accounts. She had managed to sell a few pieces of jewellery to cover what was needed, leaving the larger bills until Luc was well again and able to deal with them himself if he wished. They would not need money at Etoiles, and if they did, she was sure Jeanne would lend her sufficient to meet whatever expenses occurred during their stay. Their own carriage was still being loaded with luggage, and so she used a hired fiacre to do her shopping and then come to Belaincourt, expecting to spend only a short while there. Instead, she had been waiting in the drawing-room for over two hours, most of the time

seated before an inviting fire. A dozen times she had
risen to leave, and changed her mind. Luc had been insistent that she thanked Alain for his help, and she would
do so and then would walk out of the Duc's life. At
Etoiles, she would have time to compose her thoughts
and accept that what she felt for him could never become
blissful reality. And accept it she would by the time they
returned to Paris.

More than once she had fallen asleep, still tired out
in mind and body from her long vigil at her husband's
bedside. She had been startled to discover how late it
had grown, and had been on the point of giving up her
wait, when Gaston came into the room again.

'The fiacre,' she gasped. 'Is it still waiting outside? I
did not think...'

'I took the liberty of sending it back to Paris, madame.
I am sure the Duc will provide a conveyance to take you
back home. Also an escort. The roads are not safe in
such weather—indeed, not at all, lately. We have been
plagued by robberies in this area, and several houses have
been broken into and valuables stolen. He would not
want you to travel alone.'

'Gaston, where the devil are you, man? I'm chilled to
the bone. Heat some water for my bath and bring me a
drink while I get out of these wet clothes.'

Alexandrine rose to her feet as Alain's voice sounded
outside the room. Gaston hurried out, and the next
moment she heard a muffled oath, and then he appeared
in the doorway. Snow glistened on his thick black hair,
turning it almost completely white. He stared at her in
silence, pulling off heavy gloves and the coat he wore
and tossing them down.

'Bring me some brandy, and wine for the marquise.'

'No!' Alexandrine had not touched anything stronger
than apple-juice since that horrifying night, and he
frowned at his lack of thought. 'Nothing, thank you. I
cannot stay.'

'Give me a moment to get out of these clothes, and
then I'll be with you.' If her appearance at Belaincourt
disturbed him, he showed no sign. In fact his tone was

rather off-hand, as if unexpected company annoyed him. She had not expected a cordial reception, but his manner was so formal, so distant, that she felt the peace she had been experiencing, as she waited in the delightfully feminine drawing-room, vanishing at the sight of him. She could not stay. It was too dangerous. *He* was too dangerous!

'No, please do not put yourself out on my account.' She hurried after him, and he turned at the base of the staircase to frown at her. How best to go about this business of thinking him? She wanted no more complications, no more misunderstandings. A polite, but genuine, offer of thanks, and then she could take her leave. 'I did not intend to stay this length of time, but I must confess...' A faint blush rose in her cheeks as she realised how comfortable, how much at ease, she had felt in the room, 'I fell asleep. The room is so pleasant.'

'Yes, it is,' Alain agreed, allowing his eyes to wander past her to the welcoming fire, the chairs placed before the hearth. It was a very special place for him—and now for her, too! He should have regarded it as an invasion of his privacy, but he could not. He could imagine her curled in a chair, her fair head laid back against the cushions, watching the snow falling through the large french windows. How often had his mother done the same thing. The two of them could sit for hours without talking, and yet know what was in each other's minds. With his father he had shared a turbulent relationship, always fighting to please him, to be both soldier and landowner. He had succeeded in both worlds, and his father had died satisfied that his inheritance would be carried on by a worthy son. But never did they speak of love, only of strength, power, money. His gentle mother had been the bridge between them, and he missed them both beyond words. 'It was my mother's favourite room. I have changed little in here since her death, and it is beginning to need a woman's touch again.'

'I am sure Madame de la Fontaine will have great success with it. I have been told she has excellent taste,'

Alexandrine replied, unable to contain the words which betrayed her curiosity as to the woman's whereabouts. What was the matter with her? She had not come here for this!

'I should have said, the touch of the *right* woman. Claudia is not that woman. She will never set foot in Belaincourt again?' What a startling admission! 'To what do I owe this totally unexpected visit, Madame la Marquise? As you can see, I am not prepared to entertain anyone.' He ran a hand over his unshaven chin, grimacing. 'I have been buying horses, and enjoying the company of a friend—the only man I call that, apart from Luc. I am wet through and in need of a drink and a bath.'

'I—I did not come here to ask you to entertain me, Monsieur Ratan, especially as it is obvious that you are in no mood for company,' Alexandrine answered stiffly. 'I came at Luc's request to thank you for what you did for him, and for us. He wanted to do this himself, but I believe, the last time you saw him, he was not quite himself.'

'That is hardly surprising! And his thanks are not necessary, surely you know that? I would never desert a friend in need. Is that your only reason for being here?' One dark eyebrow arched quizzingly.

'Of course.' What was he suggesting? 'I shall take up no more of your time, for I am sure you are tired. Your steward has sent my fiacre back to Paris, but would you be so good as to provide transport for me?'

'Gaston, find Jules and get him to hitch up the horses. I shall take madame back to Paris,' Alain ordered the hovering servant. He did not sound too pleased about it. 'Fetch me a dry cloak.'

'There is no need...' Alexandrine began, but a look silenced her. Whether she liked it or not, he was going to accompany her.

'It has stopped snowing, so would you care to see my new acquisition? My mare foaled safely, thanks to Selim's medicine. In future, I shall know where to come for sound advice,' he said, when Gaston reappeared.

Alexandrine was only too pleased to accept, to change the subject of conversation and ease the tension she felt creeping between them. Alain's magnificent black stallion turned his head as she passed and watched her progress to the back of the stables where a fine-looking mare stood.

'Motherhood agrees with her,' Alain murmured, going down on one knee beside the small foal at her feet. 'My stallion Midnight Blue is the sire, Lady Blue the proud mother, and now I have to find a name for this little thing. Isn't he delightful? Perfect in every way—thanks to Selim.'

'Yes, he told me he had given your man some advice. I am glad he could help.' Alexandrine stole a look into the dark face so close to hers as she knelt beside him. Such pride in his voice when he spoke of his horses and how gentle was the hand stroking the coat of the tiny animal. It reminded her of how his fingers had touched her cheek where Martin had slapped her, and the look in his eyes then had set her heart racing... That same look was in his eyes now as he sensed her scrutiny, and he raised his head. She knew she should move back, but she could not, even when his hands fell upon her shoulders and she was drawn against him.

'Why did you really come, Alexa?' The anger was gone from his voice. No longer were his eyes dispassionate. They gleamed like pale emeralds in the lamplight, searching her face, her very soul, for his answer.

'I have told you...'

'Don't you think it was rather foolish to come alone?' he mocked. 'To walk into the lion's den unprotected?'

'Foolish? Of course not!' She gave a shaky little laugh, not liking his choice of words.

'Dangerous, then?' he insisted, bending his head to hers.

'Please! Please, I must go back home,' Alexandrine pleaded. He raised his head, and stared down at the lips quivering from his kisses into the eyes where tears brimmed like silver drops of early morning dew.

'Really?' he whispered back, touching his lips to her hair, the lobe of her ear. 'Don't lie trembling in my arms, Alexa. Touch me, you know you want to, as well you know that I want to do more than hold you like this each time we are together. That is why it is dangerous for you to be here.'

'I could not go away without doing as Luc asked...' The words slipped out before she could contain them. She had not intended to tell him she was leaving Paris.

'Away? Where?' Alain's tone was unexpectedly harsh. 'For how long?'

'Jeanne d'Etoiles has asked us to stay. We shall remain there until Luc is really well again, no matter how long it takes.'

'Do you think staying away will change what is between *us*?' Alain tilted back her head, his gaze challenging her to deny his words. She could not, and her silence brought a tight smile to his lips. At last! He lowered his mouth to hers, parting her lips with kisses that sent her pulse racing and with no thought of the consequences of his madness. He wanted her! He had forgotten what it was to desire a woman so completely, so blindly! *Now* was all that mattered—this moment shared with her.

'Alain...' His name was torn from her as she fought to control the fires he had ignited. 'Please stop!'

'Dammit, I am not made of stone. I am flesh and blood!' And once more vulnerable to a woman's trickery. He had been so sure he would never allow this one to penetrate his armour, but she had...and seemingly without making any overtures to him. He could not think of a time when she had set out deliberately to be charming or seductive. In fact, the opposite applied. Yet, with each meeting, the attraction had grown—his desire had grown—but she had not encouraged him with a single word or a smile. How had it happened? What mysterious essence did she possess which had reached out to lure him into her web—to chain him as he had once been chained to his adulterous wife? Had he not known better, he would have said 'innocence'. Many times she had appeared to be little more than a naïve girl, unaware of her own beauty, the tantalising delights offered by her young body. Then, again, there had been occasions when he had held her as he was doing now and kissed her, and had felt the woman fighting to be released and satisfied.

Alexandrine reached out to stroke the glossy brown coat of the foal. 'He reminds me of a chestnut—a fresh, gleaming chestnut just taken from the pod.'

'Then he shall be named "Marron". I shall give him to you when he is older. And you shall have Lady Blue, too. She will be an excellent animal for you to ride when you next hunt with the King's party,' Alain said as she lifted her face to his in surprise. 'Or when you come to Belaincourt again.'

'I shall never come here again. Or see you alone.' How resolute she sounded! A fierce expletive exploded beneath Alain's breath and he caught her to him again, only to have her break free of his embrace and push him away so that she could regain her feet. She backed against the wooden stall behind, throwing up her hands to ward him off as he came up in front of her, his eyes glittering at her stand. 'Take me home!'

'You cannot deny what is between us. I will not allow it.'

'Will you destroy us all? Me—yourself—Luc? When you touch me, it is easy to forget I am a married woman. You make me feel...' She broke off, colour flooding into her cheeks. 'I am ashamed to feel as I do. I will not be another of your conquests, I will not! Let me go in peace!'

'Do you think you will find peace at Etoiles?' Alain asked, and then became aware of the figure who had just entered the stables. 'The carriage is ready, Jules?' He could have struck the man for his untimely arrival!

'Yes, monsieur. It is beginning to snow again—quite heavily...'

A hint that they should not linger, he thought sardonically. One which Alexandrine seized on immediately. As she passed the man, Alain saw the look that passed between them and was frowning as he helped her into the waiting carriage.

'Do you know Jules?'

'Yes, as a matter of fact, I do. I met him one day with Jeanne. He is Francine's sweetheart. She once told me he is the best thief in Paris.'

'Is he? That could explain many things,' Alain replied, relapsing into silence. It was some while before she recalled Gaston telling her of the many burglaries and carriages being waylaid in the area. Surely not? Francine had been so sure he was making an honest living these days.

Alain was quick to notice the lack of lights about the house when they arrived, and an emptiness about the inside as he stood in the hall and took his leave of Alexandrine. It was a little after six o'clock, a time when the house should have been bustling with activity as preparations were made for the evening meal. But there was only Pierre to greet them, and no smell of cooking coming from the kitchen downstairs. Intuitively he knew all was not as it should be, but before he could comment on it, Alexandrine turned to him and said politely, as if he were some stranger, not the man who had held her in his arms less than an hour before and wanted to make love to her. 'Thank you for escorting me home, monsieur. I hope the snow will not impede your return journey.'

'I have been out in worse weather than this,' he returned, his eyes flickering upwards to the upper level. Few lights burned there. Where the devil was everyone?

'Goodnight, Monsieur Ratan, and thank you once again—from the bottom of my heart.' Alexandrine dared not say more. She fled upstairs, leaving a trail of snowflakes on the polished floor.

'Madame is very tired. You must forgive her brusqueness, sir,' Pierre said, as his gaze followed her out of sight. 'For weeks, since the master came back, she has not spared herself. A rest in the country will do her good.'

'And the Marquis too, I hope. I should like to pay my respects to him before I leave,' Alain said, starting towards the staircase.

'But he is not here, sir. He left this morning with Selim and some of the other servants. After Madame la Marquise has left we are closing up the house for a month.'

Gone, and she had said nothing! Alain stood stunned. She was alone in the house. She had not told him, because she was afraid of what would happen. And so was he—if he stayed!

'Monsieur's clothes are wet through,' Pierre exclaimed, noticing the puddle forming about Alain's boots. 'There is a fire in the study, and some of the master's good brandy.'

'You have persuaded me, Pierre. I am uncomfortable. I'll dry off a little, help myself to a drink and then let myself out. There's no need for you to stay. I am sure you have things to do if the establishment is to be closed up.'

'Indeed I have, sir. If you are sure?'

'Quite sure.' Alain dropped his wet cloak on to a chair as he entered the study, closing the door firmly behind him.

'Madame looks exhausted, and frozen!' Francine exclaimed when Alexandrine entered her apartment. 'Let me help you off with those clothes.' Her mistress looked not only pale and cold, but upset.

'I am both, Francine.' And so unhappy! It was as though part of her had died. How easy it would have been to accept what Alain had been offering. It was not love, at least not for him. For her, it would have been the fulfilment of a dream. Now it was over. Tomorrow she would be at Etoiles with Luc, safe from the enticement of *his* kisses, *his* soft words. 'It is too late to go to Etoiles today. We shall make an early start in the morning. I hope the weather improves before then, as it is snowing quite heavily again.'

'Pierre and I were beginning to get worried. Madame was—detained—at Belaincourt?' the maid asked innocently, meeting Alexandrine's penetrating look without flinching.

'The Duc was not at home, so I thought it best to wait. We shall be away for some while, and it would have been most discourteous to leave Paris without thanking him for what he did for us. Help me out of this dress, and then bring me some warm milk. I shall go directly to bed. The servants have all gone?'

'Except for Pierre and his grandson. They will close up the house and make it secure when we leave.' Francine brought her a loose robe of pale green taffeta and slippers for her feet, massaging them for several minutes before slipping them on. Her mistress did not seem to notice how cold she was. She did not see to notice much at all, Francine mused, as she paused by the door before leaving and watched Alexandrine sink into a chair and gaze into space. Her mind was at Etoiles, perhaps? Or had she left it at Belaincourt, with the handsome Alain Ratan?

Alexandrine heard the door close behind her. When it opened again some time later, she did not bother to look round, believing it was the maid with her drink. She felt utterly at a loss for something to do to occupy her mind and rid her thoughts of those moments in the stables.

'I shall not need you any more tonight, Francine...' The words died in her throat as she half turned and saw who stood with his back against the door. 'What are you doing here? I—I thought you had left?'

'I have been downstairs. I don't know how long... an hour, perhaps.' Alain gave a harsh chuckle. 'Would you believe I was trying to pluck up enough courage to leave? As you can see, I did not succeed.'

'You are drunk!' she gasped. The strong smell of brandy reached her as he came to where she sat, and she was not quick enough to avoid the hands that grasped her as she leapt to her feet.

'No, I have been drinking, but I am not drunk, Alexa. I know full well what I am doing.'

'This is madness. Go before I call the servants!'

'There is only Pierre and a young boy, and I have told them that they will not be needed again tonight. Nor will your maid return. I have sent her to fetch her sweetheart Jules and take him to the kitchen until I want him again. The poor man would freeze to death outside.'

'You—You intend to stay? You cannot!' Alexandrine felt faint at the realisation. Yet within her stirred a flicker of excitement—of acceptance. Was this not what she wanted to happen? Who would know? *She* would!

'I told you what would happen when we stopped being adversaries, did I not? The fighting between us ended that night I brought Luc back—you know it did.'

'Is Madame de la Fontaine unavailable this evening, that you force your way in here?' She flung the words at him bitterly, knowing no other way to hold him at bay.

'That is unworthy of you!' Alain chided, but without anger in his voice. 'You speak of madness. In a way, I suppose I have lost my senses. I have, since I watched you mincing about downstairs on Paul's arm. That's why I left early. I couldn't stand the sight of you laughing at his stupid, inane comments. I knew I would never be able to control my temper if I stayed. I would have slept with anyone that night. Claudia just happened to be there—and unfortunately you saw her the next morning.'

'Unfortunate for you.' She was weakening, she could feel it. *He* had been angry?

'No, for you, because you misunderstood what you saw. You did not realise that she meant nothing to me, and she never will.' He tightened his hold on her as she began to struggle feebly. 'Will you not listen to the truth?'

Crushed against his chest, she was forced to endure the kisses pressed upon her mouth. Her lips could not withstand the storm of emotion she felt in them, and softened beneath his.

'No! This is not right,' she moaned. Why was she so weak? He was draining all strength from her, all resolve not to surrender, but she had no defences against his touch, or the searing kisses that branded her mouth, her bare skin. Weak, disorientated, yet at the same time aware of being lifted to dizzy, splendorous heights that offered her delights she had never dreamed were possible, her body sank against his until the arm about her waist became her only support, and she offered only a smothered protest beneath the pressure of his mouth as he pushed open the robe and cupped her breast.

She trembled with fear, shivered with anticipation, and knew she was no longer in control of the situation. She was lost, and he too knew it, she realised, by the increasing boldness of his scalding touch.

'Right?' Alain whispered against her hair. He, too, had totally abandoned himself to the need in him—the desire to possess this untouchable woman, giving no thought to the fact this final act might very well prove all he suspected about her to be true. 'What is right in this world? Was it right for me to love as I did? To have that love betrayed by a worthless slut? Perhaps it is not right to want you as I do, but there is nothing I can do about it. It is my fate.'

Fate! Solange! It was coming true—that stupid, impossible prophecy was reality now. Luc, her husband, was the first man in her life. Alain Ratan, the second. And there it would end. There would never be another. How could there be, when she loved this man so completely?

This *was* love. Love was madness, which might well destroy her marriage, but it was love! A cry escaped her lips as the shadowy room was suddenly lit up from outside by a coloured glow. From beyond the window came loud noises and more multi-coloured flashes in the sky.

'It's nothing,' Alain murmured. 'Versailles has started its celebrations tonight. Perhaps some people in Paris have also decided to begin the festivities early. It is only a firework display, Alexa. It cannot harm you. My poor darling, your nerves are at breaking-point.'

Alexandrine barely heard the endearment. The room reeled about her. 'Beware the hunter when coloured lights fill the sky.' It was happening as Solange had predicted.

Alain was the hunter and she the hunted, the prey he had stalked—and captured!

She sagged in his arms as he lifted her and laid her down on the bed, pulling away her robe as he straightened. She watched in silence as he stripped off his damp clothes and tossed them aside. Never had she seen a man naked before!

'Share this night with me, Alexa,' he breathed, easing himself alongside her and taking her in his arms again. For a moment Alain gazed down at her with open admiration mirrored on his face—the contrast of her milk-white skin against the dark coverlet was superb. His eyes appraised the firm uplift of her breasts, the slim waist and hips, the long slender legs. A prize fit for a king, but she was his!

Alexandrine closed her eyes to shut out his burning gaze. He took her face in his hands and kissed her slowly and with great expertise, parting her lips, darting his tongue inside her mouth. The flame within her flickered again and was rekindled and he drained the last doubt, the last resistance, from her, replacing it with a hunger...a need...

As he felt the change in her, Alain made love to her very carefully, prolonging each kiss, each caress. She found herself in the arms of a man determined to explore every secret cavity of her body. Nothing was sacred to him, rendering her weak with pleasure.

She gave herself up completely to the sheer ecstasy of his touch, the sensations of fire running up and down her limbs as first his hands and then his lips continued to move over her body, seeking, exciting, dominating her with the skill of his lovemaking.

'I swear this night will be the first of many to come, Alexa. I will not let you go—ever!' The confident, possessive words whispered against her cheek drove the last inhibitions from her mind.

Her hands clutched at his shoulders as he moved over her, his hard, muscular body pressing her deep into the coverlet—trembling—eager...

The unleashing of the wild passion that consumed them both without warning left Alexandrine dazed and spent. And then, in the wake of it, as he turned on his side and drew her against his chest, to cradle her head against his shoulder, came blessed peace and such contentment that she fell asleep at once. Loving him! Loving him! At that moment she was conscious of neither guilt nor shame—only of the marvel of her fulfilment as a woman.

It was growing light when Alexandrine opened her eyes. She was alone in bed. Her sleep-filled eyes stared for a long moment at the deep indentation left by Alain's head on the pillow beside her. Fear gripped her. He had gone without a word—he had deserted her! A sob escaped her lips as she sat bolt upright.

'Alexa.'

Only then did she see the tall figure standing in the shadows beyond the bed, like some elusive apparition in a dream, about to slip through her fingers.

'You were going without waking me...' she faltered.

'I thought it best to leave before there are too many people about. The last thing I want is to compromise you,' he replied quietly. How could he tell her what last night had meant to him? She had penetrated his thick armour like a flaming arrow, inflicting a wound he suspected would never heal. He did not want it to. 'But I could not leave. I just wanted to stand here and look at you as you slept, and remember what we have shared,' he added, as she tentatively stretched out a hand towards him.

A momentary hesitation, knowing that to linger would be sheer foolishness—and then he dropped on to the bed beside her, took her face in his hands and kissed her with controlled passion on the lips.

'Never, never, forget these few stolen hours!' he whispered fiercely.

'How could I? If only they meant as much to you as they do to me,' she returned tremulously.

Alain sat up and held her at arm's length, his pale eyes searching her face. 'Never doubt it, Alexa. One day you will believe that I care for you. I shall pursue you until you do.'

'No! That is impossible.' The moment of parting had brought with it reality. She was the wife of Luc Boussières, Marquise de Mezière! She had betrayed her husband! 'This—This was a wonderful, unforgettable night of madness, but only that! It cannot happen again. Luc . . .'

'I have not forgotten. It changes nothing that you are his wife. I shall never let you go, Alexa, you are mine! One day we shall be together—always!'

His lips bruised hers in a long, savage kiss, and then he was gone, his words still ringing in her ears.

I shall never let you go—you are mine! One day—together—for the rest of their lives!

Hello!

As a reader, you may not have thought about writing a book yourself, but if you have, and you have a particular interest in history, then now is your chance.

We are specifically looking for new writers to join our established team of authors who write Masquerade Historical Romances. Guidelines are available for this list, and we would be happy to send a copy to you.

Please mark the outside of your envelope 'Masquerade' to help speed our response, and we would be most grateful if you could include a stamped self-addressed envelope, size approximately $9\frac{1}{4}'' \times 4\frac{3}{4}''$, sent to the address below.

We look forward to hearing from you.

Editorial Department,
Mills & Boon Limited,
Eton House,
18-24 Paradise Road,
Richmond, Surrey,
TW9 1SR.

THE POWER, THE PASSION, AND THE PAIN.

EMPIRE – *Elaine Bissell* _____ £2.95
Sweeping from the 1920s to modern day, this is the unforgettable saga of Nan Mead. By building an empire of wealth and power she had triumphed in a man's world – yet to win the man she loves, she would sacrifice it all.

FOR RICHER OR POORER – *Ruth Alana Smith* _____ £2.50
Another compelling, witty novel by the best-selling author of 'After Midnight'. Dazzling socialite, Britt Hutton is drawn to wealthy oil tycoon, Clay Cole. Appearances, though, are not what they seem.

SOUTHERN NIGHTS – *Barbara Kaye* _____ £2.25
A tender romance of the Deep South, spanning the wider horizons of New York City. Shannon Parelli tragically loses her husband but when she finds a new lover, the path of true love does not run smooth.

These three new titles will be out in bookshops from December 1988.

WORLDWIDE

Available from Boots, Martins, John Menzies, WH Smith, Woolworths and other paperback stockists.

STORIES OF PASSION AND ROMANCE SPANNING FIVE CENTURIES.

CLAIM THE CROWN – *Carla Neggers* _____ £2.95
When Ashley Wakefield and her twin brother inherit a trust fund, they are swept into a whirlwind of intrigue, suspense, danger and romance. Past events unfold when a photograph appears of Ashley wearing her magnificent gems.

JASMINE ON THE WIND – *Mallory Dorn Hart* _____ £3.50
The destinies of two young lovers, separated by the tides of war, merge in this magnificent Saga of romance and high adventure set against the backdrop of dazzling Medieval Spain.

A TIME TO LOVE – *Jocelyn Haley* _____ £2.50
Jessica Brogan's predictable, staid life is turned upside down when she rescues a small boy from kidnappers. Should she encourage the attentions of the child's gorgeous father, or is he simply acting through a sense of gratitude?

These three new titles will be out in bookshops from January 1989.

W❂RLDWIDE

Available from Boots, Martins, John Menzies, WH Smith, Woolworths and other paperback stockists.